Friends and Enemies

**Center Point
Large Print**

**This Large Print Book carries the
Seal of Approval of N.A.V.H.**

ॐ श्री गणेशाय नमः

Friends and Enemies

Stephen Bly

Center Point Publishing
Thorndike, Maine

For
Aaron
our youngest son

This Center Point Large Print edition
is published in the year 2002 by arrangement with
Broadman & Holman Publishers.

All Scripture citation is from the King James Version.

The text of this Large Print edition is unabridged. In other
aspects, this book may vary from the original edition. Printed in
Thailand. Set in 16-point Times New Roman type by
Bill Coskrey and Gary Socquet.

ISBN 1-58547-216-6

Library of Congress Cataloging-in-Publication Data.

Bly, Stephen A., 1944-
    Friends and enemies / Stephen Bly.--Center Point large print ed.
        p. cm.
    ISBN 1-58547-216-6 (lib. bdg. : alk. paper)
    1. Black Hills (S.D. and Wyo.)--Fiction. 2. Sheriffs--Fiction. 3. Large type books.
I. Title.

PS3552.L93 F75 2002b   0103- 43560
813'.54--dc21

                                                                2002023766

*When a man's ways please the L*ORD*,*
he maketh even his enemies to be at peace with him.

Proverbs 16:7 (KJV)

AUTHOR'S NOTES

Anyone who came to Deadwood, Dakota Territory, before the trains arrived had to hike, straddle a horse, or ride the stagecoach into town. The roads were neither straight nor smooth. It was not a place to go for a sight-seeing trip. You went there for a reason . . . gold! The early pioneers were tough, bold, determined, and a bit arrogant. They were the stagecoach aristocracy. Even today in the northern Black Hills, anyone who can trace his family back to the pre-railroad days holds a certain place of respect.

South Dakota gained statehood on November 2, 1889.

But on December 29, 1890, the railroad reached Deadwood and with it came easy contact with the outside world.

There was a grand celebration. A parade. Fireworks. And that night, when people finally went to bed . . . they locked their doors for the first time. The protection of isolation was gone.

It was a new day.

Deadwood has never been the same since.

The changing of eras brings both sadness and joy, disappointment and hope, tears and laughter. The old era will become more exciting because many boring days of the past are quickly forgotten, and only the adventurous ones are remembered, usually embellished with loving additions.

But the old era will never come back.

There will be new friends . . . and new enemies.

Most of us who live in the little towns in the West know exactly what it's like to be considered one of the "old-timers" or a newcomer. Sometimes the most important people in the community are those who can bridge those eras and find acceptance by both groups.

That's what makes people like Robert and Jamie Sue Fortune so important to a town like Deadwood. They moved to town after the train arrived. Yet they were the first couple to be married in Deadwood, fifteen years before. Robert's father was an original prospector in Whitewood Gulch, and his brothers, sister, and family had lived there for years.

They were newcomers with old-time roots.

The kind of person that gets elected mayor.

Or sheriff.

Or chairman of the school board.

Or a deacon in the church.

Or maybe all of the above.

All it takes is a strong sense of God's leading. Enthusiasm. Discipline. A listening ear. And the ability to laugh at oneself.

That is, provided you don't make too many enemies, right from the start.

Stephen Bly
Broken Arrow Crossing, Idaho
Summer of '01

CHAPTER ONE

Just north of Rapid City, South Dakota . . . June 2, 1891

Ponderosa pine trees flashed by the train window like green-needled black pickets on an endless fence . . . none distinguishable from the one before, and too many to count. Behind the tree trunks, the muted shadows of a cloudy June day kept the Black Hills black.

The rattle of steel wheels on steel tracks had sounded deafening when they boarded the train but now had become the foundation upon which all other sounds were built. And like the rhythm of a smooth-gaited horse, the movement of the train car seemed to lull, rather than jar, the passengers.

With dark brown beard neatly trimmed, Robert Fortune sat with military posture and held a Denver newspaper. But he was reading the faces of his family.

Jamie Sue's right, Lord. They are growing up. Little Frank is fourteen. Patricia and Veronica are twelve. I have gray in my hair and creases around my eyes. The days I can account for, but I have no idea how the years went by so fast. It saddens me to think how few years are really left for them to be with us. Maybe it's a good move after all. No more long campaigns into the Sierra Madres. No more hearings in Washington, D.C. No more twenty-one-gun salutes and the solitude of Taps over the grave of a good friend.

He turned to the woman next to him. She had dark brown hair parted in the middle and stacked on the back of her head. "Don't you think it's strange to be out looking for a new start and a new vocation at my age?" he blurted out.

Her high, white lace collar on her blouse was fastened with a gold-framed cameo. With the filtered light of the train car, he could see a few small wrinkles at the corners of her eyes. With a knowing countenance she glanced up at him, then patted the knee of his gray wool trousers. Her blue eyes danced as she pointed to the emergency brake cord at the top of the Pullman car. "Perhaps you'd like to stop the train and go back to Arizona."

"I've thought about it," he concurred.

She leaped to her feet and reached up for the cord.

"Jamie Sue! I was just ponderin', and you know it."

"You weren't pondering. You were fretting," she corrected as she plopped back down beside him.

"Doesn't this move bother you? At least in the army we usually knew what was expected."

"Captain Robert Fortune, retired. I rather like that." She reached over and ran her finger over the brass button on his vest.

"Maybe I should have stayed in for a full thirty years. It seems rather foolish to be moving at our age."

"At our age? We are barely considered middle-aged, Robert Fortune."

"But to be starting over?"

"We aren't starting over; we're moving on." She rolled her eyes at the light green ceiling of the Pullman coach. "If I remember right, Daddy Brazos was near fifty when he moved up here from his beloved Texas."

"They took away the ranch. He had to move."

She slipped her fingers in his. "Bobby, we've been all

8

through this, remember? The West is settling down . . . army life has turned routine. . . . General Crook, rest his soul, is gone . . . since Wounded Knee last December, hostilities are at a minimum . . . and you were told flat out you would not make colonel until you were fifty."

He stared out the window at the speeding forest. "If then."

"Well, your letter to the secretary of war concerning the government's incompetence in dealing with Chirachua Apaches most certainly slowed down your prospects."

The back of his neck flushed. "Every word of it was true."

"Of course it was; that's why their reaction was so vindictive. No one wants to be reminded so graphically of failure they are already quite ashamed of. It really is all settled," she reasoned. "It was time for us to find new challenges."

A sagging strand of mostly dark hair drooped across her eye. He reached over and brushed it back.

Robert again studied his wife and children. The twins wore identical chocolate brown dust cloaks of satin merveilleux that covered their identical white, lacy cotton dresses. Both wore saucer-shaped white straw hats with identical large green silk ribbon bows. Little Frank sat wearing leather braces holding up worn ducking trousers and a boiled cotton shirt. Each looked as if they had indeed lived in the same clothes for a week. "None of you know what it's like to live so close to my family. It's different from just seeing them for a couple weeks a year."

Veronica bounced on the leather train seat as she talked, her light brown bangs flopping across her forehead. "It's the most exciting thing we've ever done in our whole lives," she insisted.

"Finally, we don't have to be the ones that load up and go home after Christmas." Patricia leaned forward, her elbows on her knees. She bit her lower lip right before she spoke. "Daddy, did you know that Aunt Dacee June promised to teach us how to ride jumping horses bareback?"

The thought of young girls' skirts breezing up in the wind caused Jamie Sue to glare. "You will ride sidesaddle," she insisted.

Veronica slumped back against the wide leather seat.

Jamie Sue smoothed down the small crocheted blanket in her lap, then laced her fingers on top of it. "Ladies always ride sidesaddle. You know that."

"But we're just twelve years old," Veronica protested. "Do we have to act like ladies?"

"We aren't living alone out on the desert. We will be in a town built in a narrow gulch where everyone sees everyone else. It is time you learned proper manners."

"But . . . but it's Deadwood we're moving to . . . not Denver or San Francisco," Patricia added. "Things are more relaxed up here, Mama."

"Proper manners are never out of style, no matter where you live," Jamie Sue insisted.

"But Amber straddles a horse and rides bareback!" Veronica's left foot still kept time with every word.

"And she's nearly sixteen years old. But her freedoms are not a measurement for you to follow. Your cousin Jehane sucks her thumb, but that doesn't mean you are allowed to."

"Jehane is only two!" Patricia murmured.

Robert Fortune gazed into the identical round faces of his daughters. Often, it seemed like there was only one girl, and his vision blurred. "Now don't provoke your mother, girls. You must do what is proper for your age and for your position in Deadwood."

Veronica wrinkled her small, round, upturned nose. "At Fort Huachuca we were Captain Fortune's kids. What is our position in Deadwood, Daddy?"

"You are a member of one of the largest and most prominent families in the northern Black Hills. You've got a grandpa, three uncles, three aunts, and ten cousins who preceded you to that location, and you have to live up to a family standard."

"Well, I can't wait to move into our new house," Little Frank added. "It will be a lot different from our adobe down in Arizona."

"The Lord's timing was quite gracious," Jamie Sue added. "When Professor Edwards passed on, Louise moved in with her sister and insisted on selling the house to us."

Patricia chewed on her lip, then spoke. "Do we really get the whole second floor of the house to ourselves?"

"Yes, Little Frank gets the back bedroom, and Mama and I will have the one off the dining room," Robert added.

"Daddy, how long will you keep calling him Little Frank? He's fourteen years old," Veronica said.

"I don't mind," Little Frank shrugged.

"I suppose as long as the Dakota sun reflects off Big River Frank's silver cross up at the Mount Moriah Cemetery, he will be Little Frank to the whole Fortune clan."

Little Frank stared out the window as the train slowed to climb through rocky boulders and small scattered trees. "I am anxious to work at the lumberyard this summer. I've never had a real job like that before. I'll have to learn how to do it."

Robert pulled off his new Stetson hat and ran his fingers through slightly oily hair. "We all have a lot to learn. I've never run any business before, let alone a mill and a lumberyard."

Jamie Sue slipped her arm into Robert's and for a moment thought about a time they had picnicked alone on a blanket on the beach at San Buenaventura. *Lord, how I like being with this man . . . whether it's the beaches of California, the deserts of Arizona, or the gulches of the Black Hills.* She squeezed his arm. "Todd didn't see any problem with your ability when he bought the mill from Quiet Jim."

"Big brother could run a business in his sleep. He's been organizing and bossing since the day he was born."

"You certainly know how to organize, give orders to others, and follow instructions. You were one of the youngest captains in your company."

"And now one of the oldest."

"Perhaps I should run the lumberyard," Jamie Sue grinned, revealing dimples at the horizon of her crescent smile. "And you raise the children."

She started to pull away from Robert, but he clamped her arm to his side. "Oh, no . . . we already discussed that. You aren't running anything."

Veronica danced the heels of her lace-up boots on the floor of the railroad car. "What's the matter, Daddy? Don't you think Mama could operate a business?" she asked.

Robert folded his arms across his chest. "From the day I met her, I have never known a more quickly decisive woman than Jamie Sue Milan. I am sure she would do much better than me at running a business. But, she has a job."

"Yes," Patricia admonished, "but what will Mama do after we're grown?"

Robert leaned his head back against the smooth brown leather seat. "You two aren't gettin' married until you're thirty, are you?"

"Thirty?" Patricia moaned. "I'm going to get married when I'm eighteen."

Veronica dropped her chin and batted her eyes. "Oh? Is it anyone I know?"

Patricia sat up and shoved her chest forward. "Well, I haven't met him yet. And I wouldn't tell you if I did."

"You intend to keep a secret from your sister?" Jamie Sue challenged.

"Hah!" Patricia heckled. " 'Nica never knew anything about Horace."

Jamie Sue felt a slight twinge of pain in her lower back as they continued to rattle and rumble along the tracks. "Was he the red-headed boy with the crooked teeth?" she quizzed.

"They weren't all that crooked," Patricia insisted.

Robert rolled up the Denver newspaper and swatted a fly on the seat beside him. "What kind of secret do you have with Horace?" he questioned.

Veronica's feet now uncontrollably tapped the floor of the Pullman car. "It was probably that time he followed her out to the cedars and helped her when she got bucked off.

She pretended she hurt her ankle so he would lift her back on her horse."

"How did you know that?" Patricia pouted.

"A twin always knows!"

Patricia chewed on her lower lip. "Did you spy on me?"

"Spy? I can ride out to the cedars if I want."

"You spied on me, didn't you?"

Veronica's knees bounced up and down beneath her full cotton skirt. "She wouldn't turn loose of his neck," she added.

"My ankle hurt!"

"You were well by that evening."

"I'm a fast healer," Patricia insisted.

"You're a fast worker!" Veronica laughed.

"Girls . . ." Robert interjected.

"Grandpa Brazos said he would take me hunting this fall and I could use his Sharps .50 caliber," Little Frank said.

"I told you kids, Aunt Rebekah wrote that Grandpa's been sick lately. He might not feel like goin' hunting this year," Robert cautioned.

"I can't imagine your father not hunting," Jamie Sue commented.

"Todd says he and Quiet Jim spend most of the day at the woodstove in the store talking about the old days. It's just the two of them left," Robert murmured.

Little Frank reached under the seat and tugged out a worn baseball bat. "Grandpa Brazos will come watch me play baseball. That is, if we can find a field big enough." He gripped the bat with both hands and held it out in front of him.

"Don't swing that in the train car," his mother cautioned.

Little Frank clamped the bat between his knees and surveyed the mountainside out his window. The trees had thinned out and massive boulders littered the hillside. "I think those men are wanting to catch up to the train." He pressed his face against the cold glass window.

"What men?" Veronica's dark bangs bounced with each word as she leaned over her brother and tried to see back down the tracks.

"Back there, see?" Little Frank pointed.

Patricia scooted over to the window and Robert leaned toward his wife as they all stared at the oncoming riders.

"Oh, my, they have bandannas over their faces," Jamie Sue exclaimed. "Are they highwaymen?"

"Nah, they just want to keep the dust out of their mouths and noses," Little Frank explained. "Uncle Sammy said he used to do that all the time."

Jamie Sue glanced at Robert. He reached down and unfastened the leather keeper on his holstered revolver. Then he pulled off his suit coat and laid it neatly on the back of the seat. *And your Uncle Sammy robbed more than his share of trains and stages in his younger days.* A few of the other passengers stared out the window. Up front a baby cried. Across the aisle an old man muttered. In the rear a woman with a high-pitched voice called for the conductor.

"The one with the curly blond hair is going to jump on the train!" Veronica clamored. "He looks very strong."

"I suppose he missed the train back in Rapid City," Patricia called out. "I hope he has a ticket. They won't let you ride the train without a ticket."

Robert yanked open the brown leather dufflebag under

his seat and pulled out a Colt .44 single-action engraved pistol with carved ivory grips.

"What are you going to do with your presentation gun, Daddy?" Little Frank questioned.

"Your mother's going to keep it under her lap robe."

"Do you expect trouble, Robert?" Jamie Sue asked.

Robert jammed the gun into his wife's hands. "Keep this out of sight. Don't use it unless you must. You kids stay seated! Girls, be smart. We've got some snakes to deal with. Little Frank, if you have to use that bat, don't bunt. Go for a home run."

The train suddenly braked. The passengers lunged forward. Robert loosened his black tie and swung out into the aisle. He plucked up the Denver newspaper, pulled out his holstered .45 pistol, then scooted to the back of the crowded railroad car. Most of the passengers were picking themselves and their belongings off the floor with shouts, whimpers, and curses.

"Daddy!" Veronica called out. "What do you want us to do?"

"Be patient, darlin'," he called back. "You'll know, when it's time."

Robert leaned against the back corner of the train car, the newspaper hiding the drawn revolver. The rear door banged open and a masked gunman with curly blonde hair barged in and shouted, "Everyone sit still! Don't nobody try to be a hero. Hold your hands way up high in the air and all you'll lose is some dollars and jewelry!"

Men gasped.

Women trembled.

Girls screamed.

And the moment the gunman relaxed his thumb off the hammer of the single-action revolver, Robert lunged toward him.

The man never saw the barrel of Fortune's revolver fly through the air, but he felt the skull-cracking pain as it creased his faded gray hat. The man sprawled on the aisle of the railroad car.

"Everyone keep seated!" Robert yelled. "There are at least two more!"

He lugged the man behind the last seat just as the train came to a complete stop. Another man burst in the front door of the train car waving a short-barreled shotgun. Reddish-yellow trail dust covered his brown hat and worn leather vest. "Butch?" he yelled.

Robert stepped out in the aisle, his hands in the air, still holding the newspaper. "Is he the blond man?"

"Where is he?" the dark-haired gunman snarled. He took a step down the aisle, pointing his gun straight at Robert Fortune.

"He's back there, mister," Robert pointed. "I think he bumped his head on something."

The passengers were perfectly quiet as if they were all holding their breath in unison, waiting for the gallows door to drop.

"What do you mean, bumped his head?"

His hands still in the air, Robert moved to the far side of the car opposite the downed gunman. "Yes, sir, I think he hurt himself. Do you want me to take a look at him?"

"You stay away and keep your hands in sight!" the man growled. "Get over in that far corner. I don't want anyone in this car moving a muscle. You all understand?"

"Yes, sir . . ." Robert mumbled and edged to the back of the car. *I surely hope he falls for this humble routine. There's no threat in this car . . . just take your finger off that trigger. Relax the hammer. You have us all buffaloed. That's it . . . let the gun sag toward the floor.*

When the gunman barged down the aisle, the passengers scooted close to the windows like hen-house chickens with a dog in the coop. That is, all but Veronica and Patricia who, along with Little Frank, had their backs to the gunman and their eyes on their father. Robert nodded at them.

Veronica's polished black lace-up boot stayed neatly tucked under the train seat until the gunman reached her row. A swift kick tripped the man. Patricia jumped up and stomped on the man's right hand with an identical boot, pinning his wrist to the floor. Little Frank's homemade hickory bat doubled off the back of the man's head. The gunman dropped unconscious in the aisle.

The passengers' cheers muzzled to silence when the front door of the car crashed open again.

"What are you doing?" a winded, wild-haired third gunman screamed as he crashed into the car. His bandanna drooped down, revealing a sagging brown mustache, an unshaven narrow face, and angry brown eyes.

Little Frank dropped the bat and slouched next to the window, his back to the gunman. The girls spun around and plopped down on both sides of their mother.

The furious gunman dashed toward them. "What happened to Clinton?"

Veronica clutched her mother's arm and stared down at the man sprawled in the aisle. Her shoes tapped on the floor with the rapidity of a young child needing a quick trip to the privy. "I think he tripped," she replied.

At the back of the car, Robert lowered his right hand toward his holstered revolver.

"He tripped?" The gunman glanced toward the back. "Keep those hands up high!" he shouted. He slowly worked his way down the aisle of frightened faces and raised hands. His eyes on Robert, he reached down and plucked up the baseball bat and waved it at Little Frank. "You bushwhacked him!" he screamed.

"Don't threaten my children," Jamie Sue replied in a nervous, yet soft voice.

"What did you say, lady?" the gunman bellowed.

Robert moved up the aisle.

"Stay where you are, mister," the gunman roared. Once again, he waved the bat at Little Frank. "Where in Hades is Butch?"

Jamie Sue's lower lip quivered. The girls clutched each arm. *Lord, sometimes we have to be bold against evil. And this man is evil.* She cleared her throat. "I told you, don't threaten my children, and don't curse at them," she blurted out.

He spun around to face her and the girls. Robert inched his way up the aisle. "Shut up, lady!" His hands sagged in disgust. "I'll cuss when I want to, and I'll threaten anyone I choose. What are you going to do about it, shoot me?"

Only the barrel of the presentation revolver peeked out from under the multicolored lap blanket. The gunman never saw it at all.

But he heard the blast from the firearm.

Smelled the acrid gunsmoke.

And felt the two hundred grain bullet rip through his right boot and plow a hole through his foot as it exited into the rail car floor. His scream made every hair on the back of Robert's neck stand on edge. He drew his own revolver and charged.

The gunman staggered back. He collapsed to his knees and grabbed his bloody boot. "Lady, you shot me in the foot," he cried. "I can't believe you'd shoot me! What kind of woman would just up and shoot a man like that! Why did you have to shoot me?"

Robert shoved the man to the floor and held a gun at his head. "Mister, never . . . ever . . . threaten that woman's children."

As if orchestrated by a secret signal, the passengers stood up and cheered again.

Tears trickled down the man's grimy cheeks as he clutched his bleeding foot. The train conductor and fireman burst into the car.

"What happened!" the conductor called out.

"These men frightened our children," Jamie Sue replied. "We do not tolerate such behavior."

"This ain't no good!" the wounded man wailed. "She jist sat right there proper like and then shot me! What's this world comin' to? Train robbin' ain't no fun anymore!"

🥾

The passengers disembarked slowly. Most waited among the boulders and trees as the train crew toted the injured and unconscious gunmen to the caboose, where they were chained into leg-irons.

Robert Fortune assisted them, then hiked over to his family perched on a log worn slick by wind and weather.

"They telegraphed back to Rapid City. We have to wait for the sheriff to come out and pick up the train robbers."

"They didn't actually rob anyone," Little Frank added.

Robert plucked up his suit coat from Jamie Sue's lap and slipped it on. "Thanks to you three and Mama . . ."

"It was you, Daddy," Veronica insisted.

"If you wouldn't have encouraged us, we wouldn't have done anything," Little Frank added.

Patricia bit her lip. "I was too nervous even to be scared," she admitted.

"I suppose it looks rather rash and foolish to others, but it seemed like the right thing to do at the time," Jamie Sue added. "I pray that's the last such adventure we have to go through."

A short man with a pin-striped gray wool suit ambled over to the log. His hair was the color of the thick gray clouds. "I couldn't believe my eyes back there on the train. I've never seen a family like this before. The husband cold-cocks one robber, the kids pounce on the next, and the wife shoots the third! This is the most lethal family in the West. Where did you all learn to respond to crisis like that? You struck so quickly and thoroughly. There was no hesitation whatever."

"Did you ever live around snake country?" Jamie Sue quizzed.

"No ma'am, not really."

"We lived for the past several years at Fort Huachuca in the rocky desert country of southern Arizona. We averaged killing a rattlesnake a week," she reported.

"Sometimes even in the house!" Veronica added.

"At first it was terrifying, but as soon as you learn how to kill a snake, you find out it's not so scary," Jamie Sue explained. "You just do it quickly before the snake has a chance to think or harm you."

"Then you skin 'em, and tan the hides," Little Frank added. "I sold them to soldiers for hat bands and such. 'Course, the meat was good too."

"You ate rattlesnake?" The man's face turned pale.

"Sometimes Mama would make a stew out of them, but I like them grilled right over the flames," Little Frank explained.

The man with the green face turned to Robert Fortune. "What do snakes have to do with these train robbers?"

"You have to strike fast before they get a chance to think or harm you," Robert explained. "Some things you have to do quickly, before you rationalize yourself out of them."

"Of course, train robbers don't taste as good as snakes," Veronica offered.

"And when you skin 'em you can't hardly get nothin' for their hide," Little Frank concluded.

The man's hat dropped. His face whitened.

Robert grinned. "The truth of the matter is, this is a pretty stubborn family and we just don't push around very well. Never have. Kind of an inherited characteristic."

"Yes," Jamie Sue concurred. "All the Fortunes are that way."

"Fortune?" As the man retrieved his hat, Robert noticed he packed a small revolver in a shoulder holster under his suit coat. "Your name is Fortune?"

"I'm Robert Fortune. This is my wife, Jamie Sue, and

our children."

The man rubbed his round chin as if contemplating a weighty decision. "You related to that Deadwood bunch?"

"I'm afraid so," Robert laughed. "They have quite a reputation, don't they? Are you a friend of Daddy Brazos or my brothers?"

"Eh . . . well . . . I've never actually met any of them."

"I bet you read that book about my Uncle Todd and his 'Flying Fist of Death'!" Veronica added.

The man took several small steps backward.

"It wasn't all that dramatic. You know how those dime novels play things up," Robert reported. "That was about the only time Todd had to face a gunman of the caliber of Cigar Dubois. Daddy Brazos, on the other hand, has made a lifetime gettin' himself in and out of tight squeezes. He was the one who brought down Doc Kabyo and that gang."

"You don't say?" The man cleared his throat. "Actually, I was hoping to meet the one called Samuel Fortune," the man explained.

"Uncle Sammy is a real gunfighter!" Patricia added. "He isn't scared of anything. Some say he was the toughest man in the Indian Territory."

"They call it Oklahoma now," Veronica corrected.

"But it's still a territory," Little Frank added.

"Sammy's served his sentence in prison and retired from all that now," Jamie Sue added. "The Lord has made him a changed man."

Robert leaned back on the log and surveyed the other passengers. A large woman chased a two-year-old boy, naked from the waist down, through the boulders. He glanced back at the short man. "Are you in the telephone business like Sammy?"

Even though it was cloudy and cool, beads of sweat popped out on the man's forehead. "Eh, no."

"Well, what do you do?" Little Frank quizzed.

The man took out a soiled white handkerchief and sponged his forehead. "You might say I'm a retired bounty hunter."

"No foolin', you used to be a bounty hunter?" Little Frank added. "Boy, that must have been an exciting life. I'd like to be a bounty hunter, but Daddy says all the important outlaws are dead or in jail already."

"When did you retire?" Jamie Sue asked.

The man pulled out a gold-plated pocket watch from his vest and studied the time. "About thirty seconds ago," the man mumbled.

Robert glanced over at his wife, then back at the man. "You were after Sammy?"

"Eh . . . well . . ." He looped his thumbs in his belt. "A family in Ft. Smith, Arkansas, said that Samuel Fortune owed them $400 for the wrongful death of four horses and two mules. If he doesn't pay, I'm supposed to arrest him and bring him back for trial."

"If Sammy truly owes them something, he will pay, I know that," Robert said. "But they had better show up in person and have some proof of their accusation, because lots of folks want a piece of Sammy's bank account nowadays."

"Are you really going to try to arrest my Uncle Sammy?" Veronica quizzed.

"Can we watch?" Patricia pleaded. "Mama, you've got to let us watch."

The man wiped the sweat off his forehead. "Actually, I don't think I'll go to Deadwood after all. In fact, maybe I'll ride back to Rapid City with the sheriff's posse." The man backed down the slope of the hill toward the train, his hat in his hand.

The passengers were given the option of waiting out on the hillside or reboarding the train and waiting there. Most of them, like the Fortunes, remained out in the fresh air of the Black Hills.

Little Frank tucked his boiled cotton shirt into his ducking trousers, and tugged his worn, wide-brimmed hat down low across his eyes. "Daddy, can I go look at the horses while we are waiting?" He stared toward the far end of the train.

"What horses?" Jamie Sue queried.

"The two horses that are going to Deadwood for the big race," Little Frank reported. "It looks like they're unloading them to give them some exercise."

Her narrow eyes pinched; her thin lips tightened. "I will not have my son hanging around that racehorse crowd," she insisted.

Robert reached over and hugged her narrow waist. "He only wants to see the horses, Mama, not run off and join the circus," he laughed. "Besides, it will be a history lesson."

She folded her arms across her chest. "And just how is this going to be a lesson in history?"

Little Frank rocked back on the heels of his worn brown boots. His blue eyes danced. "The big gray is a descendant of Traveller, General Lee's favorite. And the other is a descendant of General Grant's horse, Cincinnati!"

"Oh, my . . ." Jamie Sue reached up and tried unsuccessfully to tuck a wild strand of brown hair back under her straw hat. "I can see how this will be a horse race of epic proportions and national significance."

"Does this mean I can go watch them exercise the horses?" Little Frank pleaded.

She reached over and brushed his hair off his forehead. "How can I refuse such a historic event? It would be unpatriotic."

When Robert attempted to withdraw his arm, she clamped it around her waist. They watched Little Frank sprint back toward the livestock car.

"The girls are right," Robert admitted. "I should stop calling him Little Frank. He's almost as tall as I am."

She pulled his hand over to hers and laced his calloused fingers in hers. "No matter what we call him, Daddy Brazos will call him Little Frank."

"Mama, we want to go for a walk too," Veronica insisted as she stood and brushed down her lacy white cotton dress.

Jamie Sue raised her thick dark eyebrows. "You want to go look at some horses?"

"No, she wants to go look at that young blond boy with the curly hair that's standing by the big lady and the half-naked little boy," Patricia announced.

"I do not."

"Yes, you do."

"How do you know?"

" 'Cause I want to go see him too! So there!" Patricia stuck out her small, pointed pink tongue.

"Please, Daddy," Veronica begged, "can we just walk around?"

He glanced at the milling crowd of impatient passengers. "As long as I can keep you in sight."

Patricia jumped up next to her sister. "Why do we have to stay in sight, Daddy? Little Frank doesn't have to keep in sight."

"Because Little Frank isn't one of the two cutest girls on the face of the earth," Robert replied.

Patricia and Veronica grinned and wrinkled their identical round, upturned noses in unison.

"Daddy is one smooth talker, Mama," Veronica beamed.

"Yes, he is." Jamie Sue drew his fingers up to her lips and brushed a kiss across them. "It's a Fortune characteristic."

The girls held hands and giggled their way over to a stand of short ponderosa pines. Soon, they wormed their way close to the blond curly-headed boy.

"Well, Daddy, you sweet-talked them this time, but they won't fall for that forever," Jamie Sue lectured.

"Can you imagine what life's going to be like when Veronica and Patricia are sixteen?" he said.

"You'll have solid-gray hair, Robert Fortune, just like your father."

"And Sammy. He's been gray since he was twenty-five." Robert took a deep breath and let it out slowly. "We haven't all lived in the same place since . . . since Mama died."

Jamie Sue stretched her arms out and could feel stiffness and pain at the base of her back after several days on the train. "I predict you'll make a quick adjustment."

"How about you?"

"I'm looking forward to settling in. But I'll have to get used to it," she admitted. "I'll be only one of many Mrs. Fortunes. Rebekah is the queen. Abby's the one with stunning looks, . . . and Dacee June . . . well, there is no one on earth like Dacee June Fortune Toluca."

"The whole family is defined by our relationship with Lil' Sis, aren't we?" Robert concurred.

"Yes, and I'm just not quite sure where that leaves me." She stood and rested her hands on her lower back. "Where do I fit in?"

Robert pulled her over toward his knees, tugged her around, then began kneading his thumbs into her lower back. "You're my darlin' Jamie Sue, the original heartthrob of the Black Hills. There wasn't a prospector in '75 who didn't stare at that handbill of yours and dream," Robert grinned.

"That was a long, long time ago." She flinched. "Just a little higher."

"Not for me, it wasn't," he replied. "It seems like yesterday that I came through that blizzard on the prairie and you bushwhacked me. How's that?"

"Bushwhacked you? You wrestled me to the ground, and we hadn't even been introduced. Oh, yes . . . right there . . . oh my, I think I'm in heaven," she moaned as he continued the massage.

"Wrestled you to the ground? You tried to bust my skull!"

She sat on his knee as they laughed.

"We've been bushwhackin' and wrestlin' ever since, haven't we?" He slipped his arms around her.

She leaned her back against his chest. "Are you bragging

or complaining, Robert Fortune?"

"I am continually amazed that a woman of your beauty and charm ever wanted to put up with the likes of me."

"Are you trying to sweet-talk me like you do the twins?" she pressed.

"Did it work?"

"Yes, it did." She turned her head back and kissed his narrow, slightly chapped lips. Then she scooted over on the log next to him and surveyed the crowd until she spotted her daughters. "But I'll never know how in the world you three Fortune boys turned out to be such smooth talkers growing up with Daddy Brazos's rough, blunt ways."

"Ah, Jamie Sue, you never knew our Mama."

Some of the passengers had pulled out dinner baskets and were picnicking on the hillside by the time the sheriff and his men drove up. They brought a doctor, two train officials, a buckboard wagon, and several outriders with them.

Robert spent a half-hour explaining the entire capture scene to the lawman and officials of the Fremont, Elkhorn, and Missouri Valley Railroad. Soon after, the engine was stoked, the whistle sounded, and the livestock and passengers, including the Fortunes, were reloaded.

"His name is Harold McGinnis, but everyone calls him Curly Mac," Veronica reported, her lace-up boots dancing with each word.

Patricia bit her lower lip. "He's almost as old as Little Frank."

"He used to live in El Paso."

"And Las Cruces."

"And Santa Fe," Veronica added.

"And Durango," Patricia blurted out.

"And Denver."

"And Ft. Laramie."

"And Custer City."

"But now he's going to Central City," Patricia declared.

Veronica untied the lacy bow at her waist, then retied it. "And he's going to visit his aunt in Central City."

Robert glanced over at his wife. "I presume we're talking about the blond-headed boy."

"No doubt." Jamie Sue squinted at Veronica. "You have a smudge on your chin."

Both girls wiped their faces.

"He can't tell us apart," Veronica added.

"Very few people can." Jamie Sue studied her daughters. *How can that same wisp of hair fall out of their hats at the same time and droop in identical fashion across their foreheads?*

"Veronica pinched him and then said she was me," Patricia reported.

"You did what?" Jamie Sue gasped.

"He was showing us his muscles and he . . ."

Robert felt his neck stiffen. "His what?"

"The muscles on his arms, Daddy. He bet I couldn't even pinch him there he was so strong. So I pinched him."

Patricia chewed on her lower lip. "Veronica made him cry."

"I did not. He said some dust got in his eyes."

"Well, why did you tell him you were me?"

"I was afraid he would get mad."

"Did he get mad?" Jamie Sue asked.

"No, but he did quit bragging about his muscles," Veronica announced.

"Well, you shouldn't have touched him. Touching could produce sinful thoughts," Jamie Sue warned.

Veronica grinned. "In me, or in Curly Mac?"

"The only thought in his mind was pain!" Patricia added.

Jamie Sue tapped Veronica's bouncing knee. "You are not building a ladylike reputation, Veronica Ruth Fortune."

Veronica stopped bouncing her knee. "That's OK," she smirked. "He thought I was Patricia." Her toes began to tap.

"Tricia and 'Nica should have come down with me to look at the racehorses."

"We are not allowed out of Daddy's sight!"

"Veronica!" Jamie Sue scolded.

"Sorry."

"Did you know that dark chestnut is over sixteen hands?" Little Frank continued. "I bet he's going to win the race!"

"You will not wager on the horse race." Jamie Sue sighed. "Robert, your children have lived around too many forts and too many soldiers."

As the train picked up steam and resumed full speed, a man with a dark brown wool suit and leather vest strolled into the car and down to their seats. "Mr. Fortune, may I have a word with you?"

Robert turned to Jamie Sue. "This is Mr. Vanborg, a railroad supervisor."

The man with a thick gray mustache tipped his round hat. "Actually, I'm the vice-president of the Fremont, Elkhorn, and Missouri Valley Railroad. I just happened to be in the Rapid City office when we got word of the attempted holdup. Mrs. Fortune, I want to thank you and the children personally for assisting in capturing the train robbers."

"Mr. Vanborg, I confess I thought only about protecting my children, not your railroad."

"I completely understand. Thank you for your courage, anyway." He leaned closer to Robert Fortune. "I thought perhaps we could step to the back of the car where we could have some privacy."

"Why don't you just sit down on the seat across from us?" Robert suggested. "Jamie Sue and I have never kept anything from each other. This way I won't have to repeat what you say word for word."

"Well . . . yes . . . certainly . . ." Vanborg perched himself on the edge of the leather seat across the narrow aisle. "Mr. Fortune, I believe in getting to the point. I'd like to hire you to go to work for the railroad."

Robert didn't even look back at his wife. "Thank you, Mr. Vanborg, but I'm not looking for a job."

"I'm glad for that. The unemployed are not always the most stable workers. But I do have an offer I'd like you to consider."

"What do you want my husband to do?" Jamie Sue asked.

"As you probably know, this route is new, just completed

right after Christmas. I'd like to hire you to be in charge of train security between Deadwood and Rapid City. It's our most troublesome division of the line, and often we have shipments from the mines. We need to be able to tell the mine owner this is the safest stretch of railway in the West."

"I suppose today's adventures will not help your reputation for safety," Jamie Sue offered.

"Yes and no," he replied. "Thanks to you folks, not one penny was lost, not one passenger hurt. We can't do anything to stop people from trying to rob our trains. However, we can do a lot to see that they don't succeed."

"And it would help you to hire the man who stopped the robbers today?" she asked.

"Precisely."

"You want me to ride shotgun for a train full of gold?" Robert asked.

"It's much broader than that. I see you as running the security operation. I'd want you to hire two men. Then you would set up a schedule where one of the three of you is on every train, providing the first line of defense against attacks."

"It sounds dangerous," Veronica added.

Vanborg glanced at the children. "It's no more dangerous than any lawman's job. I think once the word of what happened today gets around, there will be very few who want to take on the man who stopped the Wild Bunch."

"The Wild Bunch?" Patricia quizzed.

"That's what they like to call themselves."

"I never heard of them," Robert admitted. "They've actually been successful?"

"Mainly in Nevada and Wyoming," Vanborg reported.

33

"I understand your need, but I'm committed to helping out in a new family business," Robert declared. "I don't believe I could consider backing out without discussing it with all of them."

"Let me make the full proposal, then you and Mrs. Fortune and any others can think and pray about it for a while."

"Why did you say, 'pray about it'?" Jamie Sue quizzed. "Are you a Christian, Mr. Vanborg?"

He pulled off his hat and nodded, "Yes ma'am, I am. I sensed that about your husband as well. That's what makes me even more convinced he is the right man for the job. I don't need a violent man. I need a compassionate man that won't tolerate violence."

"I appreciate your explaining it that way," Jamie Sue said.

Vanborg pulled some folded papers out of his suit pocket. "Here's my offer. You would get an office in Deadwood and could share our office in Rapid City. It's very modern with a typewriting machine and all. That way you'll have one at either end of your run. Like I said, you would be able to hire any two men you want to work with you to rotate duty on every train that runs through the Black Hills. In exchange, we will pay your total expenses, furnish guns, ammunition, room, and board while away from home . . . plus . . ." he glanced over at the three children.

"It's alright, Mr. Vanborg, we don't keep secrets from our children either."

Vanborg cleared his throat. "I would like to offer you $350 per month and $250 a month for each assistant."

Jamie Sue sat back in the seat. "That's a lot of money."

"It's an extremely important position, and we need to hire the best man available. Plus, you and your family would have a free pass to ride on the Elkhorn, Fremont, and Missouri Valley Railroad any time you please," Vanborg added.

"That's a generous offer, Mr. Vanborg," Robert insisted. "But I do have a commitment to my family in Deadwood. It's not something I could back away from easily, even if I wanted to."

"Mr. Fortune, the mines in the Black Hills are some of the richest left in our country. We would like to be able to guarantee that gold is safe on the Fremont, Elkhorn, and Missouri Valley. But even more important to me, I don't want any women or children ever threatened or in peril as yours were today." Vanborg stood and replaced his hat. "I saw the results of your quick thinking. Anyone else will be pure speculation. I believe you are the exact person for the job. May I contact you in a few days in Deadwood?"

"Yes, but I'm not sure I'm your man," Robert replied.

"Where can I find you?" Vanborg asked.

Robert glanced over at Jamie Sue. "I'll either be at Fortune & Son Hardware . . . Fortune and Troop Lumberyard, or S. Houston Fortune's Telephone Exchange."

The nobby dressed, gray-haired man pulled out a white linen handkerchief and wiped his forehead. "My word, it sounds like your father and brothers run the whole town."

Robert leaned back against the stiff, slick leather rail car seat. "Oh no, Daddy and my brothers just own the businesses. It's my sister and my sisters-in-law that run the whole town."

CHAPTER TWO

Patricia, Veronica, and Little Frank had their faces pressed to the clear glass window as the train slowed down entering Deadwood.

"I don't see them yet," Veronica whined. Her straw hat tumbled off the back of her light brown hair as she scooted away from the window. She retied the green hat ribbon under her chin.

Little Frank tapped the baseball bat against the side of his worn brown boot. "Maybe they are all on the other side."

Patricia chewed her lower lip. "How many do you think will be waiting for us?"

"Everybody will be here. I just know it!" Veronica reached under her long white dress and tugged up her white socks.

Patricia checked her own socks and pulled at them even though they didn't need it. "I had a dream that everyone was waiting for us and there was a big parade for us down Main Street . . ." she began.

". . . and we were riding on top of a stagecoach pulled by . . ." Veronica interrupted.

Patricia waved her hands as she continued the dream, ". . . six white horses and Grandpa Brazos . . ."

Veronica bounced up and down on the heels of her shoes. ". . . was driving it and . . ."

"I was sitting right next to him!" Patricia triumphed.

"You were not. I was sitting next to him and you were next to me," Veronica insisted.

"Whoa!" Little Frank interjected. "You two even share

the same dreams?"

Patricia and Veronica glanced at each other and blushed. "Eh, sometimes . . ." Patricia murmured.

"Anyway," Veronica glanced out the window at brick buildings slowly passing by, "I'll bet everyone in the family will be waiting for us."

"Not everyone," Robert cautioned. "Remember, there are businesses to operate. They aren't going to close down the stores just to greet us at the train. We aren't coming for a visit. They'll get to see us most every day from now on."

Jamie Sue folded her lap blanket and stuffed it into the brown satchel. "I would guess Uncle Sammy, Aunt Dacee June, maybe Rebekah, and some of the older cousins will be there."

"How about Grandpa?" Little Frank pressed. "I bet I'm taller than him now."

"If he gets any more stooped, we'll all be taller than him," Jamie Sue offered. "If he's feeling well, he will certainly be here."

"Grandpa will," Veronica said.

"Grandpa is always the first to greet us," Patricia added.

Robert pulled various satchels out from under the seats. "Remember, we're three hours late. They have other chores to do, I'm sure, besides sit on a depot bench and wait for a train. So don't be disappointed if only a couple of them are waiting for us."

A whistle pierced the air. Steam flew from the sliding wheels and the steel tracks rattled as the train rumbled to a full stop.

"But the railroad telegraphed ahead and told them we were delayed." Veronica stared across the passenger-clogged aisle of the train.

Little Frank stared out the window toward the west. "Daddy, how come there is so much smoke in the gulch?"

Robert glanced at the buildings on Main Street. "Perhaps it's drifting down from the mines."

"It's not like living in the clear, clean air of the desert." Jamie Sue rubbed her eyes. She could feel the taut, dry skin of her cheeks and forehead.

Little Frank was last down the aisle, his baseball bat slung over his shoulder, a satchel clutched in his hand. "I don't remember this much smoke other times we've been here."

"Perhaps there is a fire." Veronica fingered the silver necklace draped around her neck.

"Most of the downtown buildings are now built of brick." Patricia seized her bag with both hands. "Grandpa told me fire wasn't as big a worry as it used to be."

Robert motioned back toward the seats. "Make sure we gathered up everything, then let's go find the Fortune family welcoming committee."

Jamie Sue, Veronica, and Patricia sat on the dark green painted wooden bench in front of the depot. Little Frank leaned against a street lamp pole when Robert stomped back from the baggage car.

"What's the matter, Daddy?" Veronica called out.

He rubbed his beard, then propped his hands on his hips. "Our trunks and suitcases are not on board the train. I can't believe the inefficiency of such an outfit. If I had a quartermaster do this to me, he'd be a private by now!" Robert fumed.

"At ease, Captain Fortune," Jamie Sue cautioned.

"This is no light matter!" he grumped.

"And there is absolutely nothing we can do about it," she countered.

"You mean, they lost all of our belongings?" Veronica gasped.

"I don't suppose they are lost." Jamie Sue's voice was soft. "They just aren't on this train."

"I can't believe this! Everything in my satchel is dirty and wrinkled," Patricia wailed.

Jamie Sue glanced around the platform and tried to smooth down the white lace yoke on her dress. "I'm sure our things will arrive on the next train."

"Do you see Uncle Sammy or Aunt Dacee June or anyone?" Little Frank pressed.

Robert surveyed the depot. "There doesn't seem to be a Fortune in sight."

In the distance, the rattle of fast-rolling wagons and the shouts of men could be heard.

Patricia rubbed her nose with the back of her hand. "This isn't the way I thought it would be." Veronica began rubbing her nose too.

Robert plucked up a satchel in each hand. "Let's walk over to the hardware. We can't expect they would just sit here all day long."

Thick clouds of gray smoke drifted down the White-wood Gulch. They gathered up suitcases and string-tied cartons, then hiked toward Main Street. They waited at the curb as a water wagon rumbled by them. Robert tugged down his hat and led the troupe across the empty dirt street.

A lone rig rumbled along behind them.

"Look in that carriage . . . it's Curly Mac . . ." Veronica called out.

"Who's that woman with him?" Patricia quizzed.

"It must be his aunt," Little Frank added. "Didn't you say he was going to visit his aunt?"

"Wearing a dance hall girl's dress?" Veronica sat the brown satchel at her feet. "No one's aunt is a dance hall girl!"

"She doesn't look too young," Jamie Sue said. "She looks older than I am."

"Mama, you're pretty enough to be a dance hall girl," Little Frank suggested.

"Thank you, young man, but I don't think beauty is a prerequisite for the job."

Robert began to hike up the boardwalk. "I'll bet Daddy Brazos is at the woodstove in the hardware."

"In June?" Veronica questioned.

"It's a cloudy day," he replied.

"Mostly smoke," Little Frank said.

The windows at Fortune & Son Hardware displayed everything from horseshoes to bathtubs, from cream separators to gold pans.

Robert crashed into the front door of the hardware when he turned the latch.

"What's the matter, Daddy?" Little Frank probed.

"It didn't open. The door's locked." Robert pushed his hat back and leaned into the glass. "I don't think there's anyone in there!"

"They probably closed down the store to come meet us

at the station!" Patricia exclaimed.

Veronica stood on her tiptoes and peered in. "No one was at the depot. Remember?"

Jamie Sue searched up and down the empty boardwalk. "Is it a holiday?"

Robert stepped into the dirt street. "No, and they didn't even put up their 'Closed' sign. Not all the employees were going to come greet us. I don't know why they closed the store."

"Are you sure we're in the right town?" Jamie Sue laughed as she slipped her arm into his. "Come on, let's go over to Abby's dress shop. She'll know where everyone is."

"Promise you won't tell Amber about Curly Mac?" Veronica scurried to keep up. "If she goes after him, we don't have a chance."

"She's too old." Patricia tugged on her earlobe, and her sister did the same.

"That's what you told me last summer when she stole Quintin Troop from me." Veronica transferred her satchel from one hand to the other.

Patricia sat her satchel down on the sidewalk. "From you? Quintin liked me."

"That's only because he thought you were me," Veronica purred.

As they waited on the boardwalk, a wagon full of men raced up the street from the badlands.

"What's happening?" Robert called out.

"There's a fire at the mill," one of the men shouted.

"Which mill?" Robert hollered, but the men were already out of shouting distance. He turned toward Jamie Sue. "One of the reduction mills at Lead must be on fire."

41

"And it all drifts right down the gulch?" she inquired.

"I suppose so." He led the family across the street toward Abby's Fine Paris Fashions dress shop.

Veronica stared in the window. "Look, Mama, at that beautiful green dress on the hanger. Can I have a dress like that some day?"

"Not until you can fill it out," Jamie Sue insisted.

"Tricia and 'Nica couldn't fill out that dress if they both got into it at the same time," Little Frank murmured.

The twins stuck out their tongues at their brother.

"You could fill it out, Mama," Patricia added.

"Don't embarrass me," she replied.

"Aunt Abby has such beautiful clothes," Patricia sighed.

"Amber fills out her dress," Little Frank muttered.

"Little Frank!" Jamie Sue scolded.

"Well, she does . . ."

"She's your cousin," his mother reminded him.

"Can I help it if all my girl relatives are so handsome?" he countered.

"Good reply, son," Robert said.

"Don't you school him in sweet talk, Robert Fortune!" Jamie lectured.

Little Frank tried the door. "It's locked, too, Daddy!"

All five stared through the glass window at the darkened, empty dress shop.

"What is going on?" Veronica sniveled. "Did everyone move and forget to tell us?"

"I know what it is. This is a charade. They are all gathered together to give us a surprise welcome." Patricia chewed on her lower lip for a moment. "It's just like that party you gave Mama when she turned thirty."

"Oh, yes," Veronica danced on the boardwalk. "We'll walk into the room and they'll jump out and yell, 'Surprise'!"

"What room?" Little Frank pressed. "Where are they all hiding?"

"At the Telephone Exchange!" Jamie Sue suggested. "They have that big foyer."

"That's two blocks away," Veronica moaned. "My satchel is getting heavy!"

"You tried to pack too many things," Patricia said.

"I packed the very same things you did!"

"Not exactly. I didn't pack a . . ."

"Tricia!" Veronica blurted out. "Don't you dare . . ."

"What are you two fussing about?" Jamie Sue pressed.

The answer came back as a duet. "Nothing."

"Come on," Robert insisted. "We can all make it two more blocks. Everyone be sure and look surprised." He glanced back down the street. The entire badlands were now totally obscured by smoke.

Little Frank trotted ahead of them, then turned around and walked backward. "Do you think they'll have orange punch and cake? We had orange punch and cake at Mama's surprise birthday."

Jamie Sue jogged to catch up with her husband's long strides. "Robert, don't you think this is going to extremes? If this is a Fortune brothers' joke, I think they've carried it too far."

He looped his arm in hers. "Brothers? You know Lil' Sis . . . I bet this was all her idea. We should have checked at the Telephone Exchange first thing."

"Maybe we should have hired a hack," Jamie Sue huffed.

Robert slowed down to let the girls catch up, their satchels in one hand and their straw hats in the other. "I haven't seen a wagon or a carriage go by since that one that was going up to the mill," he added.

"This reminds me of the time we had to run to catch the trolley in Denver," Little Frank said. "Maybe everyone is up at Lead fighting the fire."

"Lead is three or four miles up the canyon. I don't think Abigail or Dacee June would be out fighting a fire in Lead," Jamie Sue said.

"If Daddy Brazos is there, Lil' Sis is there." Robert resumed his trudge down the wooden sidewalk. "She won't let him go anywhere out of town without her any more."

"I've never seen a daughter so devoted to taking care of her father."

"The commitment is mutual," Robert murmured.

"Well, Rebekah is not one to fight fires," Jamie Sue said. "Fires are much too dirty." *I can't imagine soot on those beautiful fingernails of hers. Forgive me, Lord, that sounds so petty and jealous.*

"Rebekah has a tough streak . . . just like all the Fortune women," Robert said.

"If the Telephone Exchange is closed, are we goin' to hike up to Uncle Todd and Aunt Rebekah's?" Little Frank quizzed.

"That's seventy-two stair steps above Main Street!" Veronica whimpered. She stopped in a slump.

Patricia leaned her back against her sister's. "I'm tired, too, Daddy."

"I'm sure the Telephone Exchange is open . . ." he insisted. "Come on, it's just around the corner."

The blind was pulled on the glass-and-oak front door of the Deadwood-Lead Telephone Exchange. And, like the others, the door was bolted.

Robert Fortune and family trooped back out to the curb of the boardwalk. The girls collapsed on their satchels.

"What are we going to do now, Daddy?" Veronica asked.

"I think that fire must be getting worse," Little Frank reported. "The smoke is so thick we can't see the homes up on Forest Hill."

"Look, Daddy, here comes some men up the middle of the street," Patricia pointed back down Main Street.

Veronica scooted her satchel to the curb and sat facing the street. "It's like a parade!"

A string of twenty men, each carrying a bucket in one hand and a bottle of beer in the other, serpentined up the center of the street.

"Where are you headed?" Robert called out.

The lead man pulled off a greasy felt hat and staggered toward them, then shouted as if they were a hundred yards away, instead of ten feet. "We're goin' to fight the fire!" he hollered, almost tipping over backwards.

"Free beer at the Piedmont Saloon for all who fight the fire!" another shouted.

"I thought we was goin' to get a whole bucket of beer, but all we got was a bottle," a third reported.

"Where's the fire?" Robert questioned.

"At the mill!" another hollered.

"In Lead?"

"Shoot, mister, we ain't hikin' to Lead. This fire is right up there where the road turns toward Central City." He swayed and wobbled back to the column of volunteers.

"There's a reduction mill there?" It was as if Robert had swallowed a lit firecracker and was waiting for it to explode in the pit of his stomach.

"Reduction mill? Mister, it's the sawmill that's on fire."

The internal explosion went off. "Sawmill?" The word shot from his mouth like a Fourth of July cannon.

"Yeah, the one them Fortunes bought from Quiet Jim Troop. We hear it's burning to the ground and a-threatenin' to jump the yard to miner's hall and even the church."

"Oh, no!" Jamie Sue gasped.

The cortege of drunks continued their haphazard march up Main Street.

"That's our mill!" Little Frank moaned.

Patricia's tongue stuck out the side of her mouth and she chewed away. "What are we going to do, Daddy?"

"Go fight a fire," he replied.

"Do I have to carry this satchel?" Veronica pleaded. "I'm really tired, Daddy." There was no dance in her step.

"You and the girls stay here. Little Frank and I will . . ."

"Oh, no you don't. If we can kill snakes and catch train robbers, we can fight fires!" Jamie Sue blurted back. "You've made the point about the toughness of your family's women. We do not intend to be stranded on the streets of Deadwood while the rest of the family is in peril. Come on, girls, it's time to join the Fortunes of the Black Hills."

They were all winded by the time they rounded the corner by the Belmont Hotel and could see what was left of the Troop-Fortune Lumbermill and Yard. A tall, thin black smudge-faced woman with tangled hair half unpinned stared at the charred remains. Her hands, with grimy fingernails, were on her hips, and two small dirty boys were at her side.

"Is that Rebekah?" Jamie Sue whispered. "I've never in my life seen her dirty."

"Aunt Rebekah!" Patricia called. "What happened to our lumberyard?"

The woman spun around and a white-toothed smile glowed out from the grimy face.

"Veronica! Oh . . . Robert . . . Jamie Sue . . ." Rebekah started to cry.

"It's OK, Mama," the taller of the two boys tried to console. "It's alright."

"Little Frank, take Stuart and Casey over to those white-wood trees for a minute. . . . Show them your baseball bat and your leather glove," Robert motioned. Then he held out his arms to his sister-in-law.

"I'm filthy," Rebekah whimpered.

"Who cares?" Robert grabbed her and held her tight. "What happened, darlin'?" he asked as Jamie Sue stepped up and also hugged her weeping sister-in-law.

Tears cut furrows into the grime on Rebekah's high, square cheek bone. "There was an explosion in the sawdust burner. It just blew up like dynamite, scattering flames all over the mill."

Even in the heat and smoke of the dying cinders, Robert felt a chill run down his back. "Who got hurt?"

"No one seriously, praise God. That part was a miracle. Some of the men were singed bad and some were hit with flying boards, but no one has reported anything more than a broken arm so far." Rebekah took the blue bandanna Robert offered her and began to wipe her eyes and cheeks.

"What do you mean, so far?" Patricia asked.

"Oh . . . girls!" Rebekah clapped her hand over her chapped, dirty mouth. "You are so grown-up looking!" She held out her arms and they scooted next to her.

"What did you mean, no one is hurt so far?" Veronica echoed the challenge.

"There's always a possibility someone was at the mill we don't know about. Todd's trying to determine that now."

Patricia chewed on her lip. "You mean they could have burnt up, Aunt Rebekah?"

"Oh, no, I'm sure there was no one else there." She stared at the boys by the trees. "Stuart and Casey spent yesterday down at the mill with Todd. I shudder to think what would have happened if the fire was yesterday." She began to cry again and tried to hold the tears back with the bandanna.

"The 'what ifs' of life will drive us insane," Robert counseled. "It's only a mill. The family is safe."

"That's exactly what Todd said. We didn't even try to put out the mill, just kept it from spreading," Rebekah added. "It's been a gruesome afternoon."

"We've had quite a day as well," Jamie Sue said.

"We heard there was a hold-up attempt on the train," Rebekah replied.

"Yes, and then this man from the railroad offered Robert . . ."

"Enough of that," Robert interrupted. "We'll have plenty of time for talk later. What can we do to help?" he asked.

"I think there's nothing left but to make sure the fire doesn't start back up." Rebekah surveyed the ruins, then her eyes rested on the boys by the aspens. "How did Little Frank get so tall? I can't believe how much he looks like a young Todd," she added.

Jamie Sue pointed at the taller of Rebekah's boys. "And your Stuart looks so much like Robert."

"I know it. Todd often forgets and calls him Bobby."

"Which Fortune do I look like, Aunt Rebekah?" one of the twins asked.

"Why, darling . . . you look . . . you look identical to . . . Patricia!"

"Aunt Rebekah, I am Patricia."

A wide, relaxed smile broke across Rebekah's dirty face. "You see, I'm right."

A fortyish-looking gray-haired man, with a dirty white shirt, no tie or suit coat, and an empty wooden bucket jogged up toward them. "If it isn't the Fortunes of Arizona! Just like little brother to show up after all the hard work is done."

"Sammy, you look like the time you got stuck under Lesa Bufford's front porch with that family of mad raccoons," Robert greeted.

Samuel Fortune threw an arm around his brother's shoulder and purposely rubbed soot on Robert's forehead. "The raccoons were nothin' next to the whippin' ol' man Bufford gave me when I finally crawled out."

Veronica's blue eyes widened. "Really?"

Samuel stepped back and surveyed the twins. "Say, Bobby, you didn't introduce me to these two fancy ladies from Paris."

Patricia bit her lip, then giggled. "It's me and Veronica, Uncle Sammy!"

Samuel pushed back his hat and spread open his arms. "Patricia? Veronica? I can't believe it! You both look so charming and mature."

"Uncle Sammy, don't you try to sweet-talk us. We know all about you!" Veronica giggled.

"You do?"

"Yes," Patricia continued. "Mama said if we ever meet a boy like Daddy we should marry him, and if we meet one who reminds us of Uncle Sammy, we should run the other direction."

Sam laughed. "You've got a very wise Mama."

"That wasn't exactly the way I worded it," Jamie Sue protested.

With one arm around Robert's shoulders and the other around Jamie Sue's, Samuel stared at the ruins. "Well, little brother . . . what do you think about the lumberyard? Think you can make a go of it?"

"Sammy, it's not a laughin' matter," Rebekah protested.

"Rebekah, darlin', Fortune men aren't very good at cryin', so we might as well laugh. Right, Bobby?" Samuel insisted.

Robert studied the ruins and shook his head. "You're right about that."

Samuel Fortune dropped his arms and turned to the twins. "Amber took most all the other kids up to the school-yard. Do you want to go up there?"

"Can we, Daddy?" Veronica asked.

"Take Little Frank and the boys with you. We'll be up in a bit," Robert instructed.

All five children scampered down a smoke-filled Main Street.

To the north, clumps of bucket-toting men huddled around smoldering ashes. Two dark-haired ladies, soot-covered and sweaty, scurried out of the alley.

"Bobby! Jamie Sue!" the younger called out as she threw her arms around Robert's neck and planted a sooty kiss on his cheek.

He hugged her tight, then pulled back. "Well, Lil' Sis, I do believe you have a slight smudge on your face."

Jamie Sue hugged the other woman. "Abby, it looks like you've had an exciting day."

"It started out peaceful enough. We all hiked down to the depot right before noon to meet lil' brother and his family," she explained.

"And she does mean everyone . . ." Samuel added. "Abby actually had Garrett's cowlick combed down and his face clean. Rebekah had her gang slicked up like military school cadets."

"Sammy, don't exaggerate . . ."

"Lil' Sis and Carty even dressed up those three little princesses of theirs."

"Where are your girls now?" Jamie Sue asked Dacee June.

"Thelma Speaker and Louise Edwards are with them."

"Anyway," Sam continued, "Daddy shaved, washed his hair, and put on a new boiled shirt for the occasion."

"How's he doin', Sammy?" Robert pressed.

"Oh, you know Daddy." Samuel stared down at his dirty boots. "He just keeps goin', no matter how he feels."

Robert turned to Dacee June. "How's Daddy really doing?"

The near-permanent smile dropped off Dacee June's face. Her chin sagged. "He hurts every time he takes a breath, Bobby. You can see it in his face and his eyes. He doesn't hike up to Forest Hill any more."

"Is that apartment over the hardware workin' out for him?"

"Yes, but some mornings Todd comes in and Daddy's asleep on the cot by the woodstove. He couldn't make it up one flight of stairs the night before." Tears trickled down her cheeks.

Robert clutched Jamie Sue's hand. *Did I come to Deadwood just to watch Daddy die? Lord, maybe that's the real reason You drew us to this place.*

"I trust you all are speaking kindly of me!"

A tall man with grayish-brown goatee and mustache strolled toward them.

Todd Fortune slipped an arm around Jamie Sue. She kissed his cheek. "Jamie Sue, where are Little Frank and the girls?"

She squeezed his hand. "At the school with the others, Todd."

Todd stared out at the smoldering embers and slapped Robert's shoulder. "Well, lil' brother, just think . . . it's all yours!"

"From the description in your letters, I was expecting it to be in a little better shape."

"Oh, no," Todd protested. "Didn't I tell you it would need a little work?"

"Little? I don't think there is one thing that is salvageable!"

"The dirt didn't burn," Samuel laughed. "You still got the dirt, Bobby."

Todd glanced back at the women. "I suppose they told you about us all waitin' for you?"

"I was just describing it," Rebekah said.

"Twenty of us were lined up at the depot when word came about a delay." Todd pulled out a clean white handkerchief and handed it to Rebekah. She returned Robert's bandanna. "Something about a hold-up attempt?"

"What happened?" Samuel asked.

It was the first time Robert noticed he was the only one wearing a gun. "Three old boys tried to rob the train, that's all. But they were dispatched quickly enough."

"Who stopped them?" Abigail asked.

"The Robert Fortune family," Jamie Sue explained.

"No foolin'?" Samuel laughed. "Who were the hombres?"

"They called themselves the Wild Bunch," Robert explained. "I never heard of them. They aren't friends of yours, are they?"

"Oh, no, not those." Abby stepped over and slipped her arm into Samuel's. "That's the bunch of rustlers that hang around over near Sundance, Wyoming."

"Are those the ones you stopped?" Dacee June prodded.

"I reckon. But it was a family activity," Robert reported. "I clobbered one, the kids coldcocked the second, and Mama here shot the third one."

Dacee June turned to Jamie Sue. "You did? You shot one! I think every Fortune woman has shot an outlaw, except me!"

"They're all afraid of you, Lil' Sis," Samuel teased.

Jamie Sue dropped her chin and spoke softly. "I shot him in the foot. He was harassing my children."

"And you didn't even have to use the flying fist of death?" Samuel teased.

Todd sucked in a big breath. "Don't you two start in with the dime novel parody."

"No sir," Robert added. "We won't argue with our big brother."

"Bobby!" It was the shout of an old man.

Robert spun around. The man's hair was pure white, his shoulders slumped, his big hands hung at his sides. The wrinkles around his eyes were leathery tough. *Oh, Lord, he looks so tired. So very worn out and tired.*

But his eyes danced.

"Daddy!" Robert met him with a handshake, then a big hug. When they pulled back, Brazos Fortune wiped his eyes with thick calloused fingers. "That blasted smoke's been makin' my eyes water all afternoon."

"Hi, Daddy Brazos."

He stepped over and hugged his daughter-in-law. "Jamie Sue . . . you haven't changed one iota in fifteen years! Still the pride of the men of the Texas Camp. Where are Little Frank and my twins?"

"At the schoolhouse with the others."

"Well, if you grown-ups will excuse me . . . I've got me some grandkids to hug." He turned and shuffled back across the street. He stopped to let a water wagon pass, then turned back. "Welcome to Deadwood, Bobby."

"Thanks, Daddy," Robert replied.

"I've been waitin' for this day for a long time!"

"So have we."

The old man reached up and brushed across his eyes. "It's that lousy smoke," he called out.

"He seems old," Jamie Sue murmured.

"He is old," Todd offered.

"He's only 65," Dacee June added.

"Sixty-five hard years of chasin' cattle rustlers, runnin' Union blockades, gunfights with outlaws, Indians, frigid streams, and burnin' deserts," Todd said.

Samuel pulled off his hat and watched the old man in the distance round the corner. "Plus, losin' a wife, twin daughters, and a ranch that he dearly loved didn't help either."

"Daddy will do alright. He's got us all together. He's been praying for that since the day Mama died," Dacee June said.

"Well, we're all here now," Rebekah added. "But I do believe what he likes most of all is having the grandkids together."

"Where's Carty?" Robert asked.

"He just took the men and went back to open the hardware," Todd reported. "We were going to leave it closed for the day, but the hourly help needs the wages, so Carty said he'd open it."

The three Fortune boys, their wives, and sister Dacee June stared out at the rubble that had once been Troop-Fortune Lumbermill and Yard.

"What a mess, Bobby. I'm not sure what the Lord is tryin' to tell us. You can work with me at the hardware until we get her rebuilt, of course," Todd offered. "It might take a few months to get it goin'."

"I think the Lord's tellin' you to take that job with the

railroad," Jamie Sue blurted out.

"What job?" Samuel asked.

"I already told them no," Robert replied.

Jamie Sue slipped her arm in his. "You told him you'd pray about it."

"What are you two discussin'?" Todd pressed.

"It was nothin' . . ." Robert insisted.

"Why are you talkin' that way?" Jamie Sue stepped back, her hands on her hips. "It was a very good offer, and you know it, Robert Fortune."

Rebekah slipped her fingers into Todd's and tugged him toward the street. "Would you two like for us to take a walk so you can discuss this mystery?"

Robert's reply was tense, curt. "Jamie Sue, we will talk about this later."

Her reply was fiery, determined. "I don't know what the big secret is."

"Whatever it is, Jamie Sue, this is probably not a good time," Todd reasoned. "You're tired from a long trip, movin' your family, an attempted hold-up, and now the mill burned to the ground. It's a natural reaction to be edgy."

She glared at the tallest of the brothers. "Todd Fortune, are you calling me short-tempered and pushy?"

"Jamie Sue . . ." Robert hollered.

"I'm talking to your brother," she snapped.

"And I'm talking to you!" Robert blared.

"Whoa . . ." Abby slipped her arm into Samuel's. "I don't know about anyone else. But I'm beat, and I need a bath. The mill is gone, but we've saved the rest of the town, which is quite a rare feat for this narrow gulch. Let's all meet at the Merchant's Hotel for supper." She tugged her husband toward Main Street.

"That sounds wonderful," Rebekah added as she and Todd inched along behind them. "We had better go relieve dear Amber from her baby-sitting."

"And I've got to get back to my babies . . ." Dacee June added. She waltzed over and grabbed her brother's hand. "Bobby, you and Jamie Sue come with me. I'm sure Mrs. Edwards wants to personally give you a tour of your new home."

"Wait a minute!" Jamie Sue bellowed. Her face flushed. Her temple drawn tight. "Is this the way it's going to be? I want to discuss something and everyone shuts me out? My opinion gets totally ignored? I don't even get to complete a sentence?"

"You've had a long day, darlin'." Robert tugged at her arm. "Let's go look at our new house."

She turned to the others and roared, "Robert was offered a very good job by the railroad to supervise security between here and Rapid City that would pay him $350 a month and expenses and a staff, but he won't consider it because he feels obligated to his family, to work for you."

"Jamie Sue!" Robert barked. "I said we'd talk about that later."

She folded her arms across her chest and glared back. "Well, I talked about it now!"

Robert stomped off toward the burning embers, stared up at the smoky clouds, sighed, then jammed his hands into the front pockets of his light wool trousers.

"Oh, no you don't, Robert Fortune." Jamie Sue paced after him. "Don't you go into that silent routine with me!"

Samuel Fortune began to laugh.

"Sammy, that's very rude," Abigail insisted.

Samuel glanced over at Todd. "Isn't this the way he always was?"

Todd nodded. "Sammy's right. Bobby argues, clams up, goes off and thinks about it, then comes back with his mind made up. Just like Mama."

Jamie Sue's eyes widened. She paused and turned back toward the others. "Really? He's always been this way? We've been married fifteen years, and you never told me that before. Your mother acted the same way?"

"All Fortune women are strong-willed and spirited and handsome . . ." Samuel replied.

"And all the Fortune men are stubborn, opinionated, and . . ." Dacee June added.

"And sweet talkers?" Rebekah finished.

"You can say that again," Abby grinned.

"Are you telling me things like this happen to you guys too?" Dacee June asked.

"Arguments?" Rebekah asked. "You better believe it."

"Shouting, yelling arguments?" Abigail added. "Honey, I was an actress too many years to be demure or shy. Why do you think Sammy and I live out of town?"

"And I thought Carty and I were the only ones who ever disagreed."

"You mean Carty Toluca has actually disagreed with his darlin' Dacee June on somethin'?" Samuel jibed.

"I don't always get my way," Dacee June insisted.

"Now that must have come as quite a shock," Todd grinned.

"Alright . . . you two are ganging up on me." She looked

out at Robert, still by himself near the water-soaked ashes of the lumberyard. "Bobby, I need your help. They're picking on me! Bobby!" Dacee June's voice turned into a high-pitched whine.

Slowly, Robert Fortune turned around. His arms dangled at his sides. He shook his head and let out a long, deep breath. "This is really going to be just like old times, isn't it?"

"Some of them were good ol' times, Bobby . . ." Samuel insisted.

Robert stepped back over to Jamie Sue. "I guess I am kind of bound up and tired. Forgive me for snappin' at you."

"I'm sorry, too, Bobby. I guess I'm more nervous than I thought about moving to Deadwood," Jamie Sue admitted.

"Nervous?" Rebekah questioned.

"Well . . . you see how these Fortune boys act. They know exactly their place in family life. And Dacee June has her role clearly defined. You and Abby have been living here long enough to find your place too . . . but I'm the last."

"You were the first of us to become Mrs. Fortune," Rebekah said.

"But the last to move in with the clan."

"Jamie Sue, you are our example of the ideal wife and mother," Rebekah insisted. "For fourteen years I've tried to live up to your standards."

"You're kidding me? You . . . you're . . ."

"Older? Yes, I am. But the way you take care of Robert . . . the way you raise Little Frank and the girls . . . well, it's quite a tough act to follow," Rebekah continued. "I have to admit, I feel a little intimidated having you in town."

"Now you're trying to sweet-talk me just like the boys."

"You'll never know how many times I've heard, 'That's nice, but I don't reckon Jamie Sue would do it that way,'" Rebekah replied.

"I . . . I can hardly believe that," Jamie Sue murmured.

"You two think you have it bad?" Abigail added. "Look at me. On the one hand is the stylish Rebekah Jacobson from Chicago . . . on the other, the model mother Jamie Sue Milan. And then there is Dacee June Fortune, the uncontested queen of the Black Hills. Now, how on earth do I compete with that?"

Jamie Sue shrugged. "I guess we all have adjusting to do. I am really sorry for blowing up in front of everyone. Maybe I am just too exhausted."

"That's completely understandable," Rebekah added. "Now, do you want us to leave so you can kiss and make up?"

Abby's smile would have lit up an opera house full of grumpy old men. "That's always the best part, isn't it?"

"Carty and I always . . . whoa . . . I mean . . . forget it!" Dacee June's face blushed.

"Lil' Sis always was demure and shy, wasn't she?" Samuel laughed.

"You all don't need to leave." Jamie Sue marched straight over to Robert and threw her arms around his neck. "I'm sorry for blurting everything out." Then she pressed her wide full lips into his.

"Quick!" Samuel hollered. "Get me another bucket of water, Todd, I think little brother's about to ignite!"

"Jamie Sue . . ." Robert protested. "I forgive you. Maybe

we should wait until . . ."

"Wait to argue . . . wait to make up," Abby teased. "I'm glad I married the Fortune who doesn't wait for anything!"

"I think we should all wait until supper," Todd added. "How does six o'clock sound?"

"You make sure Daddy Brazos comes with you," Samuel insisted.

"Oh, no," Todd replied. "I'll have the twins insist that he come. There's no way on earth he could turn them down for anything."

"Sometimes he does treat them as if they were his own Veronica and Patricia," Jamie Sue concurred.

"I can guarantee you in Daddy Brazos's mind, they are his twins," Todd added.

Louise March Driver Edwards gave them a tour of her former Ingleside home, a block away from where she now lived with her sister, Thelma. She led them through the backyard, naming each plant her husband had so carefully planted.

"It is my great delight to sell this house to you and Jamie Sue. It's like keeping it in the family."

"There has never been a time, Mrs. Edwards, when you and your sister weren't part of our lives. You were Mama's best friends . . . you were there when Jamie Sue and I met . . . you've looked after Daddy . . . and mothered and grand-mothered all of us. You are family."

Louise's dark brown hair showed no sign of gray. She reached up and pushed the tears back from the corners of her eyes. "Robert, you have your mama's spirit, through and through. I never knew a woman in my whole life who could lift me up and make me glad to be alive like Sarah Ruth."

"We'll take good care of your place," Jamie Sue insisted.

"Oh, no, it's not my place now. It is the Fortune home."

Robert and Jamie Sue walked with Louise toward Lincoln Street in front of the house. "There are other houses around town that are called Fortune houses. We've decided this should always be called the Edwards house."

Shoulders back, chin raised, Louise Edwards paused. "Grass . . . I mean, the Professor, would like that. You boys and Dacee June were the only 'children' he ever had." Louise patted his hand, before continuing her stroll.

"Would you like me to walk you home?" Robert asked.

"My heavens, no, I'm not that old . . . yet."

When Robert and Jamie Sue returned to the living room, the twins sprawled on the box bench windowsill.

Veronica pressed her nose against the glass and stared up and down Lincoln Street. "Mama, we really like this house."

Patricia sat with hands folded and chewed her tongue. "Do you like it, Mama?"

"I think it's perfect for us!" Jamie Sue said. "I didn't know that we were buying so much furniture in the purchase price."

"Mrs. Edwards was very generous," Robert replied.

"And no wonder, what glowing things you told her." Jamie Sue eased down on the charcoal gray sofa.

"They were all true," he insisted.

"And that, Mr. Fortune, is exactly why we have so many

pieces of furniture left to us." She patted the sofa seat and he sat down next to her.

Veronica rocked back and forth on her knees. "We don't have any beds or dressers."

"Mrs. Edwards never had anything but her sewing supplies up in your room. We'll all go shopping tomorrow and see what we can find," Jamie Sue announced.

Veronica spun around and plopped down beside her sister. "We want French provincial furniture, with separate four-poster beds and matching wardrobes painted white with gold trim," she blurted out, keeping time with each word by tapping both shoes on the hardwood floor.

Jamie Sue surveyed the high ceiling of her new living room. "You will get one bed . . . comfortable and sturdy, and well within our budget, and share a wardrobe as you did in Arizona."

"Mother . . ." Patricia paused and wrinkled her nose. "When do we get separate things?"

Immediately Veronica wrinkled her nose also.

"When you get married," Robert grinned.

Veronica sighed. "But we'll have to share a wardrobe even then!"

"There are worse things in life. You wear each other's clothes every day of the year. Why would you need to separate them?" Jamie Sue challenged.

"You just don't understand what it's like to be an identical twin," Veronica whimpered.

"Of course I don't. I never will. But some day you will both understand what it's like to be a mother."

Little Frank ran into the living room. "I really like my room! I have my own door to the back porch. I can go outside without . . . eh, bothering anyone."

"What you mean is, you can go outside without anyone knowing it," Robert said.

"Yeah . . . that too. Can I go look around the neighborhood? I think I saw a boy my age. Maybe he plays baseball."

Veronica jumped up and brushed her bangs out of her eyes. "What did he look like?"

Little Frank jammed his hands in the back pockets of his brown ducking trousers. "He didn't have blond curly hair."

"Maybe we should go for a walk too." Patricia brushed the bangs out of her eyes.

"You girls know the rules. You need to stay where I can . . ."

"Robert!" Jamie Sue corrected.

He ran his fingers through the back of his hair and could feel the tense neck muscles. "Mama's right. We live in town now. Things will be different. Be careful. I don't have to keep you in sight, . . . but you girls keep each other in sight. Look after each other. That's the special blessing of being a twin."

All three children scooted toward the front door.

"Can we walk with you, Little Frank?" Veronica asked.

His baseball bat over his shoulder, he paused at the doorway. "No, that would spoil everything. You two stay way back and pretend you don't know me," he insisted.

"Why?" Patricia prodded.

Little Frank trudged out to the porch. "I don't want to scare the boys off on our first day."

In unison with her sister, Veronica folded her arms across her chest. "Are you saying we're so ugly we'd scare boys off?"

"No, just the opposite," he shouted back as he scooted down the sidewalk. "You two are so pretty, most boys will be too embarrassed even to talk to me."

Veronica stuck her head back into the living room. "You're right, Mama, all the Fortune boys are sweet talkers."

Jamie Sue took Robert's hand. "Well, Mr. Fortune, I do think the children are adjusting quickly."

"How about you?" he questioned.

"I think we've found a home."

"I felt the same thing. In fifteen years of army life we've lived in twenty different houses, none of which felt like home. But this one . . . the minute I walked into the living room, I knew it was home." He glanced at the oak stairway that led to the second floor. "We will need to get the girls a bed."

"We can make pallets on the floor tonight."

"This has been a long day, Mrs. Fortune. It's like a life-time of adventures in only eight hours. I still can't believe that the lumber mill burned down on the day we arrived in town."

"And I can't believe we got into an argument in front of your family the minute we got off the train. I feel mortified about that."

"I didn't realize how nervous I was about being in the same town as Daddy Brazos and my brothers. For all my life I've been 'little brother,' the one who could never quite compete with them. That's one reason I joined the army: they didn't. I was on my own, with no constant compar-isons. But now . . . I feel like the little brother having to prove myself again."

"You remember the advice you gave me this afternoon?" she challenged.

"To just be yourself?"

"Yes. Well now, Mr. Robert Fortune, it's your turn."

He leaned his head against the back of the sofa. "What does that mean?"

Jamie Sue stood and paced the polished wood floor. "If your family didn't live in Deadwood and you were moving us up here and had that conversation with Mr. Narborg about the railroad job, and then got to town and found your previous job burned to the ground, what would you do?"

"I'd take the railroad job, of course. It's the kind of thing I would enjoy. But my family *is* here," he replied.

"Robert, if you decide to operate a business in town, you will forever be comparing yourself to Todd and Sammy. If you work for the railroad, you can just be yourself, and maybe make a stand against lawlessness, which is your greatest passion in life."

He raised one thick, dark brown eyebrow. "Oh?"

"OK," she grinned, "your second greatest passion in life."

"I'd be away from you and the kids sometimes."

"I'm an army wife, with army kids. We know that Daddy has to be away from time to time," she replied. "At least you won't have three months' duty chasing Apaches through northern Mexico."

"And I will have a couple of deputies, so I can schedule myself to be home on important dates."

"I think it's a wonderful opportunity."

"It does seem to be a natural for me."

"It's ironic that the lumber mill burned down." She paused her pacing. "Almost as if it were the Lord's timing. You don't suppose He burns down buildings, do you?"

Robert reached out and took her hand. "I don't think so."

She held onto his fingers. "So, are you going to take the job?"

"Yes, I believe so." He tugged her over until she sat on his knee.

"Believe so?" She slipped her arm around his neck. "You mean, you'll take it if your family gives you permission? Robert, you need to decide on your own. Don't ask them what you should do. Tell them what you decided."

His arm encircled her waist. "Jamie Sue . . ."

"Oh, are we going to start up where we left off downtown?"

"Jamie Sue, I cannot be the way you want me to be. I am the youngest son in a family that dominates western South Dakota. I have to do this my way. No decision I make is completely separate from my family."

She remained perched on his knee. "Do you promise to decide what you know in your heart to be right?"

He reached over and brushed a strand of her brown hair out of her eyes. "I promise you."

"Then I will accept that." She held his hand to her cheek. His calloused fingers felt warm.

"Thank you," he replied.

"You're welcome."

Jamie Sue started to giggle.

"Is something funny?"

"Why is it we couldn't have this nice friendly discussion in the presence of your family, instead of yelling and pouting at each other?"

"We didn't yell and pout," he insisted.

"We most certainly did."

"That is not what I call yelling and pouting."

Jamie Sue leaned back but kept his hand at her cheek. "What do you call it?"

"We were a tad argumentative and surly."

"Which is a man's way of saying 'yell and pout'?"

He smiled. "That's correct."

She looped both hands around his thick, muscular neck. "Is it time to kiss and make up?"

"I think you took care of that in public."

"Oh, no, Robert Fortune, you promised we would wait to kiss and make up in private! Everyone knows that Fortune men always keep their word. And this is very, very private."

"Well, if you put it that way, I guess I'll have to . . ."

"Have to?" she pulled away.

"Eh, want to."

"Really want to?"

"Really, really, really want to."

She snuggled back up to where her lips were within two inches of his. "That's better . . ."

His lips had just pressed against hers, and she was wishing they had closed the living room curtains and locked the front door, when there was a stiff knock.

They jumped to their feet. Jamie Sue brushed down her dress.

"Is that the kids?" he probed.

Jamie Sue peeked out the front window. "It's someone with a freight wagon."

"Is the railroad bringing our trunks? Maybe they have them after all." Robert swung the front door open to find a short man with broad shoulders. Another man waited out near the team of mules that were hitched to the wagon.

"Are you the new Fortunes?" he asked.

"I suppose you could say that. I'm Robert Fortune."

The man glanced down at the invoice. "I'm lookin' for a Miss Veronica Ruth Fortune and Miss Patricia Sarah Fortune."

"They aren't home at the moment," Jamie Sue explained.

"I've got a big delivery here from Central Furniture," the man announced. "Shall we bring it in through the front door?"

Robert rubbed his clean-shaven chin. It felt flushed. "I don't think we ordered anything yet."

"No, sir . . . these items was paid for by Brazos Fortune. He said the girls were his daughters, or maybe it was granddaughters; he wasn't too clear on that."

"They are our daughters . . . his granddaughters. Just exactly what do you have?" Jamie Sue asked.

The man began to read the invoice in his hand. "Two spring boards, two feather mattresses, four feather pillows, two pink comforters and matching pillow slips . . . two mirrored dressers, two wardrobe closets and two four-poster beds."

Jamie Sue's mouth dropped open. "They wouldn't happen to be in French provincial, painted white with gold trim?"

"Yep, them is the ones. What room do you want them set up in?"

CHAPTER THREE

Jamie Sue's perfectly parted brown hair was curled and pinned above each ear. "Well, Mr. Railroad Inspector, are you ready for your first day at work?"

Robert stopped by the cook stove and planted a soft kiss behind her ear. There was a strong aroma of rose perfume. "It's not exactly like the first day of school." He strolled over to the doorway to the dining room.

"You're right. I didn't have to pack a lunch bucket for you." Jamie Sue scooted by carrying a copper pan with a hotpad. "I do wish I had my serving dishes."

Robert carefully hung his gray suit coat on the back of the chair. "It is somewhat ironic that we left the army to have more time together as a family, and on my first day of work I'm going to be gone for a couple of days," he murmured.

"It is logical that they need you to set things up at Rapid City." Jamie Sue fluttered back to the kitchen, taking the rose fragrance with her. "Besides, you aren't facing renegade Chirachuas, but railroad rules and bookkeepers," she called out.

Robert took a deep breath of crisp fried bacon. "I'd rather face the Indians."

She waltzed back in carrying a napkin-covered basket of biscuits. "It should be a pleasant enough trip. You don't have to take control of train security for a week or so. Let's sit down. There's no telling when the children will get up. I thought they should get their sleep this morning."

The back door slammed shut as Little Frank sprinted into

the dining room.

"Slow down and wash your hands, then come eat," Robert insisted.

Little Frank disappeared into the kitchen. "Guess where I've been?" he called out.

"In the backyard, I presume?" his mother answered.

Little Frank appeared at the doorway, towel in hand. "No, I was down at the livery and . . ."

Jamie Sue laid her fork on her plate. "You were where?"

Little Frank scooted into the chair between his mother and father. "Down at the Montana Stables and . . ."

"At 7:00 A.M.?" Jamie Sue challenged.

"Actually, I was down there at daylight and . . ."

Jamie Sue took the milk pitcher and poured Little Frank's glass full. "Wait a minute . . . you took off downtown and didn't tell your parents?"

Little Frank scooped out a large mound of scrambled eggs. "I hollered at you, Mama. Would you please pass the Tabasco?"

His mother passed the hot sauce. "When did you holler at me?"

"About 5:30."

"You yelled at me at 5:30 in the morning?" his mother challenged.

The bite of eggs towered out of his fork and into his mouth. "Yeah, didn't you hear me?" he mumbled.

Jamie Sue took a sip of strong, bitter coffee. "I couldn't hear a stick of dynamite if it exploded under my bed at 5:30 in the morning!"

Little Frank waved his empty fork as he talked. "Daddy was already gone down to the hardware. So I headed that way but met up with Quintin Troop and he . . ."

"What about Quintin?" Patricia, clad in pink cotton robe and matching slippers, scooted into the dining room. Her long brown hair hung down her back, almost to her waist.

Little Frank clanked down his fork and rubbed his long, thin nose. "I was just saying that Quint and I . . ."

"Quint? Do you really call him Quint?" Patricia quizzed.

"Will you let me finish the story?"

"I wonder if he'd get mad if I called him Quint?" she replied.

"I can't imagine Quintin getting angry about anything," Robert offered. "He's too much like his daddy." He motioned for Patricia to pass the pomegranate jelly.

Veronica, clad in pink robe and matching slippers, brown hair combed out and hanging almost to her waist, scurried up to the table. "Who is like his father?"

"We're talking about Quint . . ." Patricia grinned.

"Quintin Troop? You call him Quint?" Veronica gasped.

"This conversation doesn't seem be going anywhere," Jamie Sue protested. "Sit down. Now that we're all here, Daddy can pray a blessing for the day."

When Robert finished, Little Frank spooned into a bowl of grits. "Quint and I swung by the livery so I could show him the racehorses . . ."

"You're wearing my robe," Veronica challenged her sister, who sat next to her.

"I am not. This is my robe," Patricia insisted.

"Girls!" Jamie Sue scolded. "Little Frank is telling us something."

Little Frank gulped down a fat wad of grits. "We thought we would just peek at the horses, but the trainer was exercising them and we got to see the way they . . ."

"That is too my robe. This one has a tea stain on the cuff. See?" Veronica held up her arm. "You were the one that put your arm in the tea yesterday."

"Yes, but I was wearing your robe when I did it because you had taken my robe."

"I did not!"

"Yes you did. When Grandpa brought them over, he gave me the first robe out of the box. And when we carried them up the stairs and laid them on the bed, you switched robes."

"I did not." Veronica had one small spoonful of eggs on her large, otherwise-empty plate.

"You know you did. So the robe I got the tea on is not my robe but your robe and . . ."

"Girls!" Robert barked. "This is the silliest discussion I have ever heard in my life. Sit still. Eat more than one bite of eggs. And let your brother finish his story."

Little Frank took a slice of bacon in his fingers, folded it into a small square, then crammed the whole piece in his mouth. "Ehfm, knin mmgn . . ."

"Wait until you chew that bite," Jamie Sue insisted.

"Say, Mama, how would you like to go with me to Rapid City for a couple days," Robert teased.

"I'd love to. The children will have to fend for themselves." Jamie Sue took another sip of coffee.

"What?" Veronica gasped.

"We're teasing," Robert explained. "But I want you to mind your mama and be helpful while I'm away. Little Frank, stop eating for a minute and finish your story."

"The horse trainer said he was promised a one-mile

horse track to race the horses on if he brought them to Deadwood."

"But we don't have a mile-long horse track," Robert pressed.

"Exactly." Little Frank glanced across the table. " 'Nica, are you goin' to eat that bacon?"

"No."

"Yes, she is," Jamie Sue announced.

"Well," Little Frank continued, "the trainer is going to have to extend the track. Homestake Mine is furnishing the property free, but he has to clear it, level it, and put in some guardrails. He said if me and Quint help him for the next couple of weeks, he'll let us use the grounds for baseball after the horse racing is over. Won't that be swell to have a full-size field?"

"So, this man gets you two boys to work for free? What kind of man would employ child labor and refuse to pay them?" Jamie Sue said.

"But, Mama, we would be gettin' paid. We have us a nice baseball field. We work for two weeks and we have a place to play baseball all summer. That's a good deal, isn't it?"

She glanced over at her husband. "Robert?"

"I don't reckon it could hurt. He can't work at the lumber mill. So a little physical work and experience working with others won't hurt any."

Jamie Sue surveyed the bite piled on her fork. "I don't like the thought of him hanging around with horse-race gamblers. No telling what bad habits he could be exposed to." She took a deep breath, then crammed the grits into her mouth.

"That gambling crowd won't be out chopping brush and

shoveling dirt to make a longer horse track," Robert countered. "The only habits he'll learn will be an aching back and callouses on his hands."

"Yes, well, we do have some chores around the house. I'll expect you to continue with those," she lectured.

"Yes, ma'am. You mean, I can do it?"

"If Quintin does it too. I like having you boys work together."

"I haven't even seen Quintin since we've moved to Deadwood." Veronica's slippers tapped on the floor as she talked.

Jamie Sue scraped up another bite of grits as if it were foul-tasting medicine. "You could have gone over with me yesterday afternoon."

"My dress was dirty, and we don't have our trunks yet," Veronica complained.

"Daddy, will we get our trunks today?" Patricia asked.

Robert wiped biscuit crumbs off his neatly trimmed mustache. "That's the first thing I'm going to check on when I get to Rapid City."

"I think it's funny that Daddy went to work for the same railroad that lost our baggage," Little Frank added.

"The trunks are not lost. Just misplaced," Robert insisted.

Little Frank crammed his mouth with half a buttered biscuit, then jumped up. "Can I be excused, Mama? I want to go tell Quint that you'll let me help build the racetrack."

"Quiet Jim and Columbia have agreed to let Quintin participate, I presume?" Jamie Sue probed.

"Oh, no, he was afraid to ask them. But he said if you let me do it, then he knew they would too!" He scurried toward the back door.

"Little Frank, your father will be gone for two days," Jamie Sue called out.

Little Frank stuck his head back into the kitchen. "Bye, Daddy. Will you have to shoot any train robbers this time?"

Robert dipped his biscuit into the grits and honey. "I'm leaving that chore to your mother."

"She really surprised me when she did that," Little Frank added as he banged his way out onto the back porch.

Patricia made a roadway through her grits with the back of her fork, then brushed some biscuit crumbs off the sleeve of her pink robe. "Daddy, I really, really like my new robe and night shirt, but I was wondering," she murmured. "How come Grandpa Brazos gives me and 'Nica so much stuff?"

"I suppose because he hasn't had you close by all these years and he's wanting to make up."

Patricia bit her lip. "But he hasn't given Little Frank anything."

"He will. You wait and see. It's just that you girls needed some things a little more urgently than your brother," Robert explained.

Veronica took a big sip of milk and wiped the white mustache off with a napkin. "I think Amber is jealous of our new furniture."

"Did she say that?" Jamie Sue inquired.

"No, but I can tell by the way she sneered at it. Amber is very good at sneering," Veronica insisted.

Robert emptied the grits bowl on his plate, scraping it clean. "Amber is naturally dramatic, like her mother."

"What was Amber's father like?" Patricia asked.

"We never knew him, but Aunt Rebekah and Dacee June did for a very short time before he was killed. He was a doctor."

Patricia spooned her grits onto her father's plate. "Amber says she has some stepsisters and brothers back in Tennessee that she's never met."

Robert ladled thick honey on his mound of grits. "That's what I understand."

"That would be strange, having brothers and sisters you never met," Veronica added. "Do we have any sisters we haven't met?"

"Young lady!" Robert scolded.

"I was just teasing."

"Years ago, your Aunt Abby and Amber went through some difficult times." Jamie Sue smeared a small dollop of jelly across her biscuit.

Veronica was now rocking back and forth in her chair. "I like Amber."

"So do I," Jamie Sue added. "She makes a delightful big sister to all you cousins."

"Oh, Mama, Aunt Dacee June is the one that acts like our big sister." Patricia nibbled like a chipmunk at her bacon.

"That's true," Robert grinned. "She doesn't know how to be any other way. But it might not hurt if you girls didn't go on and on about all the things Daddy Brazos bought you," he cautioned.

"I think we should paint our trunk pink when it gets here, so it will match everything else in our room," Patricia suggested.

"I think we have the most beautiful bedroom in Deadwood," Veronica said.

"I get the bed near the window tonight," Patricia insisted.

"I don't see why we have to trade back and forth," Veronica whined.

"Alright, then I'll take the bed by the window every night."

"No, you won't."

"What is this argument?" Robert pressed.

"It seems that a certain brown-haired boy can be seen in his backyard if you have the correct angle from the girls' bedroom window," Jamie Sue explained.

"In that case, I'll nail shutters over the window."

"Daddy!"

He turned to Jamie Sue. "You know, a nice peaceful trip to Rapid City sounds very relaxing."

By ten o'clock Jamie Sue Fortune was alone in a house they had occupied only three days. She walked through the rooms carrying a cup of strong black coffee.

My linens aren't here. My dishes aren't here. My knick-knacks are in a crate somewhere . . . all those touches that will make this house mine are misplaced in some railroad depot. It's almost like being in a hotel room in a strange city. Nothing is really settled.

She rubbed her long fingers across the scalloped china cup, letting the heat warm her hands.

The girls seem settled, especially when Daddy Brazos spoils them so. And Little Frank . . . that child finds a home anywhere on the face of the earth. He loves everything he does, trusts everyone he meets, believes that there isn't any-

thing in the world he can't do. He's probably right.

And Robert's off on a new job.

Jamie Sue sat in a straight-back, leather-cushioned chair facing the sofa and sipped her coffee. There was no sound except the ticking of the round brass clock over the mantel.

Keep him safe, Lord. I suppose I'll never have a day that I don't worry about his safety. It's always been that way. But I couldn't live without him, Lord. I know we fight and argue some, but we do make up. Oh, mercy, how we do make up.

After all these years, here we are in Deadwood.

And I don't have anything to do.

There are no clothes to wash; we have them on our backs. Louise has this house so clean that dust is ashamed to come through the door. That's the trouble with living in a hotel; there's nothing to do. Even my sewing basket is in one of the trunks.

I should go to the library and find a book.

Is this the way my life will be in Deadwood?

At the fort, everyone needed me. "Mrs. Fortune, could you help me write to my mother?" "Mrs. Fortune, the baby's sick, what should I do?" "Mrs. Fortune, would you go with me to tell a young wife and mother that she's now a widow?" "Mrs. Fortune, I need your advice on how to lay out my vegetable garden." "Mrs. Fortune, my husband is drunk and mean again; can I stay in your spare room until he sobers up?" "Mrs. Fortune, could you see my wife gets to the doctor in town?"

In Deadwood no one needs me. No one needs another Mrs. Fortune. I'm not complaining, Lord. Just bewildered. Puzzled. At a loss to find my place.

OK, so I'm complaining a little. Forgive me.

Jamie Sue was staring at the blank wall above the sofa when she heard a knock. Peeking outside the window, she saw a company panel wagon that read "Deadwood-Lead Telephone Exchange." She opened the door. "Sammy!"

"Hope I'm not botherin' anything," he drawled.

"Oh, my no, I'm delighted to see you. Bobby headed for Rapid City, and the children are out and about."

"I saw the girls down at the hardware with Daddy Brazos."

"I trust he is not buying them anything else."

"Sort of goes overboard, doesn't he?" Sam grinned.

"With the twins? He's bordering on a world's record for spoiling." She glanced out at a workman at the back of the company wagon. "Is this a social visit or a business visit?"

"Both. I brought Mr. Richards to install your telephone."

"Telephone? Robert and I didn't even discuss a telephone. How much does it cost?"

"It's free," Samuel insisted.

"Sammy, we can't let you pay for . . ."

"Oh, no, *I'm* not giving it to you for free. The Fremont, Elkhorn, and Missouri Valley Railroad want their railroad inspector to have a telephone for those late-night and weekend emergencies."

"We've never had a telephone before."

"They are a wonderful invention that no home should be without." He leaned a little closer and lowered his voice, "If you want to know the truth, don't let the twins even know you have one. Amber bothers us night and day to use it. And she doesn't have anyone to call besides Dacee June. But she'll have the twins now."

"I don't think it will be too much of a problem," Jamie Sue said. "We'll use it just for business and emergencies."

"That's what ever'one says, until they own one. Let's find a good wall to mount it on, then Mr. Richards will run the wire to the pole. Oh, yes, Abby sent over a box of things for you. Let me go fetch them."

🥾

While Mr. Richards attached the awkward oak and black-steel box to the kitchen wall, Samuel sat at the dining-room table with a deep blue, gold-trimmed mug of coffee. His tie was loose; the collar button on his white shirt, unfastened.

Jamie Sue sorted through the box that was propped in the middle of the table. "Sammy, I can't let Abby give us these new dresses!"

"You'd better, or I'll be in a mess of trouble. She figures you'll need a change of clothes sooner or later, what with those trunks lost."

"Oh, I'm sure they're not lost. Robert's going to inquire of them in Rapid City. This green dress is beautiful. I don't think I've ever owned one so . . . so . . ."

"So dramatic?"

"Yes, that's it."

"Abby has a goal in life to make sure Fortune women are well dressed."

Jamie Sue watched as Sam gulped the coffee exactly as Robert did. *I don't think they all learned that habit from their mama.* "I'm a little embarrassed," she said.

"She said you might need to stitch it up in the front."

"No," Jamie Sue blushed, "that's not what I meant. I'm embarrassed by her generosity . . ." *I will definitely stitch it up in the front!*

"It's what Abby does, Jamie Sue. She has to be that way. Isn't that the way it is for all of us?" he reasoned. "Within the Lord's limitations, we have to do what we have to do. Now, your Bobby has to wear a uniform or a badge. We all know that. Law and order is in his blood. He would have made a miserable lumber-mill owner. You and I both know that."

She waltzed around the dining room holding the dress in front of her. "How do I look, Sammy?"

"Stunning, of course."

"Samuel Fortune, you are a wonderful liar."

"I am neither wonderful nor a liar. But I have developed a keen eye for spotting a handsome woman. It is common knowledge that the Fortune brothers cut themselves out the three prettiest ones in the herd."

"I always have a difficult time remembering that cattle analogies are compliments," she laughed as she folded the dress back up.

"The duckings and boiled shirt for Little Frank came from the hardware. Abby doesn't carry men's clothing."

"You mean, boy's clothes."

"Jamie Sue, you've got a handsome young man there. And he's as quiet and reserved around adults as his name-sake."

"I wish I could have known Big River Frank better," she added.

"Todd claims the day he was killed was the day Daddy's health started to slip. Big River took that bullet for Daddy and Dacee June, you know. It's a debt Daddy could never repay. They just don't make friendships like those any more."

"I don't know. . . . I know some brothers who would do the same thing," she countered.

"You're right about that. But that's because we were taught that way."

Jamie Sue pulled out a light yellow dress.

"Abby said the girls could decide who got the yellow one and who got the rose one," Samuel explained.

"Oh, my . . . they are beautiful . . . but we do have a problem."

"What's that?"

"Never in their lives have the girls had unmatching dresses."

Samuel leaned back and rubbed his gray mustache. "You mean they always dress alike?"

"Always. They even have to have identical undergarments."

"Abby apologized, but she doesn't have two of any ready-made dresses. She has this idea that no woman wants to see someone else in the same dress, so every dress she stocks is completely different. But, listen, if it will cause a fuss, let me take them back and they don't even have to know," he proposed.

Jamie Sue pulled out the rose-colored dress and ran her fingers across the cool, slick satin trim. "No . . . I think this will be a good lesson for them. They just have to figure this out." She left the two dresses draped over dining-room chairs. "I think I'll just leave them here and not say a word. It will be interesting to see what they do. You'll have to take my sincere thanks to Abby."

"You can thank her yourself, once that telephone gets installed."

"Now that will take some getting used to. At the fort not even the colonel had a telephone."

"Someday most every home in the country will have one of these."

"You sound like the president of the phone exchange."

"Isn't this strange, Jamie Sue, Sam Fortune running a telephone exchange? Todd is doing what he was created to do. And so is your Bobby. But me? What in the world am I doing running a phone company?"

She carefully stretched out the dresses on the chairs. "Making a good living, it looks like."

Samuel nodded. "That's for sure. But it's not me. You know that. . . . Todd and Bobby know that . . ."

"What is your place, Sammy?"

"Out on the range. I should have me a spread and cows to work, horses to break, and the wide open spaces in every direction. Look at me, Jamie Sue. I'm tucked into a wool suit, corralled in a gulch . . . with a bank account growing and so many belongings we have to lock our doors at night. This isn't me."

"Does Abby know you feel that way?"

"I don't want to break her heart, darlin', . . . and don't you tell her, either. She loves it here. For the first time in her life, she is surrounded by a family and friends that deeply care about her. She's had a rough life. I wouldn't take all that away from her for anything."

"So you stay miserable."

"I'm not miserable." Sam brushed his thick, prematurely

gray hair off his ears. "I've starved out on the run in the hills of Oklahoma. . . . I've been locked in little jail cells months at a time. . . . I've woke up not knowin' where I was or who I was with. . . . I know what misery is, and I'm not miserable."

"But it's not you?"

"That's about it. How about you, Jamie Sue? Is this your place?"

She paused. "I believe so."

"I'm glad. Because all the rest of us are so glad you are here."

"I appreciate that."

"And I appreciate you listenin' to me. It's funny, but ever since I came to Deadwood, I've felt like I have to watch what I say and who I say it to. With family thick as rattlesnakes in the prickly pear cactus, a person has to be careful. I don't know why I'm shovelin' all of this on you. It just seems like . . . well, I don't know quite how to say this, . . . but you just seem to see right to the heart of a person on first glance. You've always been that way."

"You're exaggerating."

"When did you decide to marry Bobby?"

"Sammy . . ."

"Answer me."

"The first day I met him in that blizzard."

"See? It's a gift, Jamie Sue. It ain't a threatenin' thing. It's relaxin' to know someone sees right through you and likes you anyway. I thank you for it."

"Thanks, Sammy. That's very nice. No one's ever told me that before. You aren't trying to sweet-talk me again, are you?"

Sam Fortune frowned. "I could never figure what you ladies mean by me sweet-talkin' you. I just look at you and tell the truth, and you all giggle and call it 'sweet talk.' I don't even have any hidden motives. I'm just tellin' the truth."

"Oooohwee, you are good at it, Sammy. You have got to be the best there has ever been at saying things that make a lady glad to be who she is."

"Maybe that's what I do best." Sam stood. "Now I need to check and see if Mr. Richards needs any help outside with the telephone wire. I'll leave you a sheet of instructions. On the back side is the directory of phone numbers."

She walked him to the front door.

He shoved on his hat, then stepped back and kissed her cheek. "Thanks for listening to me, Jamie Sue. I haven't really had someone to listen like that since . . . since Mama died."

She watched Sam Fortune stroll out. The sunlight was just peering over White Rocks, high atop Mt. Moriah cemetery to the east.

Lord, I have never known a woman who is more dearly missed by all her family than Sarah Ruth Fortune. He hasn't had someone to talk to since his mama died? What about Abby? You talk to your wife, don't you?

But not about everything. You love them, want to protect them, but you feel like you need to uphold a certain confidence.

I understand.

But who do I have to talk to?

Sammy? Abby? Rebekah? Daddy Brazos?

Maybe all I have is You, Lord.

I'm not complaining.

I just long for someone to talk to who could help me discover what is my thing to do.

Robert sat in the last seat of the last car of the train to Rapid City. With railroad maps spread on the seat around him, he studied the landscape on the west side of the tracks. He recorded every narrow gorge, every horse-hiding boulder, every building, every clump of trees that could masquerade danger.

When he arrived at the depot in Rapid City, he crammed all the papers back into his new brown leather satchel. The sky was a clear, washed-out blue. The Dakota sun seemed to explode with bright yellow heat.

As he stepped out onto the platform, he noticed the conductor was the same man he met when the attempted hold-up occurred.

"Mr. Fortune, I hear you hired on as train inspector."

"Yes, sir."

The man's white hair curled out under his cap. "That surely does make me relieved. How can I be of assistance to you?" The man tugged off his wire-frame spectacles and rubbed the red marks on the bridge of his nose.

"I'm developing a set of guidelines for railroad personnel on how to handle dangerous situations. I'll let you know when I have it complete," Robert explained.

"You lookin' for men?" the conductor asked.

"You got any suggestions?"

"My brother-in-law is looking for work. Years ago he

worked for Marshal Pappy Divide in Cheyenne."

"What's he been doing lately?" Robert studied the process of unloading the baggage car as they continued to stand on the train platform.

"Goin' broke lookin' for gold up at Cripple Crick, Colorado." The conductor pulled off his cap and rubbed the bald spot on top of his head.

"Where's that?"

"On top of the mountains behind Colorado Springs. Ol' crazy Bob Womack suckered him into dumpin' his savin's into worthless claims. Now he's needin' to work."

"Send him by for an interview tomorrow morning. I can't guarantee anything. But I'll give him a listen."

A roar of shouts rolled across the train yard. "What's happening over there?"

"Probably some bummers and drifters got into a fight."

"Does anyone stop it?"

"The sheriff don't want them stinkin' up his jail and wolfin' down supper at county expense, so he won't come near them . . . unless someone gets killed."

"Isn't that railroad property?"

"Sure is."

"Then I'd better check it out. Can you tote my satchel up to the company office?"

"I will, but you be careful out there, Mr. Fortune. It ain't a healthy place to visit."

"Neither is a mine shaft, but that doesn't keep men from doin' their job."

Robert took his time. He strolled around the east side of the freight car where a half-dozen men stood in a rough circle. A lone man with bloody knuckles and bruised face stood in the middle, daring any and all to fight.

The others scooted closer, slowly encasing him. The shouts and curses echoed the train yard and none of the men seemed to notice or care about Robert's marked approach. A big, red-haired man grabbed the skinny man in the middle from behind. A tall, bearded man threw a wild punch into the victim's mid-section. The man crumpled; the red-haired man loosened his grip. Then the one in the center spun around, catching the big man in the chin with a bone-popping roundhouse. He staggered to his knees. The tall, bearded man landed a punch to the man with the bruised face and ear. Blood trickled down, yet the man hit back with three quick blows that busted the bearded man's lip and bloodied his nose.

"Come on," the man in the middle screamed. "I'll take you all on at once. You ain't brave enough to fight me one at a time!"

Two more men jumped the man and began to swing. Several punches found their target. Yet the man in the middle fought even harder.

Robert fired his .45 Colt single-action army revolver into the air.

The fighting ceased.

"Who in Hades are you!" the bearded man with the bloodied nose hollered.

Shoulders back, gun raised, hand steady, Robert showed classic military posture. "Railroad inspector."

"I don't need no help," the man in the middle of the crowd bellowed.

"I don't care if you do or you don't, none of you are going to fight on railroad property." Robert's gun moved slowly from one man to the next.

A burly man in a tattered ducking coat pulled out a Bowie knife and brandished it. "Says who?"

The man lunged at Fortune.

Robert stepped aside. He brought the barrel of his revolver down with such force that it sounded like the crack of a whip. "I say so," he growled. The man dropped to his knees in screaming agony.

The fattest of the men tugged at a short-barreled Schofield stuck in his belt, but Robert grabbed the man's shirt collar and shoved his own revolver against the man's temple. "I said . . . there is no fighting on railroad property."

"Nobody ever complained before."

"Things have changed."

"Are you sidin' with that card cheat?" He pointed to the man catching his breath in the middle.

"I'm not siding with anyone. You can go over there along the river and beat each other unconscious. But you can't do it on railroad property."

"What about him?" another of the drifters shouted.

"I want to talk with him."

"You goin' to arrest him for cheating us out of four bits?"

This fight was over fifty cents? "Whatever it was about, it's over now." Robert waited until all but the man in the center of the ring trudged away. He turned to the bruised man.

"I ain't got nothin' to talk to you about and I didn't need your help." The man stood his ground, smearing blood across his chin. "I'm tougher than any two of 'em put together."

"I have no doubt you're right about that," Robert replied.

"But there were six of them. That's bad arithmetic."

"I didn't start it. I beat 'em fair. Two queens over an ace. But I don't back away."

"You lookin' for a job?"

"With the railroad?"

"Maybe. You ever been in jail for anything more than hurrahin' a saloon or gettin' in a fight?"

"Nope."

"Can you go two weeks without drinkin' alcohol?"

"I don't drink ever."

Robert surveyed the man from hat to boot. "Can you get a bath, a shave and a haircut, and wear a suit?"

The man took a red bandanna out of his back pocket and mopped the blood off his ear and neck. "Why?"

"I might have a job for you." Robert stared at the cottonwood trees where the men still loitered.

The man flinched when he touched the bruise on his forehead. "What if I don't want a job?"

"$250 a month, plus expenses and a free train pass. Think about it."

"What do I have to do?"

"Won't be any tougher than what you just did."

"I ain't dressin' up for nobody. I don't want your job."

"What's your name?" Robert pressed.

"Holter. Who are you?"

"Robert Fortune."

"You related to Sammy Fortune?"

"He's my brother."

The man's brown eyes relaxed for the first time. "I'll take the job."

"Why the sudden change?"

" 'Cause I owe Sam Fortune a favor and I'd like to pay him back."

"What kind of favor?"

"He helped my sister when she was hurt and in trouble. I never met him when he was alive . . ."

"He's still alive."

"No foolin'? Everyone in the territory claims he's dead."

"Trust me."

"Well, ain't that somethin'! I look forward to shakin' his hand. He treated my sister kind and gentle like, then gave her money for a train ride home. A man don't forget somethin' like that. What kind of job did I just agree to?"

"I didn't hire you yet."

"You said . . ."

"You show up at the train office above the depot tomorrow morning at 9:00. Have a shave, bath, and haircut. Put on your best clothes. Then we'll discuss the job," Robert explained.

"I said, I don't dress up for no one."

"That's up to you, Holter. You can discuss it with those six guys waitin' over by the trees. Or are you walkin' with me back to the depot?"

Holter hesitated. "Yeah, I think I might walk with you."

There were four sets of tracks to cross, and a slow-moving train on the ones closest to the depot. They waited for it to pull out.

"How come you decided to hire me when you don't know nothin' about me?"

"Here's what I know about you," Robert explained. "You aren't on the same side as some whiskied-up drifters. I can tell a lot about a man by looking at his enemies.

Second, you don't back down from a fight. You obviously don't care about the odds. And third, you'll keep battlin' even when you're hurt. If I hire someone else, I might never know all of that until I really need it; then it will be a gamble."

"Is it going to be that rough of a job?"

"I'm going to do everything possible to put in place a system that keeps any such thing from ever happening. But I want to know what kind of men I've got in case it does happen. I'll see you in the morning, Holter. I don't mind callin' you Holter, but the railroad is goin' to want a first and last name. You got any problems with that?"

"Nope. The name's Guthrie Holter. Listen, I ain't doin' real good at the moment. I don't have the funds for a shave, bath, and a haircut," he admitted.

Robert pulled out a silver dollar and handed it to the man. "You got a wife and kids, Holter?"

"You're gettin' personal."

"Are you ashamed of them?"

"I got me a wife and two little boys but . . . well, they left me."

"Why?"

"You're pushy, Fortune."

"Some day my life might depend on you, Holter. I'd like to know the character of the man who's backin' me up. I'm not judgin' you. You don't have to answer if you don't want to."

"I was the one who left, sort of. She got tired of me draggin' her down, she said."

"Where is she now?"

"Probably still in Sidney, Nebraska," Holter said. "We

got in an argument and I stormed out sayin' if she wanted to see me, I'd be in Rapid City."

When the train finally passed, the men hiked on over to the depot platform. "When was that?"

"It will make a year on June 15th."

"You haven't been back?"

Holter hung his head. "Nope."

"You love your boys, don't you?"

"Yep. I love Dacinda too. But my job fell through up here, and I barely been gettin' by, so I . . ." His voice trailed off to silence.

When they reached the raised wooden platform, Robert brushed dust off the sleeves of his suit coat. "You're too proud to go back?"

"I reckon. You sure do preach at a man, Fortune."

"You might as well get used to that." Robert surveyed the land surrounding the depot as if he were the one planning a robbery.

Holter peered back across the tracks at the men still huddled in the distant grove. "After all this time, she probably don't want to see me," Holter murmured.

"I can guarantee there are two boys that want to see you."

"I reckon you're right about that."

Robert strolled toward the stairs leading to the second-story offices. "Meet me right here in the morning. Where are you staying tonight?"

"I been campin' out over in them cottonwoods, but with those hombres on the prowl, I'd better find a different tree to camp under," Holter said.

Robert reached into his pocket and pulled out two more

silver dollars. "One is for a room, the other for some food money. You all set now?"

"You mentioned puttin' on my best clothes. I hope it don't count against me, but I sort of . . ."

"Those are your only clothes and they're a little ripped and bloody?"

"Yes, sir."

Robert sorted through the coins in his pocket and pulled out a half-eagle gold coin. "Buy a good durable suit and tie and new hat and boots."

Guthrie Holter refused to take the money. "I don't take handouts."

"Holter, sounds like your pride has already robbed you of a family. You going to let it rob you of a good job? Anyway, this isn't a handout. . . . It's a loan. I expect to be repaid from your first couple of paydays."

Holter grinned. "I thought you said I wasn't hired yet?"

"You aren't."

"How do you know I won't just take this ten dollars and ride off?"

"I don't know that," Robert admitted. "But if that's the kind of man you are, I'd like to find out right now. I'd rather lose ten dollars now than lose a passenger's life later on."

"Kind of like a test?"

"Not much of one. I don't reckon you couldn't ride off with my money."

"You're mighty confident in your surmisin'. You don't know me very well."

"Am I right, Holter?"

"Yeah, you're right. You ain't one of those guys who's

always right are you?"

Robert Fortune pushed his hat to the back of his head. A tight-lipped grin broke across his face. "Yep."

Robert Fortune spent most of the afternoon getting a tour of railroad facilities in Rapid City and reviewing company policy on everything from the purchase of ammunition to official policy when a woman gives birth on a moving train.

After supper with several railroad officials and bankers at the Dakota House Hotel, he perched for several hours at the little oak desk in a back corner room of the F. E. & M. V. Railroad office building. His was the only light shining when he turned the switch, locked the door, then sauntered down the outside stairway into the dark night.

With his tie hanging loose around his neck and his suit coat over his arm, he surveyed the street. It was close to midnight, but the gas street lamps continued to give a dull glow. A distant shout. A squeaking wheel. A dog yipped in the distance as he strolled down the raised sidewalk toward the downtown hotel. His own boot heels on the wooden boardwalk was the only sound close by. Scattered clouds blocked some of the stars, but others pierced the blackness with pricks of twinkling white. The air tasted a little dusty but pleasantly cool.

He pulled on his suit coat.

Robert Fortune, railroad inspector. One office in Deadwood, another office . . . well, at least my own desk . . . in Rapid City. That's a long way from being a Coryell County,

Texas, cowboy. Lord, I believe You've been leading me. I know You led me to Jamie Sue, so You must have led me to join the army when I did. As for being a railroad inspector . . . well, I trust it's the right thing. I believe I'll enjoy this job . . . except for the paperwork.

But I'll miss the cavalry.

I enjoy havin' a strong, spirited horse under me.

I'll buy some horses in Deadwood, one for every member of the family. Then we can ride out to Cheyenne Crossing for a picnic or . . . Little Frank is a natural on horseback.

"Well, if it ain't the railroad inspector!" a man growled from the shadows of the alley.

A two-story building with balcony over the boardwalk across the alley darkened what illumination the distant street lamp was trying to provide. Robert's hand dropped to the walnut grip of his .45 revolver. The check of a lever on an unseen carbine made him hesitate.

"Don't go pullin' that gun!" the hidden man barked. "Get your hands up and get 'em up quick."

"He don't look so tough now, does he, Dunny?" The voice was high-pitched, nervous, and more than a little drunk.

"Jist another railroad suit-and-tie man about to get his head smashed and his wallet lifted. Grab his gun, Shorty," the man with the carbine ordered.

"Don't call me Shorty."

"I always call you Shorty."

"Don't call me Shorty in front of a suit-and-tie man."

"Grab his gun!"

From the shadows of the alley, a thin man about five feet

tall stepped out. His round felt hat was pinched on top with a Montana crease. He sported either a scraggly beard or a dirty face. With no light, Robert couldn't tell which.

Fortune kept his hands held high. "You boys roam the streets in packs like wild dogs and skunks?"

The short man yanked out Robert's revolver and shoved it up to his neck. The hammer clicked.

"Mister, I kin blow your head off right now!" he yipped.

Not unless you pull that hammer back one more click. Fortune ignored Shorty and peered back down the alley. "Does it take all six of you to lift a wallet? Or just you two whiskey-brave drifters?"

"Shoot no, me and Dunny did this all on our own!" the little man bragged.

"Shut up, Shorty!" the hidden man ordered.

"Don't call me Shorty!" He shoved the barrel harder against Fortune's neck. "Give me your poke!"

"My wallet's in my boot," Robert announced.

"What?"

"If you want my poke, my wallet . . . it's in my boot."

"What's it doin' there?"

"Hiding from sneak thieves."

"He's got his wallet in his boot!" Shorty hollered.

"I heard him," Dunny huffed.

Robert Fortune stepped off the sidewalk into the dirt street.

"Where are you goin'!" the little man screamed.

Fortune lifted his foot to the boardwalk. "You want me to get my wallet, don't you?"

"Oh . . . yeah . . ."

"No!" the man in the shadows snarled.

"We don't?" Shorty gulped.

"What if he has a knife or a sneak gun in his boot?"

Shorty scooted away from Fortune and back to the alley. "What are we goin' to do, Dunny?"

"You fetch his wallet."

"From his boot?"

"No!" the man hollered. "Jist have him mail it to us, you dolt!"

"But we ain't got no address, Dunny!"

"For the sake of Hades, Shorty, coldcock the suit-and-tie man. We'll take his wallet, his boots, and his gun as well."

"I got his gun. It's got a real nice feel to it."

Robert caught a glimpse of Dunny. He resembled the red-haired man that Holter had busted in the jaw.

"Depends on how much money he has," Dunny replied. "We might just sell the gun and split the funds."

Shorty inched his way back toward Robert Fortune. "You stay down there on the street," he hissed.

"Does Dunny always make you do the dangerous part, Shorty?" Fortune asked.

The man stopped. It was still too dark to see his facial features. "Ain't nothin' dangerous about it."

It's hard to read a man's eyes when he's standing in the dark. "What if I have a knife up my sleeve? You'll be the one that takes the blade."

The sound of Shorty's boot heels in retreat was the only sound for a moment. "What about that, Dunny? Let's jist shoot him."

"We ain't goin' to shoot him. The sheriff would be here before we pulled his boots. Besides, his hands is in the air, and he ain't got a knife. Don't let him bluff you."

"Keep an eye on my hands, Shorty. You don't want to take your eyes off my hands," Robert called out.

"Don't call me Shorty."

It all depends on how quickly Dunny pulls the trigger on that carbine. "I don't know your other name."

"Lester." The word came out like a spit.

"Well, Lester, if I was worried about a man knifin' me, I'd forget his eyes and keep focused on his hands. He's got to carry a knife with his hands. Can you see my hands alright, Lester?"

"Turn around," Shorty barked.

"Hurry up!" Dunny mumbled.

Robert stayed facing the two. "You aren't going to crease my new hat, are you?"

"I said, turn around!" Shorty's voice was near panic.

"I did know a gambler down in Baton Rouge," Fortune continued, "that had a spring-triggered knife in the toe of his boot. Some men fell to the ground bleeding to death and they didn't even see him stick them. Did you ever see one of those, Lester?"

"Turn around!" Shorty's cry was similar to a man falling off a cliff.

"Would you like to see one of those boot knives now?"

"He's bluffin' you, Shorty!" Dunny insisted. "He ain't got no boot knife."

Shorty mustered up a sneer. "Mister, if you don't turn around, I'll coldcock you right across the forehead."

"I'd prefer that. It will look more dramatic to the jury when they sentence you to prison. Lester, do you know if they still have rats in those tiny brick cells over in Yankton?"

In the glimmering shadows Robert could see the finger

come off the trigger as the little man raised the barrel of the revolver above his head. Fortune left his hands in the air until the last moment, then caught the man's wrist and dropped straight down in the dirt in front of the raised boardwalk.

He wrestled the gun from Shorty, even before the little man crashed face first into the dirt street. Robert rolled under the wooden sidewalk as a shot blasted from the alley.

"It's me!" Shorty cried out. "Don't shoot, Dunny, it's me out here!"

Robert fired one shot that ripped its way up through the wooden sidewalk. He heard Dunny sprint back down the alley. He rolled out and pointed the revolver at Lester, who staggered to his feet.

"Don't shoot me, mister. . . . Don't shoot me. . . . This was all Dunny's idea. . . . Don't shoot me, . . ." he cried.

"Get out of here!" Robert hollered.

"You'll shoot me in the back."

"Get out of here before the sheriff arrives."

"You goin' to shoot me?"

"You'll find out soon enough."

"Oh, lordy, I don't want to die."

"Then change your line of work."

"Yes sir . . . yes, sir, I do believe I will. . . ." Shorty staggered, fell, got up, and ran down the middle of the street. Across the street someone lit a lantern. A dog barked. A baby cried, or a woman screamed, Robert couldn't tell which.

He searched under the boardwalk for his hat when he heard a voice from the balcony across the alley.

"You lookin' for a job, mister?"

Robert stood and tried to brush the dirt off his trousers. "Holter?"

"I know a railroad inspector that's lookin' to hire. You interested?" Then, there was a deep laugh.

"How long have you been up there?" Robert quizzed.

"The whole time."

Robert jammed his hat down on his head. "Thanks for the help."

"I thought it would be an insult to assume you couldn't handle those two."

Robert strolled across the alley to the balcony. "You're right about that."

"Besides, if I called them from up here, they might have panicked and actually shot someone."

"Thanks for your restraint."

"You want that railroad job?" Holter jibed.

"What's the boss like?" Robert pressed.

"A suit-and-tie man. Keeps his nose in the books till after midnight."

Robert continued the charade. "Is the job dangerous?"

"Kind of like building a cabin over a rattlesnake den. You know you're going to get bit; you just don't know when."

"Sounds good; are you hirin' tonight?" Robert brushed dirt and rocks out of his hair.

"Nope. You'll have to talk to him face-to-face in the mornin' . . . and don't wear them dirty clothes. You have to dress nobby."

"See you in the mornin', Holter."

"Yes, sir, I'll be there. You said it was good to see me in a jam before you hired me. Well, Mr. Robert Fortune, it was good for me to see what kind of man I'll be workin' for."

CHAPTER FOUR

The loud banging at the top of the stairs was followed by a shout. " 'Nica, open the door!"

The reply was muffled, but just as insistent. "No!"

"I'll tell mother!"

"I don't care!"

With a copy of Kipling's *Plain Tales from the Hills* in her hand, Jamie Sue Fortune paused at the bottom of the stairway. "You'll tell me what?"

Patricia stood at the top of the stairway, arms folded. Her long brown wavy hair cascaded across her thin shoulders. "Mother, 'Nica won't unlock the door."

Jamie Sue folded the book over her finger to mark her place. "Open the door, Veronica Ruth!" she called out.

"It's not fair," came a muted, whiny response.

"What isn't fair?" *Did I really pine for sixteen years to have a sister?* "Patricia Sarah, what is your sister upset about?"

Standing at the platform at the top of the stairway, Patricia looked taller, more mature, than twelve. "She's still pouting about my rose-colored dress."

The reply came from a voice identical in tone and pitch. "It's not your dress. It belongs to both of us."

The girl in the slightly wrinkled off-white dress leaned toward the locked door.

"It does not! We drew straws and I got first choice!" When Patricia turned sideways, her upturned nose and flat chest definitely looked twelve.

103

"It's not fair," Veronica whimpered. "You got to draw first."

Patricia leaned her mouth to the doorjamb and hollered, "You told me to draw first!"

"I was just tryin' to be polite. I shouldn't be penalized for being polite!"

Jamie Sue marked the book with a lavender ribbon, then tossed it on the bottom step, and scurried up the stairs. Her lace-up boots tapped impatience with each ascending step. Her right hand slid up the railing; her left hand held her hem above her ankles. "Veronica, open that door right now!"

"Mother, make Patricia agree to let me wear the rose dress," Veronica sobbed.

"Open this door instantly," Jamie Sue demanded again.

"Make her promise."

Jamie Sue ran her fingers across the brass door handle. "The only thing I promise you, young lady, is to see to it you get a paddling if that door isn't opened by the time I count to three. One . . . two . . ."

The door swung open.

A red-eyed Veronica Fortune stalked toward the four-poster bed near the window. Her beige dress was identical to her sister's. Her hair was slightly matted, but it hung freely down her shoulders. "It isn't fair." She threw herself, face down, on the pink comforter.

"Give me the door key, young lady," Jamie Sue demanded.

Patricia plopped down on the other bed.

Jamie Sue marched straight at Veronica. "I said, give me the key!"

"I won't lock Tricia out again," she mumbled into her pillow.

"You have not proved to have that much maturity. I want the key now."

Patricia's blue eyes danced in triumph as she chewed her tongue and watched her pouting sister. Finally, Veronica rolled over and sat up, handing her mother the key. Her feet barely reached the floor.

"Now, what about the dresses? We went through this yesterday. The rose dress is Tricia's, and the beautiful yellow one is yours. You both agreed that when you weren't wearing the dresses, the other one could borrow them," Jamie Sue lectured.

Veronica's wild bangs masked her forehead. "Tricia won't let me wear the rose dress."

Jamie Sue turned toward her other daughter. "Patricia?"

" 'Nica wanted to wear it to the Volunteer Fireman's Bazaar. I'm going to wear it then."

"Veronica, you know your sister has first choice at the rose dress."

"But then I don't have anything to wear! They still haven't found our trunks. I'm not going to wear this same old dress."

Jamie Sue marched over to Veronica's wardrobe and flung it open. "What about this beautiful yellow dress?"

Veronica's knees bounced up and down as her legs hung over the mattress. "But I can't wear the yellow dress. It's too new!"

"So is the rose one."

"That's the problem," Veronica wept. "If we both go out wearing new dresses, everyone will say . . . 'Oh, you two got new dresses, and Tricia got the pretty one!'"

Jamie Sue pulled the only dress in the wardrobe out and hung it on the door. "This yellow dress is absolutely stunning!"

Veronica frowned at her sister. "But not as stunning as the rose one."

"Where in the world did you get that idea?"

Veronica curled her lip. "Eachan Moraine said so."

Jamie Sue stepped over to the window and looked out at the neighborhood. "The boy down the street? He saw your dresses?"

"We told him about them. He said the rose one sounded prettier," Patricia explained.

"That's only one opinion by someone who's never seen either dress. Little Frank said he likes the yellow one best," Jamie Sue encouraged.

Veronica threw herself back on the bed and shrieked. "See . . . see? My own brother likes the yellow dress. . . . It must be horrible! When do I get to wear the rose dress?"

"Whenever Patricia isn't wearing it."

Veronica climbed off the bed. "Can I wear it to church on Sunday?"

"No, I want to wear it on Sunday," Patricia insisted.

Veronica opened her sister's wardrobe. She ran her fingers along the rose satin dress, the only one in the closet. "Can I wear it to go meet Daddy at the train depot?"

"No, I want to wear it to the depot," Patricia announced.

"See? I'll never get to wear it!"

"That's all the discussion I want on the subject. This was a test to see how you two would get along with different dresses. You failed. Now, I don't want either of you girls ever locking your door on me again. Is that clear?"

"I'd never do that," Patricia insisted.

" 'I'd never do that,' " Veronica mimicked.

Jamie Sue plodded down the staircase. *Lord, I know identical twin girls are special in this world. But just as unique is the mother of identical twins. Why is it I keep thinking it will get worse before it gets better? Robert Fortune, if you were home right now, I'd leave you with your darling daughters and go for a long, quiet walk!*

She had just reached the bottom of the stairs and retrieved her book when there was one short ring on the telephone. Then another.

Patricia scampered down the stairs behind her. "May I answer the telephone? I've never answered it before."

"No, it's just for business and emergencies." Jamie Sue scurried into the kitchen.

"Don't ring central this time when you answer it," Patricia called out.

"I won't."

"And don't shout into the mouthpiece," Patricia insisted.

"I won't shout."

Jamie Sue scooted to the wall, snatched up the hand telephone, then hollered into the transmitter, "What is it?"

"Not so loud, mother," Patricia cautioned.

The voice at the other end was relaxed. "Jamie Sue?"

"Yes?"

"This is Abby."

"This is Jamie Sue," she croaked.

"You're still a little nervous with a telephone, aren't you?" Abby pressed.

"No . . . eh, yes!" Jamie Sue yelled.

"Is your telephone working? Perhaps I should send Mr. Richards over. It sounds like you're shouting."

Jamie Sue lowered her voice. "I'm sorry, Abby. What can I do for you? I trust everything is alright?"

"Oh, yes, listen, I just received a shipment of ready-made dresses from New York. Amber helped me unpack the crates, and she says they made a mistake and sent two of the same dress. Naturally, I thought about the twins."

"We'll be there in a half-hour or so."

"I'll have Amber warm up some tea. Good-bye."

"Good-bye . . ." Jamie Sue hollered into the transmitter.

"Mother, hang up the telephone and don't ring central this time. They really dislike that," Patricia urged.

"Oh, yes." Jamie Sue replaced the receiver, then backed away from the telephone as if it were a sleeping infant.

"Where are we going?" Patricia asked.

"To Aunt Abby's store to look at some identical dresses."

"Is Veronica going too?"

"Of course," Jamie Sue said.

Jamie Sue glanced down at a short list written on a scrap of heavy manila paper. "Tell your sister to hurry up."

Patricia scampered back to the base of the stairs. " 'Nica, Mama says that . . ." After a short pause, a wail, "No! No!"

"What in the world are you fussing about now?" Jamie Sue scooted over toward the stairway.

Patricia bit her lip and pointed to the top of the stairs. "She's wearing my rose dress!"

Veronica strutted down the stairway as if ushered by a

prince, the deep rose satin swishing with every step. "You said I could wear it when you weren't wearing it, . . . and you aren't wearing it today." Her round upturned nose was held high.

"I changed my mind," Patricia glared. "I want to wear it right now. Take it off!"

Jamie Sue turned and strolled toward the open front door. "You did tell your sister she could wear it, so let's go to Aunt Abby's."

"But . . . but . . . I can't . . ." Patricia cried as she tugged at her mother's arm. "I can't go out looking like this!"

"And why not?"

"Because . . . I'm not dressed up . . . and . . ." Tears streamed down her cheeks.

"Your hair is combed. Your hat is on. Your face is clean. You look fine."

"I look fine, but 'Nica looks fancy. I can't go out. I'm not going."

Jamie Sue tugged on her daughter's elbow. "Of course you are. Aunt Abby has some dresses for us to look at, and I need groceries."

Veronica ambled out into the bright sun of a Dakota June. "It's a lovely day, Mother," she smirked.

"But . . . wait . . ." Patricia protested. "I'm going upstairs and putting on the yellow dress."

"You most certainly are not. I've had all of this I can take. We are going downtown." This time she clutched her daughter's hand and dragged her out to the porch.

"Mother . . . I can't . . ." Patricia whimpered. "I will be so embarrassed, I will die. Please, I beg you, don't do this to me! It will ruin my entire life!"

"Come on, Tricia, don't be so childish," Veronica prodded from the sidewalk.

Jamie Sue led Patricia out to the street. *Lord, I wonder what it would be like to have only boys?*

Robert Fortune glanced up at the broad-shouldered man in the new wool suit. His holster was old, but the gun jammed in it was out-of-the-box new.

"Mr. Fortune, my brother-in-law's a conductor. He said you were looking to hire a couple of train guards." The man searched the wall behind Robert, as if trying to find a clue to solve a mystery.

Robert tugged at the cuffs of his white shirt as he studied the man. "That's right. What's your name?"

The man looked down at the desk and seemed to be trying to read the scattered papers. "Stillwater Taite. Folks call me Still."

Mister, look me in the eye if you want this job. "I heard you were a deputy for Pappy Divide down in Cheyenne."

"I surely was. Pappy was a good man." Taite's sagging dark mustache seemed to have biscuit crumbs or dandruff.

Robert waited for the man to look at him. *Taite, I won't hire a man quick to cower.* "Were you working in Cheyenne when Tap Andrews signed on?"

The man's thick brown hair curled out from under his hat, slightly over his large ears. "No sir, that was after my time."

"Then you weren't there when Pappy got ambushed?" Fortune leaned his elbows on the desk and studied the man's face. *Mister, you're trying a little too hard, . . . but I am glad you want the job.*

"I was there. I was the one who drug him out of that saloon after he was shot."

Robert leaned back against the chair. "I thought it was Andrews that did that."

"Pappy got ambushed more than once," Taite replied.

"But he only died once."

"Oh, that ambush. I'm talkin' about a couple of years earlier. After Pappy recovered, I sort of lost heart and figured I'd go up in the mountains and look for gold. I should have stayed in Cheyenne. I nearly broke my back and my savin's up there. It ain't fit work for any man. You have to be part mule and part beaver to make it wadin' around in them icy streams. No sir, I should have stayed a lawman. But sometimes a man has to move away from it to see how important it is, if you catch my drift."

"Still, are you a drinkin' man?"

"I don't ever get drunk on the job, if that's what you're askin'."

Robert rubbed the bridge of his nose, then stared at Taite's narrow brown eyes. "Do you have children?"

Stillman Taite brushed crumbs out of his mustache. "I ain't never been married."

Fortune waited for the whistle of a departing train to fade before he spoke again. "Have you ever had to kill a man?"

"I'll defend myself and the goods I'm guardin' any time it's needed." Taite patted his holstered revolver.

Mister, I just asked you three specific questions and you didn't answer any of them. "I see you pack a Smith & Wesson .38 caliber. How do you like that double action?"

"Works good, as long as I remember to pull clean through on the trigger and recock the sucker. I ain't got used to it yet."

"We tested those in the army, but they kept malfunctioning. Do you have any problem with them misfiring?"

"Nope."

"That's good. Then you haven't shot yourself in the leg with it?"

"No sir, I ain't had not a speck of trouble." Taite's lower teeth were stained yellow from tobacco.

"When did you buy it, Mr. Taite?"

Somewhere out on the platform a conductor shouted.

"Yesterday afternoon. My old gun was all rusted up so from being up in them Colorado creeks. I bought me a new one. I was hopin' I'd get this job."

Fortune pulled out his own gun and laid it on the table. "Well, if you had asked me first, I would have recommended a single-action Army .45. I just think they are more reliable. Do you carry a sneak gun?"

"Mr. Fortune, I'm a competent gunman. I can take care of myself, if that is what you're tryin' to figure."

What I'm trying to do is get you to answer a direct question. "Mr. Taite, you do understand that there is a one-month probation period."

Stillman Taite shoved his hat back revealing an extremely high forehead. "Yes, sir. My brother-in-law told me all about the railroad policy. Does this mean I get the job?"

"Any man that learned from Pappy Divide certainly has the qualifications, and your brother-in-law's recommendation is good enough to give you a try. But until I see you handle a tight situation, I won't know for sure it's the job for you. Not everyone is cut out for this kind of work."

Taite reached across the table to shake Robert's hand. "I won't let you down, Mr. Fortune."

"Good, Still, because lots of folks will be countin' on that." *His hands are calloused enough to have been working a claim.*

A knock on the door brought Robert Fortune to his feet, almost at attention. *At ease, captain, you don't need to salute anymore.* "Come in."

Guthrie Holter stuck a neatly trimmed mustache and otherwise clean-shaven face into the small office. "Did you want to see me now . . . or later?"

Fortune motioned with his hand. "Come in, Holter." Robert could smell the tonic water across the room. "I see you bought a new suit."

There was a slight blush in the leather-tough face. "Holter, this is Stillman Taite, the third man in this outfit," Fortune said.

Guthrie Holter nodded his head toward the other man. "You say we're all goin' to Deadwood?"

"I want Stillman to live in Rapid City and you to pitch your tent up at Deadwood. My sister-in-law with the dress shop has some rooms to let." Fortune retrieved his suit coat from the back of the chair. "That will work until you move your family up."

"I didn't say nothin' about movin' my family." Guthrie Holter glanced straight at Robert Fortune's penetrating stare. "Eh, yes sir, providin' they'll move, of course."

"We'll all go up today so I can go over the routines with both of you. Then I'll set a schedule."

"I don't need a satchel, then?" Taite asked.

"I'll send you straight back on the afternoon train. You just need your revolver and your watch. Everyone who works for the railroad should carry a good watch."

Stillman Taite pulled a gold-plated watch out of his vest pocket. "I got me a valuable presentation watch . . . this was presented to none other than Wild Bill Hickok by the . . ."

Guthrie Holter yanked a gold-plated watch out of his own vest pocket. ". . . by the grateful citizens of Dodge City, Kansas?"

"You got one like it?" Taite gasped.

Robert chuckled. "I'm not sure the citizens of Dodge City were that grateful."

"Where did you get yours?" Holter probed.

"From a little girl at the depot in Cheyenne."

Holter picked his teeth with his fingernail. "Was her name Angelita?"

"Yep." Taite shoved the watch back into his pocket. "Was her granddaddy a friend of Wild Bill?"

Guthrie Holter stared out the office window, across the tracks. "I heard he was a friend of Jack McCall's."

Taite sauntered over next to him. "Her grandmother fell off a wagon and broke her back?"

"I thought her grandma had to have her leg amputated clean to her hip," Holter mumbled.

Taite's neck flushed. "And you bought the watch for five dollars?"

"I paid six dollars for mine," Holter admitted.

Robert Fortune grabbed his hat and ushered both men to the door. "Boys, you aren't exactly instilling me with confidence in your judgment."

Patricia Fortune trudged, chin on her chest, beside her mother as they hiked down Lincoln Street. Veronica strutted ahead of them and led the way north on Sherman.

Patricia slipped her hand into her mother's. "I feel really, really strange, Mama."

Jamie Sue brushed the brown bangs off her daughter's eyes. "Because you aren't the one wearing the rose dress?"

"Mainly because 'Nica and I aren't wearing identical dresses. I think I feel safer when we are both the same."

"You knew this day would happen sooner or later."

"Why?"

"Do you know any thirty-year-old identical twins who still dress the same?"

"I don't know any thirty-year-old identical twins."

"Let your sister enjoy herself today. It will be your turn tomorrow."

"Mama, did I ever tell you it is difficult being a twin?"

"I believe you have mentioned it to me a time or two."

"About 90 percent of the time it's wonderful. I always have someone who understands exactly how I think and how I feel."

"And the other 10 percent?"

"I cry myself to sleep and wish I were dead!"

"Heavens . . . I trust that is an exaggeration."

"It's like 'Nica is always there. I can never, ever be by myself. I am never alone, except maybe in the privy."

"Perhaps we could discuss making separate bedrooms upstairs."

"Oh, no, Mama, I would die of lonesomeness. Remember that one time at Fort Grant that 'Nica got a stomach ache and went and slept with you and Daddy and I didn't know it, and I woke up in bed and she wasn't with me. I was so scared I couldn't move until daylight."

"You were only four."

"But I sometimes dream about not being able to find 'Nica. It's horrible."

"Are you saying that this is one of the 10 percent times that are difficult to live through?"

"Sort of . . . I don't think I've ever been outside when we didn't wear the same thing."

Jamie Sue gave her daughter a hug as they strolled along. "I seem to remember one Christmas when you wore Grandpa Brazos's red shirt for two weeks, and 'Nica wore his green one."

"I only wore the red for one week . . . then we switched . . ."

They strolled in front of a gray house with white gingerbread trim.

"You did? Patricia, I don't remember that part."

"We didn't tell anyone. But that was when we were little kids."

"I believe it was just two years ago." Jamie Sue glanced down at her daughter. "You really switched shirts?" *How many times have they tricked their own mother?*

The trio stopped in front of Morgan's Grocery Store. "I think I'll give Mr. Morgan my order, then he can have it ready for us to pick up on our way home."

"Can we go on down to Aunt Abby's? I want to show her how I look in this dress." Veronica bounced up and down on the heels of her black lace-up boots as she pleaded.

Patricia chewed on her tongue and pressed her face against the grocery window. "I want to stay with Mama."

"Can I go by myself, Mama? It's just one more block. I want to show the dress to Amber," Veronica pleaded.

"Yes, but go only to the dress shop. Tell Abby we'll be there in a minute."

Jamie Sue watched as Veronica crossed Main Street, where a brown rooster was chasing a small black dog. Then she and Patricia entered the store. "I can't believe you wanted to shop with me rather than go down to Abby's."

Patricia scrunched her nose and grinned. "I know something that 'Nica doesn't."

Jamie Sue picked up a turnip the size of a melon. "Oh?"

"See that woman near the counter?"

Jamie Sue set the giant vegetable back in the crate. "With the thick black hair and pale skin?"

Patricia stood on her tiptoes and whispered in her mother's ear. "Yes, that's Mrs. Moraine . . . Eachan's mother."

"My . . . and who is that young man that came over to her carrying the empty apple crate?"

"That's him!" Patricia squealed. "That's Eachan!"

Jamie Sue clutched her daughter's wrist. "Well, I think we should go introduce ourselves!"

Patricia tugged away. "Oh, no! We can't do that. I . . . I don't have on my rose dress!"

"Nonsense, come on." Jamie Sue marched down the grocery aisle past large jars of pickled herring and a half-full cracker jar. As she approached, she noticed the young boy with thick, wild dark hair fade back behind a bin of potatoes. *He is quite shy, I presume.*

The lady smiled warmly as she approached. "You must be Little Frank's mother."

"Yes, and I believe your son is Eachan. We have reached that time in life when we are defined by our children."

The woman looked around. "Yes, he was just here . . ."

"And this is my . . ." Jamie Sue glanced back. Patricia was nowhere in sight.

"I'm Megan Moraine," the woman replied, "but please call me Meggie. It sounds rather girlish, I know."

"I know exactly how you feel." Up close she could see Meggie's thick black hair was thinly streaked with gray. "I'm Jamie Sue."

"Jamie Sue?"

"Yes, I'm afraid until the day I die, I always will be called Jamie Sue."

"Eachan says you're new in town."

"We just moved here a few days ago. Our trunks haven't even arrived yet. I've been stuck with this one dress for two weeks."

"We've been here just a month," Meggie Moraine explained. Her hair was pulled back over her ears so tightly that her eyes looked elongated.

Jamie Sue snatched up a glass jar of pickled, green boiled eggs. "Now, who on earth would buy these?"

Mrs. Moraine laughed and pointed to an identical jar in her basket.

"Oh my, Meggie, I am embarrassed. You'll have to tell me how they taste."

"I like them sliced thin on a cabbage salad," Meggie explained.

"I'm afraid my crew doesn't eat much cabbage." Jamie Sue set the jar back on the shelf. "How are you liking Deadwood?"

Meggie leaned close enough toward Jamie that she could whiff peppermint on the woman's breath. "To tell you the truth, Jamie Sue, it's a very tight community. They don't exactly welcome newcomers. I haven't made any good friends yet. And you?"

"We have family here, so I probably don't sense that as much as you."

"Your family or your husband's?"

"My husband's father and brother own the big hardware and a dozen buildings downtown, another brother the telephone exchange, and a sister-in-law has the dress shop."

Meggie's hand went over her mouth. "Are you a Fortune?"

"Oh, yes . . . I see you've heard of us already."

The woman stiffened and stepped back. "I'm Irish, you know," she declared.

"I guessed as much with a name like Moraine and your beautiful pale complexion." Jamie Sue studied the blue eyes of Mrs. Moraine.

"That doesn't bother you?" Meggie challenged.

"The skin?"

"No, that I'm Irish."

"Heavens no . . ." Jamie Sue stepped closer to the woman. "Why should it?"

"Mr. Moraine heard that the Fortunes hated all the Irish."

A sinking feeling in Jamie Sue's stomach forced her to gasp out the reply. "You heard what?"

Meggie Moraine's eyes narrowed, and there was no

expression in her face. "We were told not to do business with any store connected with the name Fortune."

"That is totally absurd." Jamie Sue clutched her hands in front of her waist. "Who would tell you that?"

"My husband works in the blacksmith shop at the Barrel Band Mine. The shop foreman is from Belfast. He said that the Fortunes all hated the Irish."

"Well, he lied to your husband."

"I will not tell Finnigan that you called him a liar."

"I don't know why anyone would start such a vicious rumor. He is mistaken, but I do apologize for calling him a liar."

"Riagan, that's my husband, is quite convinced it's true. He won't let me shop at any store with the name Fortune on it."

"But . . . but . . . this is absurd. All of our closest friends in the army . . . the Connors, the Sullivans, the Walshs . . . were all Irish. My word, my sister-in-law, Abigail, was an O'Neill. She's as Irish as they come. You must have us confused with someone else."

"Is your sister-in-law's family Protestant?" Meggie probed.

"Eh, yes . . . yes, they are. Presbyterians, I believe."

"Then she's an Orangeman, not truly Irish. I won't mention that fact to Riagan, either. He gets quite grumpy when you mention the Orange."

Jamie Sue let out a deep sigh. Perspiration drops cooled her forehead. "Mrs. Moraine, you must come over for tea so we can discuss this." *Lord, I have never in my life been accused of bigotry.*

"I don't know if Mr. Moraine would allow it."

"Do you mean he would judge us without any of us ever being given a chance to prove ourselves?"

"Riagan doesn't change his mind very easily."

"Mrs. Moraine, please ask him about you coming for tea. I'd certainly like to visit with you more. It is a very helpless feeling to be found guilty of something we didn't do."

"Mind you, I don't feel as strongly as Mr. Moraine, but I must support him. He is my husband." Meggie's narrow, pointed chin hung in resignation.

Jamie Sue rubbed the palm of her hand as if trying to remove an unseen blemish. "Mrs. Moraine, you mentioned you don't have many good friends yet in Deadwood."

"I haven't had time to socialize much." Meggie took a deep breath. "Actually, I'm shy when meeting new people."

"You and I have children the same age and live in the same neighborhood. Meggie, would you be my friend?"

"But how can that be? I told you I'm Irish . . ."

Jamie Sue reached over and rested her hand on Meggie's beige linen jacket-covered arm. The woman flinched. "Are you saying that Irish women refuse to make friends with anyone except other Irish women?" *Lord, I can't believe I'm having this conversation. Has one of the Deadwood Fortunes actually insulted the Irish?*

"No . . . you're right. We should at least have tea. I will ask Mr. Moraine. But I might need to wait for an appropriate time."

"I understand that, and I trust all of this doesn't interfere with our boys playing baseball. Little Frank says your Eachan is a very good pitcher."

Both women began to stroll down the aisle to the back

of the store.

"And your son is quite the hitter. My Riagan is a great fan of baseball. He says your Little Frank is a natural at the sport." Meggie paused in front of a display of cracker tins. "But it might be best if your son did not mention his name is Fortune when Mr. Moraine is at home."

Jamie Sue stopped. Her racing heart throbbed at her temples. "But . . . but . . . I can't tell my children to be ashamed of who they are. I will not ask him to hide his identity."

"Perhaps the boys should not play ball at our house until we have tea."

Jamie Sue kneaded her temple trying to get relief from the expanding headache. "Then let's get together soon."

"All of this must sound very parochial to you," Mrs. Moraine admitted.

"Yes, it does. If you hear where the shop foreman came up with such information, perhaps that would help us explain the misunderstanding."

"I hope it is merely a mistake," Mrs. Moraine added as she fidgeted with the gold ring on her finger. "I like how blunt and honest you are with me. I would like us to be friends."

"How about tea tomorrow?"

"I will think about it. Now, I must gather my order and get home. I left the babies with Kiara."

"Is Kiara your daughter?" Jamie Sue glanced around the room but couldn't spot Patricia.

"Yes, she is eleven."

"How many children do you have, Mrs. Moraine?"

"Five, so far. And you?"

"Just three. Little Frank and identical twin daughters."

Jamie Sue glanced back over her shoulder at the empty aisle. "One of whom came in with me but seems to have disappeared."

"The twins? You are their mother?"

"Yes."

"And Little Frank's their brother?"

"Eh, yes. Did he tell you otherwise?"

Mrs. Moraine started to laugh. "My Eachan is quite smitten with one of them and told Little Frank all about it. I think he was trying to get your son interested in the other twin. And that Little Frank never once admitted to being their brother."

Jamie Sue laughed. "He's convinced that the boys get so interested in the twins that he gets shoved out of the picture."

"He might be right. Eachan certainly talks about that one."

"Just which one of them does he like?"

"The one with the dimples . . . I think her name is Patricia Veronica."

"One is named Patricia, and the other is Veronica. They both have dimples."

"I'd say that's the one that interests him." Mrs. Moraine pointed across the store to where Eachan and Patricia huddled behind a butcher's block next to a full wheel of yellow cheese.

🥾

Patricia giggled and bounced her way down the sidewalk in front of her mother. "Eachan thought my name was

Patricia Veronica. Isn't that funny?"

"I'm surprised he spoke to you, what with you not wearing the rose dress."

Patricia pulled off her straw hat and twirled it around by the chin ribbon. "Mother! He didn't care what dress I was wearing."

"Now that's a good lesson to learn, isn't it?"

Both ladies paused and waited for a gust of dirt to blow past them. Jamie Sue shaded her eyes. "Is that a pig crossing the street?"

"Either that or it's a fat, hairless pink dog with an ugly face," Patricia giggled.

"Someone obviously left a gate open."

"Aunt Dacee June and Uncle Carty had a pig named Clarence."

"We ate Clarence last Christmas. Remember?"

"Oh yeah," Patricia gagged, then resumed the trek. There was a dance in her step. "I can't wait to tell 'Nica."

As they approached the dress shop, Veronica rushed out the door, her satin dress swishing. "Guess who I just saw in the street?"

Patricia glanced up at her mother, then back at her sister. "A pig?" she gulped.

"No . . . it was Curly Mac!"

"Who?" Jamie Sue probed.

"You remember . . . the boy on the train with the blond hair who was in the carriage with the woman with the dance hall dress?" Veronica danced on one foot and then the other. "He was in a buckboard with a man who looked a hundred and fifty years old."

"Did you talk to him?" Patricia asked.

"The old man?"

"No, Curly Mac."

"He just said 'Hi, Veronica Patricia . . .' Isn't that funny? He thought my name was Veronica Patricia?"

"Sounds like Eachan . . ." Patricia mumbled.

Veronica scooted over until the twins' arms were touching. "What do you mean by that?"

Patricia put her hat back on her head and began tying the ribbon under her chin. "Nothing."

"Tricia Fortune, did you see Eachan Moraine?"

Her nose turned high, Patricia batted her eyelashes. "Sort of."

Veronica grabbed her sister's hand. "What do you mean, sort of?"

Patricia burst out giggling. "I talked with him behind the potato bin at Morgan's for over ten minutes."

"You did not!"

Patricia spun around toward her mother. "I did too. Didn't I, Mama?"

"I believe you did." Jamie glanced across the street at the bakery as she smelled fresh-baked bread.

"That isn't fair!" Veronica pouted. "I had on the rose dress and everything!"

"You got Curly Mac to wave at you. I didn't even get to see him."

Veronica dropped her chin. "He was probably waving at Amber. She was standing next to me."

A young barefoot boy in coveralls ran up the boardwalk. "Have you seen Romeo?" he panted.

"Who?"

"My pet pig, Romeo. Has he come this way?"

"He crossed the street toward the bank," Patricia explained.

"If he went down to the Piedmont Saloon again, he's in real trouble," the little boy added.

The boy sprinted down the street.

"Eh, come on girls . . . let's go see what Aunt Abby has for us."

"Where is Amber?" Patricia asked.

"I'm up here!"

Jamie Sue and daughters shaded their eyes and looked up at the second-story window of the brick building. The girl leaning out had the shape of a twenty-year-old, but her face was definitely sixteen. "I've got to clean this apartment before mother rents it out again. 'Nica and Tricia, do you want to help me? Then we all can go horseback riding up to Central City."

"To see Curly Mac? Oh, Mother, may we?" Patricia pleaded.

"Yes, go help Amber. I need to talk to Abby. But Veronica can't go horseback riding in that rose satin dress."

Veronica tugged at her mother's arm. "Oh, Mother! I have to go! Please!"

Jamie Sue patted her hand. "Not in that dress."

"I wish I had never worn this dress!" Veronica announced.

"Well, I believe this has been a very educational afternoon."

"But . . . but . . . it's not fair! Everything is against me today!" Veronica moaned.

Patricia scooted beside her sister. " 'Nica, if you can't go riding, then I won't go either."

Veronica slipped her arm around her sister's waist. "Really? You'd do that for me?"

Patricia chewed on her lower lip. "Sure, that's what twin sisters are for."

"In that case, dear sister, how would you like to trade dresses?" Veronica asked.

"You mean I'd wear the rose one?"

"Yes, then I could wear yours and go horseback riding with Amber."

Robert Fortune sat on the right-hand backseat of the railroad car. Taite and Holter lounged on the bench seat facing him, their backs to the passengers. Unrolled maps were sprawled across their knees.

Fortune tapped the map with his finger. "Ninety-nine out of a hundred runs will be routine. The toughest thing we'll face is staying awake and alert. I won't tolerate sleeping on the job. I consider it grounds for dismissal. So make sure you get plenty of rest before you come on duty. I'm not telling you what to do with your time off, but hurrahing the night away isn't going to work for this job."

Guthrie Holter leaned forward, his elbow on his knee. "You reckon the most trouble will come from folks on the inside . . . or those jumping the train from the outside?"

Robert looked up the aisle at the crowded passenger car. Muted conversations bounced in rhythm to the rumble of the train. "No telling. We should prepare for both. I've marked key areas on the map where someone might try to board the train. I want us to assume something will happen at every point."

"Especially when we're haulin' payrolls or gold," Taite added.

Holter lowered his voice. "Are we going to know about the rich shipments?"

"I told the railroad supervisor not to inform us unless he thought it absolutely necessary."

"So we never know when the big shipments are on board? Isn't that a little dangerous?" Stillman Taite probed.

Fortune studied the man's narrow eyes. *Why are you so concerned?* "It's a safety precaution. If we don't know when the shipment is valuable, we'll have to protect every train like it was special. I don't want us to relax just because the cargo is less valuable."

"And if we don't know the shipment, we can't be the thieves," Holter's declaration turned into a sly grin.

"You think we're the type to rob a train?" Taite huffed.

"Still, here's a basic rule in the business," Fortune explained. "Assume every person on this train is capable of robbing it. It's a basic theological position."

"Theological?"

"It's called the doctrine of the sinfulness of man. Anyone is capable of anything."

"Even you?"

"Even me," Fortune added. "Evil should never, ever surprise you. Righteousness is the big surprise."

Stillman Taite glanced back over his shoulders. "Should we be studying the passengers?"

"Yes, but do it discreetly. I'd just as soon no one knows who we are when we ride the train. Keep your badge on the inside of your coat, a newspaper or book in your hand.

Wander down through the cars and pick out any likely looking sneak thieves or train robbers, then keep an eye on them. Like I said . . . most times it's going to be just a train ride."

Holter looked straight at Fortune. "Speakin' of passengers, did you spot that gordo hombre in the second row with the dirty red bandanna?"

Fortune continued to study the map on his lap. "The one with the .44 half-cocked in his holster?"

"What?" Taite spun around to look toward the front of the train.

"Don't stare," Robert cautioned.

"He has a bulge in his boot top. I reckon it's either a sneak gun or a Bowie knife," Holter added.

"You saw all of that when we boarded?" Taite pressed.

"I spied him on the platform back in Rapid City. He was at the Yellow Dog Cafe this morning braggin' about how he was goin' up to Deadwood to get rich. He don't exactly look like he works for a livin'. I thought maybe he was a gambler, but his fingernails was too dirty. Never did know a gambler that had dirty fingernails."

"Looks like he's headin' this way, boys." Robert leaned back and tugged his hat low across his forehead.

"There ain't no empty seats, except that one behind us," Taite said.

"Holter, you lean back and pull your hat down like you're sleeping. See if you can pick up any conversations. Taite, lean forward and study this map. I'll keep an eye on him."

Similar to a jack-o-lantern, the man's big round head was defined by chin whiskers and round mouth. His eyes were framed by dark bags, his lips puffy. He meandered down the center aisle very slowly, as if measuring each passenger. Finally, he plopped down next to a thin man with a black silk suit in the row behind Holter and Taite. Robert Fortune couldn't hear the mumbled conversation but could tell by the thin man's expression that he was not in favor of whatever the other man was demanding. The thin man stood as if to leave, but the other man blocked his way and shoved him back into the seat.

Guthrie Holter leaned way over the map, then whispered, "He's trying to force this Englishman to buy some worthless mining stock."

"I'll confront him," Robert replied softly. "You two back me up. But don't reveal yourselves until needed."

Fortune swung out into the aisle, took three steps, then spun around near the man with the dirty bandanna.

"What's you name, mister?" Robert demanded.

"What in Hades's name difference is it to you?" the man growled, resting his hand on his revolver.

Robert leaned his hand on the back of the leather seat and kept his voice low. "I want to know what to put on my report." He could smell stale whiskey and dried sweat.

The man rubbed his chin. "What report?"

Robert stood straight and glanced around at the other passengers. No one was looking their way. "I'm the train inspector. It's my job to file a report on sneak thieves, troublemakers, and solicitors who disturb the passengers."

The man attempted to dismiss Fortune with a flip of his hand. "I ain't doin' nothin' wrong, so go torment someone else."

Fortune glanced over at the thin man with black silk tie.

His face was pale. "Did this ol' boy try to force you to buy worthless mining stock?"

The Englishman straightened his tie and sat with a stiff back. "He most certainly did. My word, he said he'd shoot me in the . . . eh, intestines if I didn't purchase five hundred dollars worth of stock."

"He ain't telling the truth," the other man protested. "You cain't trust them foreigners. I was merely offering him a deal where he could double his investment in six months. But if this is the thanks I get, I withdraw the offer."

"What's your name?" Fortune demanded again.

The man folded his thick arms. "I ain't tellin' you nothin'."

Fortune pointed toward the handbills posted in the front of the coach. "There's a sign up there that says 'Absolutely no solicitation.' We will not have guests of the Elkhorn pestered by hucksters and drummers. I'll have to ask you to step to the back of the car."

"You ain't goin' to get me to do nothin' . . ." The man jerked his revolver out of the holster.

Fortune clenched the man's ear and twisted it sharply with one hand as he plucked the gun away from the yelping man with the other.

All conversation in the coach ceased. People turned to gawk.

"My word," the Englishman gasped as he scooted against the window, "I've heard of twitching horses but never seen it done on a man."

Robert kept his back to the passengers. He slid the man's revolver into his coat pocket. "Sometimes there's not a wide distinction between man and beast," he added.

"We've got a few things to discuss on the platform between the cars, one of which is your name." He motioned with his hand. "Step back there, please."

"Well, let a man pull up his socks before I go trampin' around." The man leaned over and reached for his boots.

Taite and Holter both shoved revolvers into the back of the man's head.

"You ain't goin' for that sneak gun are you?" Holter demanded.

The man sat straight up, his hands in the air. "My name's Oscar Puddin!" he shouted. "Who are them two?"

"My deputies," Robert explained. "Take out the sneak gun and lay it on the floor, Mr. Puddin. Take it real slow because my deputies are new on the job and they are counting on getting to shoot someone today. I'd rather you didn't give them the opportunity."

Puddin worked up a full sweat by the time he removed the .32 caliber snub-nosed revolver from his boot and laid it on the floor.

"Folks, I'm the railroad inspector," Robert told the staring passengers. "This old boy was trying to extort some money. We just won't let that happen on this train. Did he get money from any of you?"

Everyone sat motionless.

"Go on about your business. My deputies and I have this under control. The Elkhorn is the safest railroad in the West. We take care of our folks. Go back to your visits and enjoy the trip." He turned back to Puddin. "Now, if you'll just step out the back door."

The man rose slowly off his seat. "What are you going to do to me?"

"You not only harassed a passenger, but you also pulled a firearm on a railroad inspector. So you forfeit your ticket and will be put off the train."

"Where?"

Fortune leaned down and glanced out the window at the rumbling hillside. "Right here looks fine."

"But the train's goin' forty miles an hour!"

"No, it's going twenty-four miles an hour and slows to around fifteen at the turns. All of which is something you should have taken into account before you tried to extort Mr. . . . eh, Mr. . . ."

"Chambers. Byron Chambers." The Englishman tipped his bowler.

Fortune shoved his fingers into Puddin's greasy vest and pushed him toward the back door. Holter and Taite joined him in the aisle.

"But . . ." Puddin panicked. "Mr. Chambers, I apologize if I seemed a bit insistent in my salesmanship!" he called back.

Chambers straightened his tie. "My word, uh, yes. Apology is accepted."

"See there, he accepted my apology." Puddin stopped walking. "You cain't throw me off the train now."

Robert shoved him toward the back door. "You still drew a gun on a railroad inspector."

"But I didn't shoot no one!" he bellowed as he was shoved outside on the back platform.

A stiff summer breeze caused Fortune to shove down his hat as he stepped beside the man. The air had a dry, dusty taste and the rattle of steel wheels on steel rails forced the men to shout. The side of the hill was littered with tree stumps and granite boulders.

"If I let you get away with drawing a gun on us, then how many more will come along and do the same?" Fortune explained. "I think I should make an example of you, Mr. Puddin. Toss him off the train, boys."

"Wait . . . wait . . . I don't want to be an example."

"It's too late for that. If I don't, Mr. Puddin, as soon as we hit Deadwood, you'll go down to the badlands to a saloon like the Piedmont and start bragging about pullin' a gun on the railroad inspector, and the next thing I know we'll have every drifter and bummer in the badlands tryin' the same thing."

"No sir . . . I won't. I'll . . . I'll leave Deadwood as soon as I get there. I won't tell nobody. The fall would break my back."

"I reckon that would accomplish our purpose, wouldn't it?" Holter said.

"We can't take a chance, Puddin." Taite poked his double-action Smith and Wesson in the man's ribs. "Over you go."

"Wait! Put me off at the water tank. There's a water tank between here and Deadwood. It ain't two or three miles up the tracks."

"You seem to know a lot about this line."

"I've been on it before."

"You caught me on a merciful day, Puddin. Handcuff him to the rail. He can ride back here."

"I've got to ride outside?" the man protested.

"It's your choice . . . we can toss you out in the boulders or . . ."

"I'll ride back here."

When they returned to the car, every eye was on them.

"Everything's taken care of, folks," Robert explained. "The Elkhorn will not tolerate having its passengers beleaguered in any way. If you ever have anyone bother you with illegal, immoral, or inappropriate advances, please notify your conductor, who will relay the message to one of us."

Two young men in army blue instantly scooted away from a blonde young lady and sat at near attention.

The three men returned to their seats. Once again the rumble of conversations matched the rattle of the wheels on the tracks.

Byron Chambers turned around. "My word, I'm certainly glad you didn't toss him on the rocks on my account."

"You got business in Deadwood, Mr. Chambers?" Robert asked.

"I'm a chartered accountant for the Bank of Ottawa out of Toronto. We have an interest in the Broken Boulder Mine, and I've come to examine the accounts and ledgers."

"I've never heard of the Broken Boulder."

"That's one of the reasons I'm here. We haven't had a report in over six months, yet we've been sending systematic installments. It's located on the east rim of Spruce Canyon."

"We're going to put Mr. Puddin off the train at the water tanks," Robert explained. "But he might hike into Deadwood anyway. If I were you, I'd stay out of the badlands. If he meets you in a dark alley, he might figure he has a score to settle."

"Exactly what do you mean by badlands?"

"The lower end of Deadwood is lined with saloons, dance halls, and brothels. No offense intended, but a man with a fancy silk suit hiking around down there after dark will be a mighty tempting target for sneak thieves and extortionists."

"My word, I had no idea Deadwood was so philistine."

Robert Fortune laughed. "I've never heard it called that before. But I reckon one man's promised land is another's philistine."

CHAPTER FIVE

The only noise in the hardware store was the small brass bell that hung by a single bent lag bolt above the door. It signaled another entry. Robert's boots marked each step on the worn wooden floor as he ambled toward the back of the dimly lit store. A coatless Todd Fortune squatted down by the open door of the cast-iron woodstove.

"Just you, this morning, big brother?" Robert asked.

Todd leaned back on his haunches and rubbed his gray-flecked goatee. "Daddy's under the weather, Bobby. I took him some lemon-honey tea and told him to stay in bed."

Robert patted the side of a lukewarm blue enamel coffeepot. "Daddy drinkin' lemon tea? Seems funny, doesn't it?"

"You know what seems really strange? That he and that bunch of his aren't around this stove. They pestered me every morning for the last ten years. Now, it's crazy. I miss them." Todd struck a sulfur match on the side of the stove and held it under the crumpled newspaper and kindling. "I don't intend on being the senior Fortune in this clan for a long, long time."

Robert studied his brother. "If you shaved your goatee and grew yourself a thick, drooping mustache, you'd look just like Daddy."

"That's a sobering thought."

Robert pulled a gray ceramic mug off the shelf but didn't pour any coffee in it. "Quiet Jim isn't coming down?"

"Nah, he telephoned earlier. Said he was just too worn out."

"Quiet Jim's sort of giving up, isn't he?" Robert pondered.

"For years he planned on regaining his strength and walking out of that wheelchair. It's just not going to happen." Todd stared across the store. "It's not fair. He got shot for hanging around with Fortunes."

"He can still sing a pretty tune," Robert added.

Todd stood and jammed his hands in his back pockets. "Bobby, remember that first night we rode into Deadwood on the freight wagon?"

"The old men had come out to rescue us from Doc Kabyo."

"It was bitter cold and all we could hear was the squeaking of wheels and Quiet Jim's Christmas carols." Todd scooted the coffeepot to the center of the stove. "Might have been the prettiest tunes I ever heard."

Robert rubbed the back of his neck and glanced at his brother. "When is it our turn, big brother?"

The fire in the stove was starting to roar. Todd turned the damper down. "To sit around the stove and tell lies about the old days?"

"Do the years get faster the older we get? The last ten

137

seemed to have slipped by in a flash."

"Sammy was saying the same thing." Todd turned up the gas lantern until the back of the store was well lit. "I figure we've got another ten to fifteen years before that happens."

Robert shifted his holster, then sat down on a worn wooden bench, still holding an empty coffee cup. "By then the 'flying fist of death' will take on mythic proportions."

Todd poured himself a tin cup of coffee, took a sip, then sat it on the stove to warm up. "I imagine the fiction stories about these days will get even wilder. But I wish authors like Hawthorne Miller wouldn't use real names in their stories."

"What?" Robert laughed. "You mean all those Stuart Brannon stories aren't true?"

Todd plucked up his coffee cup again. "Now, those are the only ones that just might be true. But, no matter how exaggerated we become, we'll never compete with the Texas Camp of '75."

"Maybe that's the way it always is," Robert suggested. "The past generation is always more adventuresome than the present."

Todd stared down at his polished brown boots. "That might be, but our lives haven't exactly been boring. You were there at the Little Big Horn with Captain Benteen . . . and down on the border with General Crook. . . . I reckon it will be a long time before someone tops that."

Robert sat on the bench with West Point posture. "Look at you, Todd. You came to the gulch in Christmas of '75 and stayed. There aren't ten men in town who have been here longer. You've captured the outlaws, confronted the Sioux, fought the fires, survived the diseases. It was a wild place when you and Rebekah said your vows. And now it's as tame as Omaha . . . well, maybe not Omaha."

The ringing brass bell caused both men to stare back at the front door. With gray mustache drooping across freshly shaved chin and plaid four-in-hand tie hanging from a starched, collarless white shirt, Samuel Fortune pulled off his hat and moseyed toward them. "You two telling big windies back there?" he called out as he approached.

"Actually, we were," Todd said.

The woodstove was rapidly warming the already stuffy air of the hardware store.

"Are we all going to turn out like the old man?" Sam prodded. He pulled off his suit coat and hung it on a peg full of white canvas clerk's aprons. He headed for the coffeepot, opened the lid, stuck his finger in the coffee, then grabbed a cup off the shelf. "Can't think of too much better example to follow." He turned to Todd. "Is he still in bed?"

Todd nodded.

Sam brushed down his gray mustache with his fingers and glanced toward the stairway. "I think I'll go up and see him."

"He just got to sleep, Sammy. Said he was awake most the night," Todd added. "Daddy has a hard time breathing when he's lying down. Most nights he sleeps in that old leather chair."

Sam plopped down on the bench. "I'll check on him later. It's 1891. You'd think with all the advances in medicine they'd have something to help him." He turned to his younger brother. "What's your schedule for today, Bobby? You got to make the Rapid City train?"

"Nope. I've got Stillman Taite on the morning run.

Guthrie Holter's on the afternoon."

"I still haven't met Holter, but his sister was a firecracker. Not that I remember those things, of course." Sam rubbed the creases at the corner of his eye. "You have the day off?"

Robert carried his empty mug to the stove, then filled it with boiling coffee. "There's always plenty of paperwork. It's just like the army; . . . they want three copies of everything."

"Maybe you need to get yourself one of those typewriting machines," Sam proposed.

Robert plopped back down on the bench. "I've got one setting there staring at me. I won't touch it. Afraid I'll break it. Some day I'll get a company clerk. He can use it."

Todd parked himself next to the bolt bins and began to sort misplaced bolts. "Now you're beginning to sound like Sammy."

Sam took a deep gulp of nearly boiling coffee. "Listen, boys. I figure the real key to success is to get into a business you know absolutely nothing about. I can't make the telephone system work, so I hire a technician. I can't connect the switchboard, so I hire an operator. I can't even keep the bills and income straight, so I hire a bookkeeper. There's not much left to do . . ."

Todd laughed. "But butter up some new customers and carry the money to the bank."

"Seems almost sinful, don't it?" Samuel added. "This whole telephone exchange is just a matter of being in the right place at the right time. The Lord's been good to me . . . better than I deserve."

"That's the history of the Fortunes in the Black Hills," Todd noted.

"Timing . . . or God's grace?" Sam mumbled.

"Both," Todd said.

"Well, I do have a little work to do today," Sam added. "I've got to go check on a route for a phone line. I got a mine up on the east rim of Spruce Canyon that wants to know what it would cost to run a phone line up there from Deadwood."

"I met an Englishman on the train . . . well, he was from Toronto, actually," Robert explained, ". . . who was going to check the books at a mine called the Broken Boulder. I never heard of it."

Todd stopped sorting bolts, then wiped his hand off on a white canvas apron. "No one ever had any luck in Spruce Canyon. Remember ol' man Hacker and that Italian partner of his? They dug up there for years. That's exactly why I like the hardware business better than the mining business. We sell to those who strike it rich and we sell to those who go bust."

"Well, they better have struck somethin'. A phone line won't be cheap." Sam took another gulp of steaming coffee. "I've had a crew of Irishmen stringing a line from Elizabethtown to Doddsville, and it cost me four hundred dollars a mile."

Robert set his empty mug on the bench next to him. "Irishmen?"

Sam waved his hand toward the street. "Pinched-nose Pete hired a crew of Irishmen to put the line in."

Robert picked his teeth with his fingernail. "Did you have any trouble with them?"

"When they hit cliffs at Death Song Canyon they threatened to walk off if they didn't get a raise."

"What were you payin' them?" Todd asked.

"Six dollars a day. But I had to go to seven-fifty while they were on the canyon."

"Twelve-hour days?" Robert pressed.

"Ten-hour days," Sam replied. "They had to rope themselves to stumps and boulders to keep from tumbling off the cliff."

"That's better than miner's wages," Todd remarked.

"I needed a crew, and that's what it cost. It's not like stringin' a line in Cheyenne. Anyway, what are all these questions about?"

The edge of the bench felt splintery as Robert ran his hand along it. "Jamie Sue came home from shoppin' yesterday, saying she met a neighbor lady at the store. Her name's Meggie Moraine, and she claims all the Irish in Deadwood, Central City, and Lead have been told that the Fortunes are Irish-haters and they should avoid our stores."

Todd spun around, spilling coffee from his enameled cup. "Irish-haters?"

"Shoot, I paid them better than anyone in the Black Hills," Samuel grumbled. "Are you sure you got the story straight?"

Robert shook his head. "That's the way it came to me."

"Irish-haters . . ." Todd mumbled. "I can't believe that."

"That's stupid," Sam mumbled. "I married the most handsome Irish lady who ever came to South Dakota. That's not exactly hating the Irish. Someone's tellin' a lie."

"This Mrs. Moraine said that Abby, being Protestant and not Catholic, didn't really count," Robert explained.

Samuel paced in front of a shelf of drilling points. "Irish is Irish, isn't it?"

"Apparently not," Robert responded.

"Obviously, it's a mistake," Todd huffed.

"I'll try to talk to Mr. Moraine," Robert offered. "He seems to be the one pushing this thing. Kind of strange, isn't it?"

"I've never been accused of hating anyone in my life," Todd said.

Sammy grinned. "How about Ricardo Swartz?"

Robert broke out laughing. "Was he the one who lassoed the school outhouse?"

Samuel's hands waved as he talked. "He dallied it to the back of Mr. Tanner's milk wagon and turned over the privy with big brother still inside. It happened during recess while all the other kids were outside. Don't you remember?"

"I was too young," Robert chuckled. "I was still at home and didn't get to see anything."

"Well, all the girls saw everything!" Sammy grinned.

"OK . . ." Todd sighed. "So I did hate Ricardo Swartz. But I got over that."

"How long did it take?"

"About twenty-five years . . ." Todd gulped down the last of his coffee. "Of course, that's only because Ricardo died in a shoot-out on the Rio Grande." He glanced out at the morning shadows that darkened the street. "But, Irish-haters?"

"I'll talk to Pinch-Nosed Pete," Samuel said. "Maybe he heard that line crew mention somethin'. But I can't figure how that translated into hating the Irish."

The bell at the door jingled. A man with a thick, neatly trimmed dark mustache and deep set eyes strolled in. His cane had a brass cap, his top hat a crisp, silk shine. "I say, Mr. Fortune!"

A unison chorus of "yes" greeted him from the wood-stove.

"Oh, my . . ."

Robert stepped forward. "Mr. Chambers, these are my brothers. Todd, Sammy . . . this is Mr. Byron Chambers, who is a chartered accountant from Toronto."

"Would you like a cup of coffee, Mr. Chambers?" Todd offered.

"Eh, no . . ." the man strolled toward the iron woodstove. "Well, yes. Thank you."

"Are you looking for me?" Robert asked as he handed the man a steaming cup.

"Actually, I don't know which Fortune I'm looking for. I need to know how to get out to the Broken Boulder Mine. No one at the Merchant's Hotel had ever heard of it." Chambers took a dignified sip of coffee. His eyes widened, then watered. "They said I should come over here and ask one of the old geezers at the woodstove how to find it." He covered his mouth with his hand as he coughed. "I must say, you are not at all as old as I expected."

"Well, thank you," Sammy grinned. "Actually, big brother Todd is close to eighty."

Chambers swallowed another mouthful of coffee, then gasped out, "I say . . ."

"Only believe half of what Sammy says, Mr. Chambers. I'm near forty, but I feel that old some days. Men at the hotel were talking about our daddy and his pals who usu-ally hang out back here."

"Yes, well, perhaps one of you could tell me how to get

to the Broken Boulder." Chambers stared into his coffee cup as if looking for bugs in a sugarbowl.

"We were just talkin' about that ourselves. None of us are too sure where it is," Robert admitted. "But Sammy needs to go out there today."

Chambers set his half-full cup of coffee on the bolt bin. "What a fortuitous circumstance. Perhaps I could ride out with you?"

"Be my guest, Mr. Chambers. Just rent yourself a pony at the livery and we'll ride out about 10:00."

"I would rather take a carriage, if you don't mind. Is there a passable road to the mine?"

"I don't know. That's what I want to find out. They asked me about the cost of a telephone line to the headworks of the mine, but I've never actually seen the place," Samuel added. "It'll need to be horseback."

"Passable road is all in the eye of the beholder," Todd offered.

"Yes, well, I, eh . . . don't do well on horseback," Chambers admitted. "Not that I'm much of a carriage driver."

Robert glanced over at Samuel. "How would you like some more company?"

"You thinkin' of coming along?" Sam quizzed.

Robert chewed on some coffee grounds that had gotten stuck between his cheek and gum. "Sort of like to see what they've developed. I'll drive the carriage, Mr. Chambers."

The accountant reached into his suit coat pocket and pulled out a leather bi-fold. "Splendid. I'll pay you, of course."

"You pay for the carriage, but not me. I'm going just to keep my brother out of trouble." Robert insisted.

Chambers shoved his wallet back into his pocket. "My word, does he often get in trouble?"

"Sammy's been in trouble since the day he turned two," Todd said.

The fuzz from the peaches made her arms itch, but Jamie Sue's hands were so sticky and juice-covered that she refused to scratch. Her beige dress sleeves were pushed above her elbows as she stood at the sink and peeled the plump, orange-red fruit. In desperation, she tried scratching the back of her forearm with her nose. She succeeded in rubbing peach fuzz all over her face. She held a whole, peeled peach in each hand.

Lord, is this a joke? Are peaches one of Your sly tricks? Like the aroma of onions . . . or the spines on an artichoke . . . peach fuzz. . . . I wonder if the forbidden tree in the garden had been a peach instead of an apple, would Adam and Eve have sinned so quickly? If it had been a persimmon tree, they might not have sinned at all. Jamie Sue tried to turn her head away as she was overcome with an uncontrollable sneeze. The stark ring from the telephone coincided with her sneeze and caused her to flinch. Both slick peaches squirted out of her hands and rolled across the gray-painted wood floor.

She stared at the oak box bolted onto the wall as it rang again.

Oh dear, I will never get used to that startling noise. Why don't they make it a soft chime or a Brahms melody or something? It reminds me of a rocking chair on a cat's tail.

Lifting the receiver gingerly with two sticky fingers, she held it to her ear. "Yes?" she shouted into the mouthpiece.

"This is Mr. Landusky at the depot. Is this the Fortune residence?"

"Robert isn't home, Mr. Landusky." Peach juice dribbled down her arm to her elbow.

"I don't need to speak to Mr. Fortune."

"Then why did you ring?" she blustered. "I'm quite busy, you know."

"Is this Mrs. Fortune?"

Bending over the telephone, Jamie Sue's lower back ached. "Of course it is."

"We have your trunks."

"My what?" she shouted.

"The luggage . . . the cases . . . the trunks. Those that you've been waiting for."

"You have our goods?" she roared. "That's wonderful. Where have they been all this time?"

"The invoice said they were mistakenly shipped to San Diego."

"California?" she bellowed.

"Yes, ma'am. Mrs. Fortune, are you sick? You seem to be yelling."

"No . . . I'm . . . I'm just sticky."

"What?"

Jamie Sue tried to relax and lower her voice. "Mr. Landusky, can you deliver them right away?"

"Deliver them?"

"The railroad has misplaced our luggage for weeks. Surely, you will deliver them, won't you?"

"Mrs. Fortune, I'm here by myself this morning. I can't

bring them up until late this afternoon. Perhaps Mr. Fortune could bring them home."

"Is he in his office at the depot?"

"No, that's why I'm calling you. He said something about surveying a new telephone line. Anyway, I'm sorry for the inconvenience."

The back door flung open. Little Frank sprinted in. "How much do you think a kitchen window costs?" he blurted out.

Still holding the telephone receiver, she shouted, "Oh, no, what did you do now?"

"What?" Mr. Landusky choked. "I assure you I didn't do anything that would . . ."

"Just a minute, Mr. Landusky . . ." She turned to her son. "Little Frank, wait until I . . . watch out for the—"

Little Frank's boot heel stepped squarely on one of the peaches. His leg gave way. With a yelp, he flung his arm toward the iron stove to break his fall. He cracked his hand into the stove and knocked over a pot of simmering water that contained one small, whole chicken.

"Little Frank!" Jamie Sue dropped the phone receiver and lunged toward her son, who dove away from the steaming water and into the far wall.

Little Frank screamed in pain as his hand hit the wall. He clutched his right hand as Jamie Sue's second step landed squarely on the second peach. She threw her hands out in front of her to catch her fall, yet landed flat on her nose in the chicken water that had cooled somewhat as it puddled on the floor.

Little Frank continued to scream in pain. Jamie Sue rolled to her back but couldn't get a breath. Her hair matted in the chicken water. She tried to sit up but still couldn't breathe. Wiping the chicken water off her face, she noticed her fingers covered with blood.

Gasping for breath, she struggled to her knees just as the twins scampered down the stairs and peered into the kitchen. One glance at their mother and brother and both girls burst out sobbing.

"Girls!" Jamie Sue gasped. "Girls . . . I need your help!"

"What caused this?" Veronica hollered.

"It's the peaches!" Jamie Sue blurted out.

"Mother! My finger!" Little Frank cried ". . . what about my finger! Look at it! Look at it!"

On hands and knees, she glanced at her son. He gripped his right index finger that was bent almost straight back to his wrist.

Oh, Lord . . . oh . . . no . . .

She crawled over to her son.

"You have blood all over your face!" he wailed.

"It's just a bloody nose. Let me see your finger."

"Don't touch it . . . don't touch it . . ." he screamed.

With sticky, bloody hands she grabbed his hand, then yanked the finger back down straight. Little Frank's scream rebounded off the kitchen wall, then he slumped over in a faint.

"Grab me a towel. Veronica, hurry! Patricia, you get the smelling salts and . . ." Still on her hands and knees, Jamie Sue turned around to look at her daughters.

Both the girls stared with blank expressions and sheet-white faces.

They are going to collapse. . . . They are both going to swoon!

"Sit down, girls! Sit down right now and put your head between your knees," she shouted.

Both girls slumped to the floor.

Then, as if following an offstage cue, they toppled together backwards in a faint.

Jamie Sue crawled over to the small kitchen table. She pulled the clean white linen tablecloth to the floor. She tried to wipe off her sticky hands and bloody face. With a corner of the tablecloth pressed up against her nose, she crawled back over to Little Frank. Sitting on the floor in the chicken water with her back against the wall, she placed his head in her lap and stroked his cheeks.

Tears streamed across her face. Sniffing the best she could, she took the cloth away from her face and wrapped a clean corner around Little Frank's right hand. She pinned his injured index finger to the others. Then she rocked his head back and forth in her lap.

She stared up in disbelief as the telephone rang.

How can it ring? I didn't even finish talking to Mr. Landusky. Did I? They can't ring, if I don't hang up. Can they?

"Stop it!" she yelled. "I can't answer you! Stop it right now!" Jamie Sue tried to take deep breaths.

Lord, I can't handle this much . . . I really can't . . .

On the third ring, Veronica and Patricia propped themselves up on their elbows, looked over at her and Little Frank, then began to sob again.

Keeping Little Frank's head in her lap, Jamie Sue reached over and plucked up the small chicken off the floor. The ringing now blared as loud as a lighthouse bell. She hardly heard the back door open as she hurled the chicken at the ringing telephone and shouted, "I hate you!"

A stunned Robert Fortune appeared at the doorway. "What are you doing?" he blurted out as he yanked his revolver from his holster and surveyed the room.

"I am trying," she shouted through the tears, blood, and chicken water, "to bake a peach pie for your father!"

Then, like driftwood unable to resist the ocean wave's undertow, she slumped against the wall and began to sob.

Jamie Sue descended the staircase wearing her fancy new green dress and a flannel towel wrapped around her hair. Little Frank was propped up in a chair holding his neatly linen-wrapped hand. The twins were slicing peaches at the porcelain sink. Robert was mopping the floor.

"Are you alright, Mama?" Little Frank asked.

She bent over, kissed his forehead, then rubbed his shoulders. "I'm fine, honey. I just had the wind knocked out of me and got a bloody nose. You're the one that's injured."

Little Frank rubbed his nose with his good hand. "That really, really hurt when you straightened my finger, Mama."

"I know, darling, I know . . ." She stroked his matted hair.

"I tried not to cry. I didn't want to cry."

She stood next to his chair and cradled his curly, light brown head against her stomach. "That's alright, honey . . . it's alright."

"But boys aren't suppose to cry!" he murmured.

"That's a dumb rule," Veronica said.

"Everyone has the right to laugh, so everyone should

have the right to cry," Patricia said.

"Your sisters are right," Robert encouraged. "The Bible says there's a time to laugh and a time to cry . . . and this was your turn."

"But I'm embarrassed."

"You're embarrassed?" Jamie Sue added. "How about me? I was the one who dropped the peaches, answered the phone with sticky fingers, tripped and fell flat on my nose . . . and . . ."

"And threw the chicken at the telephone!" Veronica added.

Jamie Sue strolled over to the girls and looked over their shoulders. "If I had a shotgun, I would have blasted it off the wall."

"You can't imagine what went through my mind when I came in the back door and saw you all on the floor and the blood . . ." Robert shook his head. "I thought . . . well . . ." He turned his head away.

Veronica glanced across the room. "Is it your turn to cry, Daddy?"

He turned back with a deep sigh. "It was very close to my turn."

Jamie Sue gently rubbed her nose. "Even with my bruises, I can smell a cobbler. Did someone put one of those vicious peach pies in the oven?"

"We did, Mama," Patricia said.

"Good, we can take the first one to Grandpa Brazos as soon as it cools." Jamie Sue let her damp hair drape across her shoulders.

Wiping her hands on her apron, Patricia stepped up beside her. "You look very pretty in that green dress, Mama."

Jamie Sue held out her hands and looked at the starched white lace cuffs. "It's my only clean dress. It will be such a delight to get our belongings at last. Are you going to telephone Mr. Landusky?"

"I already have," Robert replied. "With a quite sticky telephone, I might add."

"It's lucky to be alive. When will he deliver our trunks?"

"He couldn't get away until after lunch. So I telephoned the express company. They'll have it all delivered before noon," Robert reported.

Jamie Sue threw her arms around his neck and kissed his lips.

"Mother!" Veronica scolded.

Jamie Sue pulled back. "I never thought I'd be so excited to see a bunch of old clothes and used furnishings."

"This will be the first time 'Nica and I have to put all our clothes in two different closets," Patricia reported.

"Yes, won't that be fun?" Jamie Sue continued to dry her hair on the flannel towel.

"Maybe I could go visit Quint before the trunks get here," Little Frank suggested. "I don't want to listen to 'Nica and Tricia fuss and fume."

"What about your finger?" Jamie Sue asked. "We need you here when the doctor comes by."

"Dr. Preston said he would stop by here after he checks on Quiet Jim. So maybe Little Frank could save the doc an extra stop and see him over there," Robert offered.

"Well, you have to change your shirt and comb your hair."

"I can't comb my hair left-handed," Little Frank complained.

"I'll comb it for you," Veronica offered.

"Really?"

"Yes!" Patricia added. "We comb each other's hair all the time!"

The twins scurried after Little Frank as he trotted back to his room.

Jamie Sue strolled over to Robert. "Thanks for cleaning up the kitchen while I cleaned up."

"The girls did most of the work."

"Do you know what's scary about all this?"

"Peaches?" he said.

"No, it's frightening to think that I went from a perfectly sane woman to the brink of stark raving mad in only a matter of a few minutes." Jamie Sue laced her fingers into his. "Am I always that close to complete collapse?"

"Maybe we all are."

"Even Captain Robert Fortune?" She led him over toward the doorway to the living room.

"When I saw all of you on the floor and the blood on your face, I was as close to losing all control as I ever want to be." He tugged her tight against him. "You know what brought me around?"

"What?"

Robert could smell lilac water on Jamie Sue's damp hair. "You throwing the chicken."

She rolled her blue eyes and sighed. "That is the stupidest thing I've ever done in my entire life."

"Perhaps . . . but it was obvious you were mad at the telephone . . . and mad at the chicken . . . and I knew . . ."

"And mad at myself . . ." she prodded.

"That's when I knew it had been an accident."

"I suppose your whole family will find out about this."

He kissed her cheeks. "I won't tell."

"I know, but I couldn't ask the children to be silent."

"It's completely understandable to me. Don't worry about what anyone else thinks."

Jamie Sue stepped over to the living room window and stared out at the steep slope of Lincoln Street. "You know what I was wishing while I was in the tub?"

Robert scooted up behind her. "That you were living at the fort, and you had Maria in the kitchen making pies?"

She leaned her head back against his chest. "You read my mind."

His arms circled her waist. "You're always reading mine."

She giggled. "That's because you have such limited thought patterns, Captain Fortune."

Jamie Sue could feel his shoulders stiffen.

"And what am I thinking right now?"

She spun around and they stood toe-to-toe. "You're thinking that you're late to pick up that Mr. Chambers and meet Sammy."

"OK . . . you win."

She reached up and straightened his tie. "Go on. We'll take care of things here."

"I told the express company to carry everything right into the living room. I don't want you toting around those big trunks. If the girls want to carry things upstairs individually, that's fine. But I'll move the trunks and crates this afternoon when I get home." Robert picked up his hat from the entry table. He kissed her cheek. "The girls are right. You do look much better."

With damp hair stringing down her back, and white lace collar buttoned high under her neck, Jamie Sue batted her eyes. "How much better, Captain Fortune?"

Robert plopped his felt hat on her wet hair. "That does it, Mrs. Fortune. I'm not going anywhere. Come on . . ." He grabbed her hand and tugged her toward the stairway.

"At ease, Captain . . ." she laughed.

"Were you just teasing me, ma'am?"

"Not teasing. I was testing," she insisted.

"Did I pass?"

"With flying colors, soldier."

"Now, may I be dismissed?"

She patted his hand. "Temporarily."

"Are you sure everything's alright here with the children? It's alright for me to leave?"

"Everything is absolutely back to normal."

"Mother!" Little Frank hollered from the back room above a chorus of giggles. "Make them comb my hair right!"

Robert glanced down at Jamie Sue. "Go on, Captain Fortune. This is normal. Shall I expect you home for supper?"

He brushed the palm of his hand against her cheek. "Definitely."

The road from Central City to Garden City was defined by two well-worn ruts, with water still standing in some places, although there had been no rain in over a week. The light carriage dropped in the ruts, spraying water like a muddy pinwheel on the Fourth of July. Each rock and stick tested the strength of the springs and the resolve of the passengers.

"My word," Chambers huffed. He jammed down his top hat. "I expected more of a road than this." The cleft in his narrow chin was held straight out, as if plowing a path for the words that followed.

Robert Fortune held the dual leather lead lines twined between his gloveless fingers. He sat military straight. His wide-brimmed hat was cocked slightly left. "Some say this is the good part of the road."

"I don't understand why the mining company doesn't have an office in Deadwood. I need to examine the books, not the mine site." A few droplets of mud peppered the back of Chambers's silk top hat.

"Anyone can rent a building and claim to have a mine," Robert replied. "Most legitimate claims don't rent an office until they have to. I trust your bosses want to see a gold mine, not books about a gold mine. You would have to come out here anyway."

"Yes, I suppose so." Chambers pulled off his hat and rubbed the corner of his eyes. "Where did your brother go? I can't see him at all."

Robert gazed up over the pine trees. Thick white clouds drifted across the deep Dakota blue sky. "Sammy needs to explore the best route for a telephone line. That's why he rode his horse. If they can secure a right-of-way, they'd rather have a straight line than a curving one."

Chambers replaced his top hat and held onto the iron side rail of the carriage seat as the two-horse rig bounced over rocks and ruts. He waved his arm to the north. "I say, there are more buildings than I expected. It's like a village."

"It is a village, Mr. Chambers. It's called Garden City, but I don't have any idea why. The Broken Boulder is supposed to be over there." Robert pointed to the east.

Chambers tried brushing the mud drops off his suit sleeves but only smeared them. "There's nothing to the east, save for trees."

"And rocks . . . and sooner or later a cliff that drops straight down to Spruce Canyon." The road widened and smoothed out. Fortune brought the team to a trot.

Chambers leaned forward. "Is that your brother up there waiting for us? How did he skulk ahead without our seeing him?"

"Sammy's good at skulking."

Sam Fortune sat in the saddle on his buckskin horse near the hitching rail in front of a rough-cut-pine cabin with a hand-printed sign that read "The Ittldew Cafe."

"You get run out of Garden City yet, Sammy?" Robert teased.

"Shoot, no . . . I told 'em I was Captain Robert Fortune and they gave me a twenty-one-gun salute. At least I think it was a salute."

"Has anyone here heard of the Broken Boulder?" Robert quizzed.

"Yeah, but no one has ever seen it. It's secretive out there. They don't exactly like visitors. All I was told is ride east until someone shoots at you, and you're getting close." Samuel chewed a light green stem of wild grass.

"This is absurd," Chambers fumed as he spun his top hat around in his hand. "I traveled all the way from Toronto, and I can't even get to the mine, let alone the books?"

"We'll get you there, Mr. Chambers," Samuel insisted.

"They asked me for a bid on the telephone line, so I know they are expecting me."

"Is the road east on the other side of that rock field?" Chambers asked.

"The road *is* that rock field," Sam Fortune replied.

"I reckon we'll have some dinner here. There is nothing beyond this cafe." Robert jumped down and brushed the brown horses with the palm of his hand.

Chambers carefully climbed down and straightened his tie. Then he stared at the bullet-hole-riddled sign above the restaurant. "This place looks rather primitive. How's the fare?"

"I hear it lives up to its name," Samuel grinned as he tied his horse off to the rail, then led the trio into the Ittldew.

The brass door handle banged into the wainscoting just below the light green burlap wallpaper as the girls sprinted into the house with a duet shout of "Mama!"

Jamie Sue wiped her hands on her flowered apron and glanced out from the kitchen. "Is the freight wagon here?"

Patricia chewed her lower lip. "No, it's Amber."

Veronica bounced on her toes. "She has a carriage and wants to know if we want to go for a ride."

Jamie Sue hung her apron on a peg, then sauntered to the front door. She waved at Amber, who wore a wide-brimmed floppy straw hat and a dress with sleeves that only went a few inches past her elbows. "Where is she going?" she asked the twins.

"Amber said she wanted to test the horse," Veronica

reported.

"She's going up to Central City, Lead, and back here," Patricia added. "Can we go, Mama? Please!"

Jamie Sue brushed a strand of hair out of Patricia's eyes, then did the same for Veronica. "That will take a couple of hours. I thought you wanted to be here when your trunks are delivered."

"Oh, yeah . . ." Patricia moaned.

"I'll need your help with the dishes and things. We'll have plenty of unpacking to do. Tell Amber perhaps some other time."

"Couldn't we go for a little ride, Mama?" Veronica pleaded. "The freight wagon might not get here until noon."

"I'm not sure I want you racing that horse."

"She isn't going to race it," Patricia explained, "just test it."

"Why is it that doesn't comfort me much?"

"We could take the peach cobbler to Grandpa Brazos. Daddy said he could use some cheering up," Patricia said.

"Yes, you could do that. If you three girls don't cheer up that old man, nothing this side of heaven will. Take the pie to him, then come back. With Daddy gone and Little Frank with a bum hand, I'll be counting on you two to help me unpack."

Patricia threw her arms around Jamie Sue and kissed her cheek. "Thanks, Mama."

"We'll be home before noon," Veronica added.

"You'll be home as soon as the pie is delivered."

"Don't worry about us." Patricia followed her sister out the door. "We'll be with Amber."

Don't worry about you? I've stewed over you two for twelve years, and I'm not about to stop now. "Aren't you forgetting something?" she called out after them.

"What?" Patricia asked.

"The pie for Grandpa Brazos."

Robert found that if he kept the team reined back to a slow walk they could keep the wagon rolling through the rocks and stumps without lodging a wheel or busting an axle. Sam circled the carriage on his buckskin, jotting down notes and marking trees with his knife. From time to time he rode out of sight, hidden by the boulders and short ponderosa pines.

Robert maneuvered the team through a narrow lane hacked out in a ponderosa pine grove, then broke out in a small meadow at the bottom of a sloping canyon.

Chambers's black tie now hung loose at his neck, his top shirt button unfastened. His top hat was jammed almost to his ears. "That's a strange way to pile logs."

"That's a corduroy road."

"What?"

"The meadow must be boggy. So someone's cut and placed logs side-by-side. Originally used to skid logs out to a freight wagon or sawpit. Sometimes they put dirt on top to smooth it down, but this outfit doesn't seem to want to do anything to make access easier."

"What keeps the logs from sinking in the swamp?"

"Nothing . . . if they sink out of sight, you have to add more logs."

Once they jarred their way past the corduroy road, the trees thinned and the granite boulders increased. The trail was smoother and wider, but it still had occasional boulders. To the east Robert saw Samuel's silhouette drop down over the horizon. He reined up when they reached the edge of a sloping descent.

"Good heavens, we aren't expected to drive off the edge of this, are we?" Chambers huffed.

Robert pointed ahead. "There's the road down there. They've been driving something off this, but I'm not sure it was a light carriage. More like a dead-ax wagon, I reckon."

"But . . . but . . . it's nothing but boulders," Chambers protested.

Robert rubbed his dark beard and studied the roadway. "Kind of makes you wish you were on horseback, doesn't it?"

"Makes me wish I was in Toronto. I'm just a chartered accountant," Chambers insisted, "not some Lewiston Clark."

"Who?"

"You know what I mean."

"Well, it's time for us to get out." Robert swung down from the carriage. "I'm going to walk up there between the horses to keep them creeping down this slope. You go around to the back and hold onto the rail. Let the carriage drag you along like an anchor."

Chambers eased himself down on the other side of the rig. "My word, are you joking?"

"Nope."

The accountant tried brushing trail dust off his neatly

creased wool trousers. "Where's your brother, Samuel? Perhaps he could help."

Robert surveyed the empty horizon to the east. "Now that's something Mama and Daddy asked me and Todd for years. They never could find him when it was time for chores. It doesn't look too bad, Mr. Chambers. I'll hold the horses back while you drag your feet. We'll ease on down off of here. I don't think it's more than fifty yards."

Chambers stomped toward the rear of the carriage. "I've never heard anything like this. I thought the West was settled and all that. They're building concrete streets down east, just as smooth as your front porch, and here we are trying to blaze a trail like Kit Bridger."

"Kit Carson," Robert corrected.

"Whatever." Still wearing his top hat, Chambers continued to huff his way around to the back of the carriage. "I say, this won't get my new suit dirty, will it? I just bought it ten days ago."

"If you start to get dusty, turn loose and hike on down at your own speed," Robert instructed.

Standing between the horses, Robert Fortune watched Chambers lace his ungloved fingers around the black iron railing at the back of the carriage. "You ready, Byron?" he hollered.

"Quite so," Chambers shouted back.

Robert led the horses on one cautious step after another down across the boulders. When he felt the wheels gaining momentum, he leaned back against the harnesses. One foot at a time they crept down the descent. The horses, but not the carriage, had reached level ground when Robert finally loosened his grip.

Just as he reached up to wipe the sweat off his forehead, a gunshot exploded from somewhere up ahead. Granite shreds flew up in front of the horses. In unison they reared. Fortune tried to grab their harnesses, but his hands slipped. The panicked horses' hooves came back down, and the rigging between slapped him to the ground. Then they took off on a wild gallop.

Robert pulled his arms and feet in as he tried to avoid the horse hooves and wagon wheels racing over him. Chambers's boots ran up his back. He rolled over and clutched the accountant with both arms around the knees and held on.

"Whoa!" Robert shouted and bounced along like an empty airtight can tied to a dog's tail. "Whoa!"

The team bolted to the right. The centrifugal force swung Robert to the left. He bounced free over the dirt and rocks, and rolled to a stop, holding nothing more than Mr. Chambers's boots . . . and wool trousers.

He rolled over and sat watching the white legs of the accountant being dragged toward a grove of small whitewood trees. "Turn loose!" he shouted. "Turn loose, Chambers!"

Robert struggled to his feet. His ankles ached. His knees felt raw. His legs were bruised. He had staggered about twenty feet when the team abruptly stopped.

Trouserless, Byron Chambers still clutched the back rail of the carriage. His black, gartered stockings were torn to shreds. Robert trotted toward him, but each step shot pain up his legs. "Are you alright, Byron?"

"How in the world would I know if I'm alright?" the accountant screamed. "I could be dead for all I know. The tortures of hell couldn't be much worse than what I've endured."

Fortune laid Chambers's boots and trousers on the back of the carriage. "Well, it looks like you're all in one piece."

"I'll have to take your word for that."

"And your trousers seem to be in better shape than mine." Robert could feel dirt and rocks in his boot. "You can turn loose of the railing now, Mr. Chambers."

"I can't. My hands seem welded in place."

"You might want to pull your trousers on. I believe they might have gotten a little bit dusty."

"Dusty? Dusty!" Chambers yanked his talon-like grip free from the iron railing and stared at blisters starting to form on his fingers. "My word, I could have been killed by the runaway wagon, not to mention the gunshot!" The chartered accountant reset his top hat, then fastened the buttons on his shirt and straightened his tie.

The gunshot! Robert reached for his holstered revolver. "Don't pull that pistol, mister!" a brusk voice shouted as a masked gunman rode out from the whitewoods behind them. A dirty red bandanna covered his round face. "Toss down your guns and pull out your pokes!"

Robert Fortune eased down on a boulder, his back to the gunman, and started tugging off his boots.

"I said, toss down your gun and hold up your hands!" he hollered.

Chambers snatched his trousers and held them in front of his legs.

Robert dumped the gravel out of his boots and tugged them back on. "Puddin, is that you?"

"Throw down!" the gunman barked.

Fortune stood and walked toward the masked gunman. "Oscar Puddin, it's me . . . Robert Fortune, the train inspector. Remember? Are you tryin' to hold up this Englishman again?"

The round-faced man tugged down his dirty red bandanna. "Fortune? What in blazes are you doin' out here? There ain't a train for miles!"

Robert looped his thumbs in his belt. "Oscar, I'm disappointed in you!" He turned to Chambers. "Go ahead, put your trousers on, Byron. You remember Oscar, don't you?"

"My word, I thought you threw him off the train." Chambers hobbled around on raw feet, trying to pull on his trousers.

Robert tried to brush some of the dust off his own trousers. "No, I put him off the train when we stopped for water. I should have tossed him when we went over that steep trestle. Look at this, Oscar . . . a nice pair of trousers all ruined. I think I bruised every bone in both legs when that team bolted."

Puddin kept his gun pointed at Fortune. "I didn't mean to spook the team. You was supposed to throw down."

"Now, see there, Oscar. You just weren't thinkin'. You should have known your shot would spook the team. A man has to think through these things if he's going to be successful in your line of work."

Puddin cleared his throat. "Toss down your gun, Fortune. I got the drop on you this time. I want your money, and I want it now!"

Fortune dusted off his shirtsleeves with his hat. "Oscar, anyone that works at it as hard as you do ought to make more money. I don't have any poke. This is not a good road to work as a highwayman. There's no place to spend money out here, so naturally I didn't bother to bring any along. I don't even have any tobacco or jerky to give you. It's kind of embarrassing not having anything to offer."

Puddin spat a wad of tobacco on the granite rock below. "The Englishman's got money! Gold mine money."

"He's a chartered accountant, not a mine owner. What kind of wages do you think they draw? Why, miners up at Lead make more money than accountants."

"He wears a mighty fancy suit," Puddin insisted.

"Not any more," Robert said. "He's got sore feet and skinned-up legs. You did enough damage for one day. Now, ride on out before you get yourself shot."

Puddin waved the gun at Robert Fortune. "What did you say?"

Robert turned away from the gunman. "You heard me. Go on. Get out of here!"

"I got a gun drawn on you!" he shouted.

Fortune refused to turn back and look at the outlaw. "If you were the shootin', stealin' type, we'd both be dead by now. Go on, Oscar, before my assistant gets riled and plugs you."

"You ain't got no backup this time," Puddin insisted.

A lever action carbine cocked behind him. Oscar Puddin spun around in the saddle. When he did, Robert Fortune drew his revolver.

The mounted gunman stared at the barrel of the .44 carbine.

Robert strolled over to the startled man. "Oscar, this is my brother, Sammy."

"Where did he come from?" Oscar blustered.

Robert pushed his hat back with the barrel of his revolver. "Mama and Daddy said an angel brought him, but I always sort of doubted that myself. Drop your gun, Oscar. You wouldn't be the first man Sam Fortune has shot."

"Sam Fortune from down in the Indian Territory?"

"That's the one."

"But . . . but . . . I heard he was dead!"

"Sorry to disappoint you," Sam said.

"That's no fair," Puddin turned to Robert Fortune. "You always have backup."

"Toss the gun down, Oscar. It's too pretty a day to get shot."

The big man threw the gun to the ground and slumped his shoulders. "I can't believe this. I didn't go to Deadwood. I stayed out of the badlands jist like you told me. I'm on my way to Montana and back at Garden City I heard that some city boys is way out here in the hills in a nobby carriage. So I reckon to pick up a little grocery money. That's all I wanted. And it's you! It ain't fair."

"What are you going to do with him?" Samuel asked.

"I suppose we'll have to haul him back to Deadwood and toss him in jail." Robert plucked up Puddin's gun and stuck it in his belt.

"He's a big man," Sam pondered. "I bet it'll take a lot of taxpayer money to feed him in jail."

Robert yanked up Puddin's right pant leg and snatched out a sneak gun. "I suppose you're right about that. What do you think we should do?"

Sam lowered his carbine from his shoulder to his side. "We could jist shoot him."

"You cain' do that!" Puddin protested.

Robert walked around to the other side of the gunman and wrenched a large hunting knife out of his left boot. "He's right, Sammy. With Mr. Chambers as a witness, we can't shoot him down. You got any more sneaks, Oscar?"

Byron Chambers sat on a boulder, rubbing his raw toes. "I'll turn my head and close my eyes."

Puddin reached into his vest pocket and pulled out a tiny, single-shot .22, then handed it down.

Robert rubbed his beard. "No, I don't think we can shoot him . . . unless . . ."

"Unless he's tryin' to escape?" Sam suggested.

"I ain't tryin' to escape," Puddin blurted out. "Look at me, I haven't even tried to ride off!"

"He's right about that," Robert said.

Sam rode his buckskin right up next to Puddin. "Maybe he'll try to escape after while."

"Could be," Robert pondered.

"No sir. I won't try to escape."

"Well, Oscar, just to keep my brother from shootin' you, let's tie your hands to that A-fork saddle of yours. That way, there's no chance of you escaping."

"You take all the fun out of it, lil' brother," Samuel grinned.

"You stay out of this. Let the inspector do his work!" Oscar Puddin insisted.

Byron Chambers tugged on his boots. "I trust you two will be discreet when recalling this scene," he said. "It is quite humiliating!"

"Runaway carriages are common occurrences. You didn't break your neck, your arm, or your leg. You did alright. Mind you, you'll probably want to get the trousers cleaned and have a bath before you head back to Toronto," Robert added. "But think of the stories you can tell the other chartered accountants back in Toronto."

"Yes, well . . . there will be a few adjustments in details, I can assure you of that," Chambers declared.

After Robert reset the rigging on the team, he and Chambers climbed into the carriage. "Are we ready to proceed?"

"Maybe I ought to stick a little closer, lil' brother," Sam said.

"Yep, I'll need you to shoot Oscar if he tries to escape."

"I ain't goin' to try nothin'," Puddin insisted.

"Well, then, Oscar, why don't you lead the way?" Robert suggested.

"I don't know where you're goin'."

"Neither do we. We were just told to head east, and that's what we'll do."

"If you don't know where you're goin', how will you know when you get there?" Puddin called back.

"We'll know when we're there 'cause they'll start shooting at us." Robert slapped the leather lines on the team. "Why do you think I want you to lead?"

Jamie Sue was at the sink washing out her beige dress when she heard the pounding on the front door.

That must be the express company. And the girls aren't here.

She wiped her hands on a cotton towel and smoothed down the front of her green satin dress.

The pounding on the door continued.

I would think the express company could be a little more courteous.

She scurried into the living room.

The pounding began once again. "I know you're in there!" a deep voice shouted.

"Just a minute . . ." Jamie Sue called out. When she swung open the door, a tall, broad-shouldered man with narrow eyes, drooping mustache, and tight-fitting bowler greeted her with a scowl.

"Well, just what do you intend to do about it!" he shouted.

Jamie Sue's hand flew up to her mouth. "Do about it? I want you to tote all the trunks and crates into the living room!"

"What?" he hollered. "You think I'm a servant?"

"You're from the express company aren't you?"

"I most certainly am not! I want to know what you're going to do about my window!"

"Window?" Jamie Sue had a strong urge to go back inside and slam the door between them.

The veins of the man's neck pulsed with every word. "You're Little Frank's mama, aren't you?"

"Oh, my, yes." Jamie Sue let out a sigh. "Little Frank came home and started to tell me something about a window, then tripped and broke his finger. It's been quite hectic. I'm very sorry about the window."

"Looks like someone punched you in the nose."

Jamie Sue's fingers patted her nose. "I, eh . . . also fell, while trying to help my son."

"It still looks like you been beat up. Where is that kid of yours?" the man demanded.

"He's over at a friend's house and . . ."

"Then what's all this talk about a broken finger?"

Jamie Sue crossed her arms over her chest. "Are you calling me a liar?"

"It ain't the worst name you Fortunes have been called. What are you going to do about my window?"

She clutched her hands tight. "Are you Mr. Moraine?" She could feel her heartbeat in her fingers.

"I sure am, and your boy purposely failed to catch a baseball and let it bust my kitchen window."

Jamie Sue stiffened. "I seriously doubt if he did it on purpose, but we will certainly be glad to . . ."

"Are you calling me a liar?" Moraine hollered. "You don't even know me."

Jamie Sue saw the lady across the street peek out at them from behind white lace curtains. "I know my son. He very well might have missed a ball. He might have thrown it errantly. He might even have hit the ball through your window, but he certainly did not purposely cause damage to your house. I will call the hardware and have them send someone up to fix it."

He stepped down off the porch and motioned for her to follow. "Come look at what he did!"

Jamie Sue stayed where she was. "I believe you, Mr. Moraine."

"Oh? Are you too stuck-up and arrogant to come to an Irishman's house?"

"Not at all. In fact, I trust your word completely. Does that sound stuck-up and arrogant?"

"But you won't come to my house?"

"Mr. Moraine, I . . ."

"That's what I figured."

"Mr. Moraine, if you would pause long enough to quit being so defensive, you would understand that I would be delighted to come to your house, but I'm waiting for a freight wagon to deliver some goods and I . . ."

"I told my Meggie a Fortune would never darken our door!" He stalked out toward the sidewalk.

"Mr. Moraine, I have never in my life met anyone so closed-minded as you. I will get my hat and come to your house. I will pay for having your window repaired, and I will see to it that Little Frank does not play baseball at your house again," she called out. "But I will not put up with slanderous accusations of my bigotry against the Irish. That is a vicious, hateful lie and I simply will not tolerate it from you or from anyone."

"Don't tell me the Fortunes don't hate the Irish," he shouted back. "I have proof!"

She could now see several neighbors in their yards watching the confrontation. "I will need to see the proof!"

"It's at my house," he insisted.

"I will get my hat!" Jamie Sue spun back through the open doorway.

CHAPTER SIX

The twelve-inch-by-twelve-inch rough-cut, creosote-stained beams could be seen poking above the granite boulders on the rim of Spruce Canyon well before Robert Fortune spied any buildings or people. The ever-present clouds began to stack up. The sky turned a mottled gray, but there was no smell of rain. The slow breeze drifted straight at them and slightly cooled their faces. The road smoothed, and the carriage hummed. Robert Fortune felt comfortable in his jacket, white shirt buttoned at the top.

His eyelids drooped even as his calloused hands fingered the one-inch-wide leather lead lines of the rented carriage. *Lord, I'm not sure why I'm out here. It's not train business . . . or family business. . . . It's just been so long since I could take off and do whatever I choose. In the army there was procedure to follow, rules to obey, chains of command to follow. There's something that feels extremely good about setting out with Sammy and taking in some new sights.*

Robert glanced up at Oscar Puddin riding the lead horse. *'Course I hadn't planned on gatherin' up Oscar. Now, Lord, I'm not too sure why You create men like Puddin. Maybe they are meant just to test the rest of us. I don't know what to do with him. I wish he'd just go away. But if I turn him loose, I swear, he'll end up hurting himself or someone else or me. It's a mystery, Lord. You have me stumped.*

With the same shock as a camp cook beating on a pan before daylight, a gunshot splintered a ponderosa pine stump next to Oscar Puddin's horse. Robert yanked back on the lead lines and jerked for his revolver.

Puddin's horse reared.

His hat tumbled to the dirt.

Then Oscar cursed.

Samuel Fortune rode up and yanked on the frightened horse's bridle.

"Untie me!" Puddin yelled. "I could have been killed."

Neither Fortune brother drew a gun.

"This rope kept you in the saddle instead of fallin' on

your head in the rocks." Sam Fortune stood in the stirrups and stared off toward the headworks of the mine shaft in the distance. "You see anyone, Bobby?"

"Not a soul."

"My word," Chambers mumbled, "that's the second time within an hour someone's shot at us. I thought this story was merely a hyperbole!"

A high-pitched voice hollered from the rocks. "This is private property! Go away!"

Still standing in the stirrups, Sam turned back to look at the carriage and shrugged.

"There's a woman out here?" Robert quizzed.

Sam sat down and studied the rocks. "Either that or a boy about eleven," he muttered.

The voice sounded determined, but tired. "Go away, or I'll shoot all of you, startin' with the fat one on the brown horse."

Puddin tugged at the leather straps that bound his wrists to the A-fork saddle. "Is she talkin' about me?" he gasped.

Robert stood up and raised his hands. "Ma'am . . . we're from Deadwood," he hollered. "With us is Mr. Byron Chambers, a chartered accountant from Toronto who's under the employ of the Bank of Ottawa. He has been sent to review the books of the Broken Boulder Mine. Do you happen to know where we can find it?"

"Who are the rest of you?" she shouted.

"I'm Robert Fortune. I work for the Elkhorn, Fremont, and Missouri Valley Railroad." He licked his chapped lips, then pushed his hat back. "Today, I'm just a driver for Mr. Chambers, but if there's enough business, perhaps the Elkhorn will run a narrow gauge out here."

"How about them other two?" Robert thought the voice was starting to relax a little.

Samuel tipped his gray, wide-brimmed felt hat toward the unseen woman. "I'm Sam Fortune, president of the Deadwood Telephone Exchange. I had a written request from a Mr. S. P. Raxton to give an estimate on running a telephone line to . . ."

"That's Miss S. P. Raxton!" the woman shouted.

"Yes, ma'am." Sam pulled off his hat and ran his fingers through his nearly gray hair. "Since I reckon you want the phone line all the way to the mine site, may we continue?"

"Who's the fatty?" This time the demand came with a lilt in the voice.

"I ain't fat!" Puddin shouted. "That there is muscles."

"In your head?" she replied, with a definite giggle.

"Yes, ma'am," Robert concurred. "Where ordinary people just have brains, Oscar has muscles!"

"That's right!" Puddin added.

"Why is he tied to the saddle?" she called.

"He's a recently retired train robber and highwayman. We have him tied to the saddle because we're trying to decide whether to toss him in jail or just hang him," Robert replied.

"They's joshin' you, ma'am!" Puddin called out. "I ain't stole one red cent from nobody."

Chambers pulled out a white handkerchief and wiped his face. "May we proceed, Miss Raxton? I really need to see your ledgers!"

"You want to see my what?" she hollered.

"Your accounts."

"Tie up your horses. Leave your guns in the wagon and

walk this direction," came the command.

To the east, the rolling dark green pines blanketed the mountains. To the west, the sheer granite cliffs of Spruce Canyon dropped off the canyon floor, though it could not be seen yet. In between . . . giant granite outcroppings the size of houses and barns made the crude road seem like a maze.

Robert Fortune and Byron Chambers led the way. Chambers carried a thick brown leather valise. Sam Fortune walked a few steps behind with Oscar Puddin, who hung his head low and muttered to himself as they hiked.

They had just rounded the first big boulder when a woman in a floppy, wide-brimmed felt hat stepped out in front of them. She held a Springfield trapdoor rifle. Bullet belts criss-crossed her thin chest.

The men stopped in a nearly straight line in front of her. "How come you got a bayonet pulled out on that musket?" Puddin asked.

Her thin lips barely moved. Each word skipped across the air like a slick rock on smooth water. "You git close enough and you'll find out!" she replied.

Oscar rubbed his wide, round nose. "Shoot, even a skunk cain't get that close."

She thrust forward, the bayonet just inches from Puddin's belly. "What did you mean by that?"

"Oscar just mumbles a lot, Miss Raxton," Robert explained. "Don't pay him any mind."

She stepped back and straightened her shoulders. Robert noticed she was about Jamie Sue's height. Her hair was light brown, perhaps blonde. But it hung down her back in a loose, dirty pigtail. Her face was filthy, as was her dress. Everything about her, including her hat, was coated with reddish-brown-colored dirt and mud. Her sleeves were pushed up to her elbows, her arms and hands caked with the same reddish-brown dried mud. Her dress was tattered at the hem and hung over thick brown boots caked with the same mud.

She motioned for them to keep walking toward the head-works. She followed, keeping the rifle and bayonet pointed at them. "How come the Bank of Ottawa wants to see my accounts?" she said, glaring at Chambers.

Byron Chambers stopped to glance back and leaped forward when he saw the bayonet approach his backside. "Because we haven't heard from you in months!" he blurted out.

"We been busy diggin' gold. Ain't that what we're supposed to do?" she declared in a tone of a mother scolding her children.

Chambers marched forward, his chin and square jaw set rigid. "We need to know where the funds have been spent."

"They been spent on this mine. What did you think we were doin', throwin' a dance?" Raxton barked.

"If you're the only woman, I reckon that would be a mighty lonely affair," Puddin retorted.

"What did you say?" she snapped.

Robert lagged back between Oscar Puddin and the bayonet. "You do have records of your operation, don't you?"

"We've got ever' penny accounted for, if that's your beef. Now, go on, and keep your hands up."

Byron Chambers opened his valise as he marched along, fumbling with papers.

Raxton pounced forward, spearing the valise with her bayonet.

"My word!" Chambers cried out. "What are you doing?"

Raxton yanked the bayonet out of the leather and pointed the .45-70 at Chambers. "Don't you be reachin' in there for a sneak gun!" she growled.

"It's full of papers and documents! I say, you ruined a perfectly good satchel." Chambers pulled out a thick packet of papers. "See here . . . the original loan was to a Mr. Apex MacClaren of Winnipeg. I really need to see Mr. MacClaren."

Raxton studied the chartered accountant from top hat to boots. "So, you want to see Mac?"

"I believe that's obvious, Miss Raxton," Chambers declared.

"Why didn't you say so back there? I could have saved you all a hike. He ain't here at the mine. He's got himself a plot of ground in Miles City."

Byron Chambers turned around to face the woman with the musket and bayonet. "Miles City, Montana?"

"I don't know of any others," she drawled, her tight, thin lips now drawn in a slight grin.

Chambers looked down on the sheaf of papers in his hand. "Isn't he still superintendent of the mine?"

"Nope. You might say he abdicated."

"My word," Chambers fumed. "I don't have anything in my records of his retirement. Why didn't he notify us?"

Raxton motioned for the men to keep hiking. "I reckon that's because he's dead."

"Dead?" Chambers stopped walking but quickly continued when the bayonet point brushed across the rear of his already torn trousers. "I thought you said he was in Miles City."

"He is. He's buried in a cemetery plot there."

"I say," Chambers puffed, "this is getting quite confusing."

They rounded some boulders and reached the base of the twelve-inch by twelve-inch beams that stretched forty feet in the air at the headworks. A massive iron pulley hung from a cross beam at the top of the headworks. Beneath it stretched a heavy steel cable holding an iron bucket about the size of an outhouse. The other end of the cable was wrapped around the spool on a steam-powered, idle donkey engine that barely rumbled its firebox. Yawning below the bucket was a dark mine shaft about ten feet in diameter.

Up against the rocks behind the headworks was a small cabin. The back half was carved out of a cave. On the front porch of the cabin, another woman with a long dress held a double-barreled shotgun. Although her hair was partially pinned to the back of her head, she was covered with the same reddish-brown dirt as Miss Raxton.

"My word, two women?" Chambers spouted. "What is this?"

"What do they want?" the lady on the porch shouted as they approached. "Why didn't you shoot them out at the road?"

"I didn't want to waste that many bullets," Raxton replied. "Besides, the one in the top hat and torn trousers is a chartered accountant from the Bank of Ottawa, in Toronto, who has come to review our ledgers."

The woman raised the shotgun to her shoulder. "Our ledges?" With a little more daylight creeping under the porch roof, Robert could see smudged face, blue eyes, white teeth, and a woman even thinner than the other.

"No, our ledgers, our accounts," Raxton shouted, then turned to the men. "My sister has been setting off explosives so long it's ruined her hearing."

"Are they married?" the one on the porch hollered.

"I ain't talked long enough to find out," S. Raxton replied. Robert spied another small shack back in the boulders. "Are you two ladies running this operation by yourselves?"

"We have a crew," S. Raxton reported as her sister approached the men.

Sam looped his thumbs in his belt. "Where?"

"Down in the shaft."

"We take shifts working two at a time," the other woman declared. "It's hard rock down there. When they get a bucket full, they ring the bell, and we stoke up the engine and haul it up."

"So, you have a crew of two?" Robert asked.

"Two other women?" Puddin blurted out. He was the only one who still had his hands raised.

"No," S. Raxton scowled. "You sit down on them rocks where we can keep an eye on you. If you try anything, I'll plug you and we'll just toss you down that shaft."

All the men, except Oscar Puddin, sat down. "I ain't goin' to be bossed around by no dirty-faced women," he declared.

"We aren't going to toss them down the shaft," the other second woman declared. "Last time we did, it stunk up the place for weeks!"

Oscar Puddin immediately flopped down next to Robert Fortune.

S. Raxton managed a faint smile. "Now, let us explain the situation. This is my sister, Augusta, and I'm Sandra Raxton. The two men in the shaft are Tio and Poco."

"Them sounds like Mexican names," Puddin blurted out.

Augusta Raxton folded dirty arms across her dirty dress. "Maybe that's the reason they don't speak English," she jibed.

"I say, this is highly irregular," Chambers said.

Sandra Raxton kept her gun steady on the men. "To have two women running a mining operation?"

"Well, it's . . . it's not at all what I expected," Chambers protested.

Robert Fortune leaned forward, his elbows on his knees. "Just exactly how did you two women get into the mining business?"

Augusta Raxton lowered her shotgun and strolled along in front of the men. A strong sweat-and-dirt odor preceded and followed her. "We won it in a horse race."

"What?" Chambers used his white handkerchief to rub the dust and dirt out of his eyes.

"From what we learnt from Tio and Poco, Mac had a crew of a dozen Chilean miners up here for almost a year," S. Raxton explained.

"What in tarnation is Chileans?" Puddin railed.

Sam Fortune brushed down his mustache with his fingertips. "That's men from Chile. That's in South America."

"No foolin'," Puddin replied. "I'm from Mississippi, myself. Decatur, Mississippi."

"Go ahead, Miss Raxton," Robert insisted.

"We're both Miss Raxton," Sandra Raxton added.

Robert studied the eyes of both women. "What would you like us to call you?"

"Rich!" Augusta Raxton hooted.

"I'm called Miss Sandra, and my sister is Miss Augusta."

Robert sat up straight and glanced back at the black open mine shaft that hunched behind him. "How did you come about this claim?"

Sam Fortune also surveyed the layout of the mining camp. "Did the Chileans get homesick and leave?"

"Yep," Miss Sandra reported. "Mac wouldn't let them leave the mine site until they struck the good ore. He was afraid of others moving in. So one day they just up and ran off."

"But Poco and Tio stayed?" Sam questioned.

"They were the Mexican cooks," Miss Sandra explained.

Miss Augusta stood alongside her sister. "So Mac went up to Miles City to find a crew."

"Why didn't he go into Deadwood, Lead, or Central City?" Robert asked. "There are always miners looking for work."

"He didn't want to give away the position of the mine," Miss Sandra explained. "We want this mine proved before everyone starts rushing out here."

"You can't hide gold," Puddin blurted out. "Besides, we all know you're here now."

"You're right," Miss Augusta added with unsmiling face, "and we have to kill all of you."

"That ain't funny," Puddin replied.

"It was not intended to be," she cautioned.

"Now Oscar . . . don't go rilin' a lady with a gun in her hand," Robert cautioned. "What happened in Miles City?"

Miss Sandra continued the story. "Well, that ain't no mining town. There's only cowboys and railroad men up there. Mac was discouraged. He was on a two-week melancholy when he came into the dance hall."

"He was drunk, that's what he was," Miss Augusta blurted out.

Miss Sandra pointed the bayoneted musket at her sister. "A man don't have to be drunk to dance with me."

With her shotgun looped over her shoulder, Miss Augusta glared back. "He was drunk!"

"That might be, but he didn't dance with you, even if he was drunk!" She held her chin high. "He was bragging about owning the fastest horse in Dakota, and I told him me and my sister owned the fastest horse in Montana . . . so naturally . . ."

"He wanted to race?" Samuel prodded.

"Yep. He stopped the music in the saloon and announced a horse race right up Main Street of Miles City. Said he would put up his interest in the Big Boulder Mine."

"My word, what was your collateral?" Chambers pressed.

There was a long pause. The two women stole a glance at each other. Miss Sandra's response was almost soft. "We weren't covered with dirt back then."

Under the dirt Robert thought he could see her blush.

Chambers tugged at the cuffs of his once-white shirt. "You mean to say a man would actually gamble a gold mine for a woman's eh, virtue?"

Sam Fortune cleared his throat. "Two women," he

corrected.

"Men have abandoned claims for a whole lot less," Robert added. "Daddy bought half-interest in the Andrew Jackson for half an elk and a dutch-oven peach cobbler."

Chambers sat awkward and stiff as he adjusted his top hat. "But, I say, to gamble one's chastity . . . however polluted it may be . . . for a worthless mining claim."

"It wasn't worthless, and we wasn't gamblin' anything," Miss Sandra insisted. "There was no way we could lose. Augusta can straddle a horse better than any man."

"You rode the horse?" Robert quizzed.

"Yep, and I won by a head."

"You could have won by a length if you hadn't turned around and stuck out your tongue," Miss Sandra lectured.

"There were fourteen horses in the race," Miss Augusta added. "We not only won the claim but picked up six hundred fourteen dollars and twenty-seven cents from the cowboys."

"Then what happened?" Sam asked.

Miss Sandra snickered. "We left town in a hurry. Men don't like to lose to women."

"But what happened to MacClaren?" Chambers probed. "You said he was buried in Miles City?"

Miss Sandra scratched her head from one side to the other as if chasing a tiny unseen critter. "We heard he went on a drunk and got pinched by a train the next morning."

"Pinched?" Chambers questioned. "You mean he got arrested?"

"Nope." Miss Augusta licked her fingertips and wiped the dust out of the corners of her eyes. "Mac got caught between two railroad cars . . . and was . . . you know . . .

crushed to death."

Chambers's mouth dropped open. "And . . . and . . . they buried him in Miles City?"

A sly smile broke across Miss Augusta's tight, stoic face. "Yep, they buried both parts of him. Used a shorter casket, so I hear tell."

Chambers held his hat up to his mouth. "My word, I believe I'm going to regurgitate," he choked.

Miss Sandra leaned over to watch Chambers. "He's going to what?"

Robert shoved his hand on Chambers's back and pushed his head between his knees. "So you two came up to work the claim?"

"Yep, Tio and Poco were here. So we decided we'd live off the cowboy winnin's and work the claim for a few weeks. Then we got a draft from the Bank of Ottawa in Toronto, so we kept diggin'." Miss Sandra shoved the rod-shaped bayonet back into the trapdoor musket.

A white-faced Byron Chambers sat up, holding his hat in his hand. "But the draft was signed by MacClaren."

"That's Tio . . ." Miss Augusta explained. "He's mighty good at cipherin' someone else's signature."

"But that's illegal . . . it's forgery!" Chambers blustered.

"We surmised you sent that money to keep the mine in operation. That's exactly what we did. We are the legal assigns. We won our share fair and square. We surely ain't spent it on ourselves," Miss Sandra huffed.

"That's obvious," Puddin snorted.

"But . . . but . . . you can't just take the bank's money and . . ."

"I don't know, Mr. Chambers," Robert interrupted. "I

think these ladies are right. Your company wanted a mine shaft dug, and that's what you got." Robert turned back to the ladies. "The important question is, are you finding any color?"

Augusta glanced over at Sandra, who nodded.

"We've been tracin' a favorable lead. So far we've been crushin' it out on a millstone, then pannin' out enough to pay for groceries. But if we hit the big lead, we'll be in the money," Miss Sandra explained.

"I still will have to see the books," Chambers insisted.

"We don't have any books," Miss Augusta replied.

"But, you said you had a record of expenses," Chambers sputtered.

Miss Augusta reached down and picked a tiny piece of lint off her filthy dress, as if she were about to enter a church. "Yep, we got that. We got two dynamite boxes full of receipts. Ever' time we spent a dime of that draft, we got the receipt and put it in the box."

"My heavens," Chambers roared as he shoved his hat back on. "It will take all afternoon to sort this out."

"Maybe we ought to bring Tio and Poco up and have them cook us all some dinner," Miss Augusta suggested.

Sandra Raxton, toting her trapdoor musket over her thin, bony shoulder, strolled over to Robert Fortune. "I suppose all you men are married?"

"My brother and I are married, but I do believe Mr. Chambers is unattached and so is Oscar." Robert glanced over at the big man. "If he doesn't get hanged, he might be the most eligible bachelor in the Black Hills!"

"I ain't the marryin' type," Puddin retorted.

"Now, Oscar, when the right lady comes along, all of that

will change," Samuel said.

"One thing fer sure," Puddin declared, "she'll be clean."

"Will she own a gold mine?" Robert challenged.

"I ain't dreamed that grand," Oscar admitted.

"And there is certainly no reason for you to do so now!" Miss Sandra sneered.

♜

The sounds of the steam-driven piston cranking a huge wooden spool muted all conversation until the two older Mexican men were hoisted to the surface. Their clothes and faces were the same color as the Raxton sisters. Under the dirt both had narrow shoulders, gray hair, leathery faces, and dark brown eyes. Oscar Puddin was put to building a fire, while Poco and Tio began to cook.

Sam Fortune climbed to the top of the headworks to survey the surrounding landscape for the best route for a telephone line. Byron Chambers and Augusta Raxton sat on the worn, weathered front porch of the cabin, surrounded by invoices and receipts from worn weathered board to worn weathered board.

Robert strolled over to a pile of crushed rock and gravel the size of the cabin. "Is this your tailings?"

Sandra Raxton trailed behind him, no longer carrying her long musket. "This is our good stuff. We don't sluice it out until right before we go to town. Figure no one would want to steal it in the raw form."

Robert glanced around at the yard. "Where do you sluice it at?"

"We have to pack it down to water."

"How far is that?"

"There's a trail to a spring about halfway down the cliff into Spruce Canyon."

"How do you get it down there?"

"Two mules and four donkeys." She pointed to a small corral behind the only two trees within half a mile.

Robert picked up some of the crushed rock and gravel and let it run through his fingers. "What are you making on this?"

"About four hundred dollars a ton, but we don't think we're recovering half of the gold," she admitted.

Robert whistled and shook his head. "If that's true, you've got a rich claim."

"It takes the four of us almost two weeks to work a ton. There's two in the mine, one on the wench, and one standin' guard. And it's tough packing the rock down the hill."

Robert rubbed his beard. "Miss Sandra, you need more equipment and manpower. If you can get that much with such a primitive set-up, some big outfit would pay you handsomely for this mine."

"It's our mine," she snapped. "And we don't want to sell it."

"But you wouldn't mind making more money, would you?"

She brushed her hair back across her forehead, revealing another layer of caked dirt. "It depends on how much goes back to the Bank of Ottawa."

Robert glanced over at the fussing Bryon Chambers. "I've got a feeling you could buy out their share. Then you could have all the profits when you hit that big lead."

She jammed her hand inside the collar of her dirty cotton dress and rubbed her bony shoulder. "Mr. Fatty's right about one thing."

"Puddin?"

"Yeah. If we could get more water up here, we could buy us a bathtub. I ain't always been this dirty, you know."

"I reckon there are sacrifices to make a mine work."

"That's exactly what I keep tellin' myself, only some days I jist don't want to listen."

Sandra Raxton and Robert Fortune strolled over to the edge of Spruce Canyon and stared down at the creek, thirteen hundred feet below.

Robert pointed down to the canyon floor. "Miss Sandra . . . I believe you could be a little more efficient in this operation."

"You know much about mines?"

"My daddy and my oldest brother, Todd, are the family experts on Black Hills mining. I don't know too much, but I've spent almost twenty years in the army and I know lots about logistics."

"About what?"

"About how to get from here to there. Could I give you some suggestions on how to be more efficient in getting your ore to a smelter?"

"As long as we don't build us a road all the way from Deadwood so ever' bummer and unemployed drifter can come try and steal our ore."

"If you want to avoid Deadwood and take your ore to Spearfish, then the fastest route is right straight off the side of this cliff."

"That's over a thousand-foot drop."

"Yes, but there's water at the bottom."

"What are you sayin'?"

"Build a cable line right off the side of the cliff. You can lower your big bucket and ones like it down the canyon floor with your donkey engine. Then build a stamp mill or reduction plant there where the water is. That way you can ship out the gold rather than the bulky ore."

"Now you're talking like a government man," she carped.

"What do you mean by that?"

"Like we could print our own money. There ain't no way we could afford a set-up like that."

Robert tried to look past the dirty face at the narrow blue-gray eyes. "Take in more investors."

"I'm tryin' to get rid of the ones we have."

"How about some local investors. Perhaps just a loan, not a partnership. My preliminary opinion is that you need to have a bigger operation to make any money."

She strolled back to the big outdoor table where Tio and Poco were slicing elk meat into an iron frying pan that was two feet wide. "We're gettin' by jist like we are."

"Would you be happy if this is the way things are still going ten years from now?"

"All of us will be dead, if we keep up this pace. But it beats what we were doin' in Miles City."

Robert put a foot up on a bench and brushed his dusty trousers. "At some point you two Raxton sisters have got to ask yourselves, Is this what the Lord wants me to do with my life?"

Miss Sandra jerked back as if stung by a bee. "What in the world does God have to do with this?"

"He made the gold . . ."

"I reckon I agree with you there."

"And He made the Raxton sisters."

Miss Sandra stiffened. "Where is this goin', Fortune?"

"If He made you and the gold, then He probably has a plan for both of them." He pointed his finger at her. "It seems to me the secret of a successful life is finding out what those plans are."

"Now you sound like a Methodist preacher," she challenged.

"Baptist. Ponder it a while. If you think God wants you to haul that gold out of this mountain, you have to find some backers. But if He's in it, you will."

"Are you tryin' to buy into our mine and sugarcoating it with religion?" she confronted.

"Nope. I don't have the funds. But I know people in Deadwood and Lead who might be interested. If you ever come to town, I'll introduce you to them."

"We ain't dealin' with ol' George Hearst."

"I don't know Mr. Hearst. He seems to be doing quite well with the Homestake."

Miss Sandra Raxton stared back in the direction of Spruce Canyon. "Cable big buckets right off the side, huh?"

"It can be done," he said. "I've seen them do it down in Arizona."

"But it would be like runnin' two operations. How would we coordinate it?"

"With telephones. That's where brother Samuel comes in."

"But . . . but with two camps, where would we live? Up

here . . . or down there?" she pointed.

"Why you'd live in Denver, or San Francisco or Chicago, what with all the money you'd make," Robert teased.

"Look at me, Mr. Fortune."

Robert gave a quick look at Sandra Raxton, then back at the men chopping meat at the table.

"I said, look me up and down," she demanded.

Robert's face flushed as he studied the tired weak eyes, long dirty nose, and filthy dark cotton dress that hung limp on the skinny frame of Sandra Raxton.

"Now," she said, "can you honestly say that you can imagine me living in a fine house on the north side of Chicago?"

He cleared his throat. "Eh, no ma'am. I think you're right. That's a little far-fetched. But, Miss Sandra, I can imagine you living on a five-thousand-acre spread along the Yellowstone River just out of Miles City, Montana, with a stable full of long-legged racing horses and a big, new, two-story ranch house with a wrap-around veranda and a half-dozen servants ready to do any chore you gave them."

Sandra Raxton's weak eyes slowly lit up. One lone tear braved the dirty cheek and plowed its way down to her upper lip. "You're right, Fortune. I can see myself in such a place. Do you reckon God would ever allow such a thing?"

"There's only one way to find out."

Suddenly, her shoulders stiffened. "I should have shot you before you ever reached the mine."

He folded his arms across his chest. "Why?"

"Then I wouldn't have such pretty but impossible dreams in my head."

"Well, you can't shoot me now," he declared.

"And just why not? I can still go fetch my gun."

"Yes, but shooting me wouldn't do any good. Because you're going to have that dream to haunt your mind whether I'm alive or dead."

She took a deep breath. "I don't know whether to kiss you or curse you, Robert Fortune."

He stepped back.

Sandra Raxton had such an explosive, unexpected laugh that Tio and Poco dropped their knives into the big black iron skillet. "Relax, Mr. Fortune," she hooted. "I don't reckon I'm goin' to do either."

"I'll have him hung!" Jamie Sue fumed as she stormed into the living room.

Her brown hair now in dual pigtails, Veronica danced over toward the entry hall. "Look, Mama, all the trunks are here!"

Jamie Sue tugged off her beige gloves. "No, I was wrong. He should be drawn, quartered, then diced and fed to ravens!"

"We couldn't find the key, Mama." Patricia circled the green wardrobe trunk that was taller than she was. Her hair, too, now hung in pigtails.

"I've heard of stupid men, but he is the stupidest in the entire world." Jamie Sue unpinned her straw hat and tossed it on the small table near the door.

Veronica tugged on her arm. "Every one of our trunks and cases is here. Isn't that marvelous, Mama? Not one piece was lost."

Jamie Sue stared at her reflection in the mirror. Dark hair pinned back, wide-set blue eyes, narrow cheeks, large mouth, pale skin . . . except for the blush of fury. "It's fiction," she blurted out to the image in the mirror. "Fiction stories are make-believe. Unreal. False. All fiction writers are liars. Everyone knows that!" *Lord, I have never been so unjustly accused and felt so helpless. He is not being reasonable. I don't know how to deal with people who refuse to listen to reason. Besides that . . . my mouth is too wide and my lips too full.*

"Mama, can we have the key and unlock the wardrobes?" Patricia pulled at her other arm. A small gold locket dangled at the end of a thin gold chain, resting on the crocheted lace yoke of her dress.

Jamie Sue stomped into the kitchen, squatted down next to the stove, and stuck several small sticks of wood into the dying embers of the firebox. She faced the back door and waved a stick of kindling as if lecturing an exceedingly naughty student. "Mr. Hawthorne Miller, I would advise you never . . . ever show up in Deadwood!" she declared. "You will justly suffer the consequences your actions deserve!"

Veronica now hung on her mother's arm. "Who's Hawthorne Miller?" she quizzed.

Patricia pulled a pigtail across her face and chewed on the end of it. "Is he the man that writes those dime novels?"

Jamie Sue took a deep breath and patted Veronica's head. "He's a man who is equaled in stupidity only by one named

Riagan Moraine."

"Mama, don't pat me on the head," Veronica whined.

Patricia scooted up on the other side of Jamie Sue. "You can pat me on the head, Mama. What did Eachan's father do?"

Jamie Sue's lip curled as if she had bitten into a rancid walnut. "I don't want to talk about it."

"That's all you've been talking about since you came in the house," Veronica whined.

Jamie Sue klunked the teapot over on the barely warm stove. She stared at her twins, her arms clenched across her chest. "Girls, tell me something. When you read a novel, do you think it's true . . . or make believe?"

Patricia raised her hand. "It's all made up," she blurted out. "That's what a story is about."

Veronica rocked up on the toes of her shoes. "Except maybe the book about Uncle Todd. It was true. Mostly. Sort of. Wasn't it?"

"Why did you ask us that?" Patricia quizzed.

Jamie Sue turned back toward the teapot. She took a long, slow breath through her nostrils, then let it out very slowly through her mouth. She could feel her shoulders and forehead relax. "I shouldn't talk about it. I need to wait until your father gets home."

"Is it something naughty?" Patricia murmured.

Jamie Sue stared into her daughter's bright, penetrating glare. "Naughty?"

"Sometimes you won't tell us something because it's naughty, and you wait and tell Daddy," Patricia declared. "You tell him the naughty things you won't tell us."

Jamie Sue put her hands on her hips, which felt wider

than she remembered. "I most certainly do not! Who told you that?"

Patricia stared down at her shoes. "Eh . . . 'Nica."

"I did not," Veronica protested. "I did not! I merely said, perhaps that's what Mama does. It was just speculation. Amber said that her mother won't talk about naughty things except to Uncle Sammy, and I merely said that perhaps Mama and Daddy did the same. That's all."

Jamie Sue stormed around the kitchen. "This definitely isn't naughty. I'm just very, very grieved, and I don't know what to do about it. I wish your father were home right now."

"So do I," Veronica said. "Maybe he knows where the key to our trunk is."

"Can't you even tell us about it?" Patricia prodded.

Jamie Sue laced her fingers. "You'll hear about it soon enough, I expect. Mr. Moraine, and apparently some others in this town, have the opinion that all the Fortunes hate the Irish."

"Hate the Irish?" Patricia yelped. "What's he talking about? Aunt Abby is Irish, and so is Amber, and I think she's the most beautiful girl in the world. And little Garrett is half Irish."

Veronica tilted her head and licked her thin, pale lips. "I certainly don't hate Eachan! Why would anyone say that about us?"

Jamie Sue paused her pacing and rested her hands on the back of a straight-back wooden chair. "There's a new Hawthorne Miller book called *Ambush on St. Patrick's Day* in which U.S. Marshal Ted Fortune single-handedly puts down an Irish miner's strike in the Black Hills."

"Who's Ted Fortune?" Patricia asked.

Jamie Sue brushed the hair back out of her eyes. "He's a fictional character that Miller made up. He has nothing to do with any of us. Besides, I'm not at all sure that putting down a miner's strike is always evil."

Patricia fussed with her white lace yoke collar. "Ted Fortune sounds a lot like Todd Fortune."

"That's the point. Miller tried to piggyback on the Fortune name and succeeded in alienating all the Irish in the Black Hills." Jamie Sue plucked up a tin plate from the counter and used it to fan herself.

"Does Mr. Moraine believe the story in the dime novel and think that Ted Fortune is a relative of ours?" Veronica questioned.

"Yes, he does."

"That's silly," Patricia said. "I hope you told him so."

"I tried to reason with him . . . but . . . but . . . he is an unreasonable man. He thinks Little Frank missed a baseball on purpose so that it would break his kitchen window . . . and he refuses for me to let someone from the hardware come fix it because he won't do business with Fortunes!" Jamie Sue bit her lip, then tried to brush back tears from the corner of her eyes. "It just isn't fair!"

Patricia stroked her mother's arm. "We'll just have to trust the Lord through all this. As soon as they get to know us, they will find out differently."

Jamie Sue stared at her daughter, then ran her hands along Patricia's pigtail. *Is this my little girl who's telling me to relax and trust the Lord? That's easy for her to say. . . . She doesn't have the constant burden of . . . I guess that's the point, isn't it?*

"Yes," Patricia added, chewing on her lip, " 'Nica and I never, ever hated anyone Irish."

Veronica danced up and down on the heels of her shoes. "Except Moira Fionne, and that's only because she padded the front of her dress and pretended she was fifteen."

Jamie Sue surveyed the fleeting eyes of her daughters. "Moira did what?"

"Oh . . . nothing." Veronica pulled her mother back to the living room. "Look, Mama . . . all of our trunks!"

Jamie Sue stared at the living room stacked with boxes, trunks, valises, and wardrobes. "Yes! Oh, girls, this is an exciting day. Forgive me for going on about those other things. And don't you dare tell Eachan about any of this. It is a misunderstanding we must clear up. I just wish I could clear it up today."

"We want to open our trunk, Mama. But we couldn't find a key that fits," Veronica said.

"They're all on that nail by the back door." *Lord, I just can't allow the confrontation with Mr. Moraine to dominate my every thought. I have other things to do . . . children to take care of. Supper to cook. Trunks to unpack. A gallows to build.*

"We tried all those, but they didn't fit our trunk," Patricia explained.

"It must be there," Jamie Sue said.

"The keys opened all the cases and trunks except ours," Veronica added. "And it's the most important one . . . to us anyway."

Jamie Sue approached the huge, faded green steamer trunk and sorted through the half-dozen keys. "This is it. See, I have it tagged V&P."

"We tried that one, Mama," Patricia explained.

"This is certainly it. You just slide it in this way and . . ." The large key did not slip into the slot of the shiny steel padlock. "Well, perhaps it goes . . ." Still she couldn't even get the key in the lock. "Do you suppose I mislabeled it?"

"We tried them all, Mama," Veronica announced. "Does Daddy have the key to our trunk?"

"I don't think so. He might have the key to your hearts, but not your trunk." Jamie Sue fussed with the other keys, but none fit. "This is rather odd. Is it your trunk?"

"Of course it is. See the picture I drew of a paint horse? Well it sort of looks like a horse. And look what 'Nica wrote: 'Wanted Pen Pal: write to Veronica Fortune, Deadwood, South Dakota.' "

"You did what? You put your name on a trunk?"

Veronica folded her arms across the top of her head. "Yes, but no one has written to me."

"I certainly don't like the idea of your soliciting anonymous letters and prefer you don't do it again."

"See, I told you," Patricia chided as she tugged at the handle of the trunk. "What are we going to do? How can we get the trunk open?"

"Perhaps Daddy does have that key."

Veronica hopped in front of the trunk. "But we don't want to wait!"

"I'm sorry, girls, there's really not much we can do."

"We could get the gun and shoot it open," Veronica said. Veronica tapped the lock with the key. "I read in a Hawthorne Miller book about a man who escaped while being chained to a runaway stagecoach by shooting the lock."

"That's my point entirely," Jamie Sue declared. "Fiction is unreal. No one ever shot a lock off a trunk. Meanwhile, you can help me unpack our dishes and other goods."

The twins huddled by their green steamer trunk.

"But mother!" Veronica cried. "What about our church dresses?"

"And our good shoes," Patricia added. "They are right in here and we can't get to them! It's not fair."

"And our scarves."

"And our dolls!"

"And our diaries!" Veronica blurted out. "We have to get out our diaries before we forget everything." Suddenly, both girls covered their mouths with their hands.

Jamie Sue sauntered back toward her daughters. "You girls have diaries?"

"'Nica!" Patricia murmured. "We weren't supposed to tell."

Veronica hung her head. "Amber gave us diaries last Christmas and told us we were supposed to keep them absolutely secret."

Jamie Sue slipped her hands on her girls' shoulders. "I see . . . well, you have been doing a very good job of it."

"It's OK, isn't it, Mama? I mean, I don't really have any good secrets, but if I did, it would be alright to write them in my diary, wouldn't it?" Patricia probed.

"I believe every girl needs to cherish a few secrets."

"See . . . I knew Mama wouldn't mind," Veronica boasted.

"Let me give you one word of caution. As secret as you want to make them, diaries have a habit of being known . . . sooner or later. So, keep that in mind. Perhaps not in your lifetime, but certainly in your own daughter's."

Veronica's eyes widened. "Really?"

"Certainly. What do you think your twelve-year-old daughters will do when they stumble across your diary?"

"Oh no!" Veronica gulped. "I really, really need to get this trunk open. When is Daddy coming home?"

"Probably not until dark."

Veronica danced back and forth on the hardwood floor in front of the massive trunk. "Isn't there anything we can do?"

Jamie Sue circled the baggage. "I believe if we were careful, we could unfasten the screws in the hinges and open it from the back."

"Really? Can we, Mama?" Veronica pressed.

"If we can find Daddy's screwdriver."

"Where is it?" Patricia asked.

Jamie Sue surveyed the crates and boxes crammed into their living room. "In one of these other cases."

Sam Fortune reviewed his notes scribbled across sheets of paper that were weighted with rocks and pebbles on the dirt next to the headworks.

"What do you think, Sammy, can you run a telephone line out here?" Robert asked.

"We can run a line most anywhere. Whether anyone can afford it, and whether it will work, is another matter."

"Would you follow the road we took?"

"Looks like it. From the top of the headworks you can see down there for miles."

Augusta Raxton strolled over to where they squatted on their haunches studying the notes. "You boys ready for supper?"

Robert noticed her scrubbed face and hands. There was still dirt on the back of her neck and under her fingernails, but most the rest of the exposed surfaces were scoured pink clean.

"You tidy up mighty fine, Miss Augusta," Samuel said.

"And you're a handsome liar, Mr. Samuel Fortune. I can't remember when I last had a hot bath and put on clean clothes."

The Fortune brothers strolled to the long, rustic, outdoor table where the others sat on half-log benches. Sandra Raxton, Tio, and Poco also sported clean hands and faces.

Oscar Puddin remained dirty.

"You know what I like best about the Raxton sisters?" Robert asked, as he sat down.

"It ain't our charming manners or our nobby clothes." Sandra Raxton's laugh was somewhere between a donkey's bray and a hawk's lament.

"I like your honesty. You just blurt out how you feel and what you're thinking. Sometimes it takes months to find out things from other women. But not you two," Robert declared.

"There's too much work to do to dally around visitin' about nothin'," Augusta scoffed.

On the table was a huge bowl of thick, dark, brown gravy with elk meat chunks the size of a man's fist. What first looked like potato wedges in the gravy turned out to be turnips. A stack of steaming tortillas, each about two feet in diameter, was piled directly on top of the stained wooden table. Coffee steamed in the pot, and thick-crusted apple pies sat at each end of the table.

"Sorry we're all out of eggs," Augusta said. "We used the last two in them pie crusts."

"This is very generous of you ladies," Robert announced.

Byron Chambers, still wearing his top hat, but not his coat or tie, stared at the tin plate full of gravied meat and turnips. His fork seemed welded to his unmoving hand.

"Well, Byron . . ." Robert quizzed. "What will be your report to the Bank of Ottawa?"

He laid his fork down. "It's very confusing."

"The records?" Robert questioned. He jabbed a forkful of meat and gravy into his mouth and was surprised that it tasted sweet, yet spicy.

Chambers pushed his plate away and sipped on the steaming coffee in the tin cup. "No, I maintain the Raxtons have most of the receipts in order. I believe I know where the funds went. And I'm convinced from the assay reports that this mine has wonderful potential. But I don't have a set of books to bring back and convince the bank to pump in more money. Without that, my employers will pull out of the project and attempt to sell their part. They weren't happy with this situation before. But now that . . ."

"Now that women are running it?" Miss Sandra asked.

"It might be a sad commentary, but it's true," Chambers declared.

"We won't get any more financial backing?" Miss Augusta pressed.

"Not from our bank. They would deem that a woman could not run such an operation."

"You mean two of us ain't even as good as one drunk man like Mac?" Miss Sandra challenged.

"I'm afraid some would see it that way."

"How about you, Byron?" Robert said. "Do you think they can run it?"

"That's the confusing part. Indeed, I believe they can run it. But the Raxton sisters, in their present splendor . . . eh, nothing personal I assure you . . . make it quite inconceivable to arrange financing."

"What do you mean by present splendor?" Miss Augusta asked.

Oscar Puddin wiped gravy across the back of his hand. "He means if you two women go marchin' into a banker's office looking dirty and smellin' like a hog, you ain't going to get no loan." The big man grinned and looked over at the cooks. "This might be the best Mexican gravy I ever et."

"But, if we sit back and do nothin', we could end up with new partners that want to chase us off our claims?" Miss Augusta speculated.

"Depends on who buys the Bank of Ottawa's shares," Robert added.

Miss Augusta stabbed a huge bite of elk meat as if it were a rat about to attack her. "I don't like it. I don't like it one bit. We did all the diggin' and blastin', and right before we hit it big, someone comes in and takes it away from us. That ain't right, and you boys know it."

"But we've got to have partners to get the real riches out of this mountain," Miss Sandra declared. "How about you Fortunes? You want to buy the bank's shares?"

"I told you, Miss Sandra, I don't have the funds. But we know some who do," Robert added.

"You could talk to them for us, couldn't you?" she asked. "You could tell them how hard we work and how close we are to the big lead."

Robert glanced over at his brother. "You two sisters would have to come to Deadwood and make your pitch."

"We couldn't do that. We can't leave the mine," Miss Sandra declared.

Sam pointed at the Mexican cooks. "Poco and Tio could watch it."

Miss Augusta dropped her head and said, "We wouldn't know who to talk to or how to talk to them."

Robert glanced over at Byron Chambers, who continued to avoid his meal. "Your bookkeeper could go to town and arrange things before you arrived. He could schedule a big dinner at the hotel. You could bring in samples and assay reports, then make your pitch."

"We ain't got no bookkeeper and no one is goin' to lend us money. Mr. Chambers made that quite clear," Miss Augusta insisted.

"I've spent my life organizing battles and campaigns that work," Robert insisted. "I have seen your ore. I can tell you how it would work."

"Do tell us how, Mr. Fortune," Miss Sandra said.

Robert rolled up a tortilla and pointed it toward the mine shaft. "You keep a crew diggin' out here as much as you can so you'll have a little spendin' money when you come to town."

Miss Augusta rubbed the back of her neck. "We're workin' as hard as we can and just breakin' even."

"No offense, ma'am, but two tired women and two old men are not the healthiest of crews. You'll need some big strong bruiser of a man to do the heavy work," Robert suggested.

"Someone like Oscar." Sam slapped the big man on the back.

Oscar Puddin wiped gravy off his chin with a steaming tortilla. "I ain't lookin' for a job, and I ain't goin' to work out here for no women."

Robert turned to his brother. "Sammy, you were on the wrong side of the law a time or two when you were younger. What kind of jail time do you think Oscar will get for that stunt he pulled back there on the trail?"

"Attempted robbery and murder?"

"I wasn't tryin' to murder nobody," Puddin insisted.

"You came extremely close to murdering me!" Byron Chambers blurted out.

"With that kind of testimony," Samuel pondered, "Oscar will get one to two years in jail. They'll send him out to Ft. Pierre. I hear those cells are might tiny for a big man."

"But," Robert added, "if none of us press charges, he could work out here for a couple of months and everything would be settled. Right, Mr. Chambers?"

"My word, is that the way justice is done out here?"

"Look, we'd be helpin' Oscar, and he'd be helpin' the Raxton sisters," Robert explained. "And I wouldn't have to look at his big round face for eight weeks. Everyone would benefit."

"I ain't no slave," Puddin muttered.

"Keep track of your hours and they'd pay you as soon as they get the loan. Maybe even let you buy in," Sammy suggested.

"I ain't goin' to buy into no gold mine."

"It beats stealing gold," Robert said.

Puddin's grin revealed yellow, tobacco-stained teeth. "What if I jist up and run away?"

"Then one of the Raxton girls just climbs this headworks and shoots you dead. You know they can do it," Robert cautioned.

"Well, the grub's good," Oscar replied, gravy dripping down his whiskered chin.

"That still don't get us a loan . . ." Miss Augusta added.

Robert slung his arm around the banker's shoulder. "Now, that's where Mr. Chambers comes in."

"My word, I'm not staying out here!" he insisted.

"Nope. Byron, you need to telegraph your bosses that the money has been correctly spent. The Raxton sisters, who have no experience in mining, won the claim in a horse race and are now running the outfit."

"That don't sound very impressive," Miss Sandra said.

"But they just might be willing to sell cheaper," Sam offered.

"Exactly," Robert added. "And then Mr. Chambers can tell them he'll stay in Deadwood to secure buyers for their shares."

"Why would I want to stay in Deadwood for any reason?" Chambers huffed.

"Because the Raxton sisters will give you a share of the mine if you work with them on it."

Miss Sandra's eyes squinted, "You're givin' away lots of shares of our mine."

"But you'd have a fine Englishman chartered accountant for a bookkeeper. You have two of the Fortune boys who have examined the site firsthand. I can guarantee between the three of us we can stir up a room full of backers. Then when you come to town, bring your ore samples and plans on how you will cable the ore off the mountain and mill it in the bottom of Spruce Canyon."

"We ain't got no plans," Miss Sandra retorted.

"Draw some up."

"We ain't no good at draftin'."

"Sammy is," Robert said.

Miss Augusta stared at Sam Fortune. "Do we have to give him a share of the mine too?"

"Nope," Sammy grinned. "Just give me the telephone franchise."

"There's just one thing." Robert looked each Raxton sister in the eye. "Oscar is right. You two will have to soak in some hot water, fluff your hair up fancy, and buy yourself new dresses. A successful mine is owned by successful-looking people."

"We ain't had new dresses in years," Miss Augusta told them.

"Sammy's wife just happens to own the nicest store in Deadwood for ready-made dresses. When you leave her place, you will feel like the queens of Spruce Ridge."

"We're the only women on Spruce Ridge," Miss Sandra said. "We are the queens right now."

"See . . ." Robert laughed. "My plan's working already."

Robert could see through the thin gauze curtains into the living room as he walked up the Lincoln Street sidewalk in front of their house. Though it was well past everyone's bedtime, the gas lamps in every room were still lit. The trunks and cases were visible, still scattered around the room.

There was the noise of pots and pans rattling in the kitchen when he came in the front door. He could smell butter frying in an iron skillet.

"Anyone home?" he called out as he hung his hat on a peg and unfastened his holster.

"Daddy, you're late!" Veronica squealed as she dashed out of the kitchen.

"Sorry about that, darlin'."

"Daddy, it's horrible," Patricia added.

"What's so horrible now?" He threw an arm around each daughter. "It looks like our trunks arrived. Everything's here, isn't it?"

Patricia's small, soft fingers snuggled into his as she tugged him into the living room. "Not everything!"

Veronica hung on to the other hand. "Our goods are gone!"

"But there's your trunk," Robert noted.

"They even took our diaries!" Veronica moaned.

Robert held up his hands. "Whoa . . . whoa . . ."

Jamie Sue appeared at the doorway. A white-frilled apron covered a wheat-gold sasheen dress.

"Nice dress, Mama," he greeted.

"I thought I would never see it again."

"Do you know what this talk is about?" he asked her.

"It's a great mystery, Mr. Robert Fortune, railway inspector. All of our trunks arrived. Only the girls' big trunk had a different padlock on it. When we took the hinges off the back we found all their belongings were missing."

Robert strolled into the living room. "The trunk was empty?"

"No, that's part of the quandary. It was crammed full of money."

"What?"

"She's right, Daddy," Veronica whined. "All of our clothing and earthly possessions are missing, and it's full of brand new, dumb money!"

CHAPTER SEVEN

The air in the hardware store was stuffy as Robert Fortune swung the tall oak-and-glass doors open. Somewhere to the east the sun had risen on the Dakota prairie. Its reflection could be seen on top of the tallest pines left standing on Forest Hill. But down below in Whitewood Gulch, the narrow streets of Deadwood crouched in shadows.

He strolled toward the woodstove. The stovepipe ascended upward like the shaft of an arrow until it pierced the fourteen-foot, soot-dusted ceiling. He recalled when there were no aisles or neatly arranged shelves . . . just the stove and goods littered across the floor.

Four men clustered near the stove. Two were elderly. All were older than he. Three carried his last name. One carried a bullet that had crippled him for ten years.

Robert tugged at his tie and unfastened the top button of his white shirt. "It's hot in here, Daddy," he reported.

The gray-haired man with a big-brimmed, round, felt hat with Montana crease stared up with narrow, penetrating eyes. "These bones of mine haven't been warm since I left Texas," Brazos drawled. "Ain't that right, Quiet Jim?"

The man in the wheelchair rubbed his neatly trimmed gray mustache and clean-shaven, narrow chin. "I don't know. . . . It was purdy warm the other day when the mill burned down." A sly grin crept across the rugged man's narrow lips.

"There ain't nothin' hotter than a lumber mill fire," Brazos added.

"Unless it was when the Nugget Dance Hall burned down the first time." Quiet Jim's voice could barely be heard above the pop and snap of the fire.

"The Nugget radiated a lot of heat, even when it wasn't on fire," Brazos roared.

"I got to say, you two are taking the burning of the lumber mill rather well." Robert paused by the woodstove and warmed his hands, even though they were already sweating.

"Bobby, a man cain't cry too long. When me, Quiet Jim, and the boys rode into this gulch, there was nothin' but down trees, a couple tents and a one-room log cabin. Someday, it will all burn down and we'll just ride off. Won't we, Quiet Jim?"

"Your daddy's right. 'The Lord giveth, the Lord taketh away . . . blessed be the name of the Lord.' " Even when he merely spoke, Quiet Jim's melodic voice sounded like a tune.

"Yeah, but that's an expensive way to keep warm," Robert said.

Todd broke open a crate of factory-made carriage bolts and sorted them into the bins. "I told Daddy he should take a vacation to some sandy beach and just lay in the sun until he's good and warm."

Sam Fortune yanked off his hat and whacked his youngest brother on the backside. "Bobby's got a trunk of cash money Daddy can spend."

Brazos pulled the green wool blanket over his shoulders as he huddled near the roaring woodstove. "What did you find out about that money, son?"

Robert poured a cup of coffee, then backed away from the fire. "Southern Pacific Railroad traced it to San Diego. It seems our bags were in the freight room there for over a week until they figured out where they were to be shipped. They surmise someone who thought all the trunks were going into Tiajuana, Mexico, jammed that one full of money."

"Brand-new money," Todd added.

"Worthless money," Sam declared.

"It ain't worth nothin'?" Quiet Jim stared at the bottom of his empty coffee cup.

Brazos stood, the blanket like a cape on his shoulders, then carried the coffeepot over and filled Quiet Jim's cup.

Robert rubbed his dark brown beard. "There isn't any such thing as the Republic of Lower California. At least, not yet. The treasury department and the war department were very curious, though. There have been rumors of privateers from the States wanting to take advantage of the political confusion in Mexico."

"Do you mean someone from San Diego was, or is, planning on invading Baja, California, and declaring independence?" Todd questioned.

"That's exactly what our government wants to find out," Robert said. "I've been down there. There isn't anything but rock, sand, sunshine, and a few nice beaches. Don't know who would want it."

"Someone who's cold," Brazos commented.

Sam Fortune was the only one wearing spurs. He rolled the rowels across the hardwood floor. "How much money was in that trunk?" he asked.

Robert pulled off his wool suit coat and laid it across a crate marked "pick handles." "Little Frank stayed up past midnight counting it. There was somewhere close to a half-million dollars."

Sam let out a loud whistle. "In that one trunk?"

"Some of the bills are quite large denominations." Robert chewed on the coffee grounds before taking another sip of coffee. "They make our greenbacks look dull. There were purples and yellows and pinks in the big denominations."

His suit coat off, his white sleeves rolled up to his elbows, Carty Toluca emerged from the back room. "Todd, I'm going down to the depot and load up that freight that came in from Chicago."

"You need some help?" Todd asked.

Carty laughed. "I'll take one of the clerks. I wouldn't want to bother you old men!"

"Old men?" Todd hooted. "If Lil' Sis wouldn't pitch a fit, I'd turn you over my knee and bend a willow on your backside."

"What's my Dacee June doin' today?" Brazos asked. "She hasn't come by to see me."

"She's bakin' you a raisin pie and teaching the girls how to speak French," Carty reported.

"French lessons? But two of them are still in diapers, and one can't walk yet," Brazos challenged.

Carty shrugged as he trudged off toward the back room. "You know Dacee June."

Robert glanced at his brothers . . . his father . . . then Quiet Jim. "Yep," he mumbled, "that sounds like Lil' Sis."

"What happens to the money now?" Sam probed. "You going to wallpaper with it?"

"We're shipping the whole works back to San Diego. The government wants to see if someone comes inquiring about it. They sent the girls five dollars to buy their old trunk."

Quiet Jim took his hand and lifted his right leg back up on the footrest of the wheelchair. "Little Frank said the twins was missin' their belongin's."

"Jamie Sue and the girls will be shopping for ready-mades to replace what they lost. They're excited about all new clothes, but there were some personal items that they're grieving over," Robert said.

"You buy them all new things, Bobby, and I'll pay for it," Brazos insisted.

"No you won't, Daddy Brazos," Robert insisted. "I can provide for my family, and you've got to stop spoilin' those girls of mine. It's appalling the way you cotton to them."

Brazos rubbed his drooping gray mustache. "I ain't got that many years left to spoil them."

"Old man, you're tougher than a piece of old salmon pounded out and left for jerky," Todd insisted. "You'll be here when the Homestake is played out and sheep are grazing on Sherman Avenue."

"Besides, Daddy," Robert added. "Some day you're going to meet Mama up there in heaven and she'll say, 'Henry, it was shameful the way you spoiled Robert

Paul's twins.' "

Brazos stared up at his youngest son. He rubbed his tongue slowly across chapped lips, then reached up and rubbed the corners of his eyes. "She will, won't she?"

"You know she will," Robert insisted.

"Well, you boys know I've never really gotten over your sisters' deaths. I look at them girls of yours, Bobby, and it's like the Lord gave me a second chance. I hope the rest of the family understands that and don't take no offense."

"It doesn't bother us," Todd reported.

"Course," Robert continued, "those two will have husbands some day that will be distressed something fierce."

"Right now, I just can't look at them without smilin'," Brazos said.

"You wouldn't be smiling at them today. They were going at each other tooth and nail when I left home."

"What are they scrapping over?" Brazos asked.

"Eachan Moraine."

"You mean all Fortunes don't hate the Irish?" Todd chided.

Sammy continued to roll his spurs on the wooden floor. "We're all a lovable lot, except for ol' Ted Fortune."

"That worthless Hawthorne Miller," Brazos mumbled. "Why in the world does he lie, then try to make it sound like us? If that man walked through the door . . ."

"I reckon you'd pull that Sharps .50 caliber off the wall over your bed," Quiet Jim suggested.

Brazos let the blanket slip off his shoulders. "I believe I'm warmin' up to the task already!"

"Now, Daddy, what does the Bible say about how to respond when we're wrongfully accused?" Robert pressed.

" 'For this is thankworthy, if a man for conscience toward God endure grief, suffering wrongfully . . .' " Samuel recited.

"And," Robert continued, " 'if, when ye do well, and suffer for it, ye take it patiently, this is acceptable with God.' "

Brazos looked over at Quiet Jim and both men grinned. "What's a man to do when the boys go oratin' Bible verses at you?"

"It's Sarah Ruth's fault," Quiet Jim added. "All those days you were out chasin' wild cattle over south Texas, she lined them up and made them memorize Scripture."

Brazos shuffled over to the coffeepot. "The worst part is, they're right, of course."

Samuel stood and straightened his coat. "Maybe I'll find out soon enough. I need to line up a crew to install a line out to the Broken Boulder, so I thought I'd check with the Irishmen again."

Todd tossed the last of the carriage bolts into the wooden bin. "Pinch-Nose Pete's dead, you know."

"What do you mean, dead? I thought he just went down to Hot Springs to sit in the mineral baths?" Sam replied.

Todd stood on the bench and reached up to adjust the gas lantern. "Nope. Ol' Billy Walston came through here last Tuesday and said that . . ."

"What's Billy peddlin' now?" Brazos quizzed.

"Watches, mostly," Todd reported. "Anyway, Ol' Billy said Pinch-Nose Pete showed up in Cheyenne a few weeks ago spendin' and braggin' about how much money he could make in Deadwood. It wasn't three days before he was robbed and shot dead out behind the Baltimore Club."

Samuel set his cup down and shook his head. "When he was sober, he was a good man. He surely kept that Irish crew workin' when they hit tough goin' in the canyon. But he didn't make enough wages off that job to whoop it up in Custer City, let alone Cheyenne."

Quiet Jim cleared his throat. "Talkin' about havin' money is as dangerous as actually havin' it."

Samuel shoved his cup back on the shelf and headed to the door. "I'll just see if I can find any Irishmen to work for me. Maybe one of them wants to be crew boss."

"I've got to head out too," Robert declared. "I've got a trunk of money to ship back to San Diego."

"You guardin' it yourself?" Brazos asked.

"Nothin' valuable to guard. We'll just toss it in the baggage car with the rest. But it is my turn to ride. It will give me a chance to catch up reading those Pinkerton Reports."

Robert reached the door, then turned back to his oldest brother. "If that chartered accountant, Byron Chambers, shows up today, introduce him to the ol' men at the wood-stove and tell him I'll be back by tomorrow."

Todd walked with him out onto the shadow-blanketed boardwalk. "How's he going to get here? You brought back his carriage."

Robert tipped his hat at a tall lady who crossed the dirt street near them. "The Raxton sisters have a freight wagon. I reckon one of the Mexican cooks will bring him in."

Todd looped his thumbs in his vest pocket. "You really think the Broken Boulder is worth something?"

"Look at the ore and the assay. It's been years since they found something that good near the surface."

Todd lowered his voice. "Are you going to talk to Raigan Moraine about that Hawthorne Miller novel?"

"Yep. I hope he's sober."

"Does he drink?"

"I don't know . . . but I hope he's sober. Jamie Sue has decided never to speak to him again. Todd, you figure there will ever be a time when there are too many Fortunes in Deadwood?"

"Never."

"Mama, did you know that Eachan quit workin' with me and Quint at the racetrack?" Little Frank shouted as he burst in through the back door.

"Was he mad at you?"

"Nope. He just said his daddy wouldn't let him work with us 'cause we were a bad influence. I don't think I've ever been a bad influence on anyone before, except maybe that one time I talked 'Nica and Tricia into sellin' spoiled meat to old Sonora Zeke. But Daddy whipped the bad influence right out of me."

"You are not a bad influence. At least, I trust you aren't. Your father's going to talk to Mr. Moraine and get it all cleared up. How is your work coming?"

"We got the track cleared, but the carpenters haven't finished the rail yet. Mr. Meyers—he's the one that's in charge—says we can come help the carpenters if we'd like."

"Yes, I imagine he would like the free help. How is your finger today?"

"Sore, but as long as I don't bump it too hard, it's alright." Little Frank grabbed a cold biscuit and crammed half of it into his mouth. "The big race is set for Sunday!" he mumbled.

"Don't talk with your mouth full, young man. You're spraying biscuit crumbs like they were chicken feed out by the henhouse. Now, the girls and I are going over to Aunt Abby's. They're trying on some more clothes. Would you like to come?"

"I'd rather get run over by a train than have to listen to them fuss about clothes." Little Frank grabbed another biscuit. "Can I go down to the hardware and play cribbage with Grandpa Brazos?"

"Yes, and come by Aunt Abby's before you come home. We might have some packages for you to carry."

"I think Daddy had a good idea. 'Nica and Tricia should have sewn dresses out of that fake money. Then they could march in the Fourth of July parade." Little Frank crammed more biscuit in his mouth.

"It's not fake exactly. It's just worthless at this point," Jamie Sue added. "Someone spent money to engrave the plates and print all of that up."

Little Frank's eyes lit up. "I wish that lady photographer, Miss Fontenot, had been in town. We could have had our pictures taken sprawled across all that money."

Jamie Sue retrieved a broom and began sweeping the gray wooden floor of the kitchen. "Aunt Rebekah said that Miss Fontenot is now Mrs. Kaid Darrant."

Little Frank paused at the back door. "No foolin'? She got married? It don't seem fair. All the good ones are either married or related to me."

Guthrie Holter's hat was pushed back. His dark hair drooped across his forehead, parallel to his mustache. His chair leaned back against the wall and he was reading an illustrated *Police Gazette* when Robert entered his office above the depot.

"You about to head out?" Guthrie asked.

Robert shuffled through some papers on his desk. "Yes. I wanted to talk to Mr. Moraine before I left, but he's working days. I can't seem to find him at home."

"If you need to stay and talk, I'll take the run," Holter offered.

"It's my turn," Robert insisted. "It's your day off."

"It's not like I have a lot to do. Let me take the run."

"Holter, you're a good man. And I don't intend to abuse your enthusiasm. It will be best if we stick to our schedule, unless it's an emergency. Now, if you told me your wife and boys were waitin' for you in Rapid City, and you wanted to go get them and bring them to Deadwood, that would be . . ."

Holter leaned the chair forward, then stared down at his boots. His voice was so soft, Robert could barely hear it. "She made up her mind she don't want to live up here."

Robert pulled a box of .45 cartridges out of his top right drawer and dropped them in his pocket.

"You going to need that many bullets?" Holter said.

Fortune laughed as he strolled toward the door. "No, I suppose I'll wear the writing off this box before I ever have to use them. But we just have to be prepared."

Robert shuffled down the wooden steps, through the depot, and out to the platform among a half-dozen waiting passengers. He heard someone shout his name.

It was a man's voice.

An angry man's voice.

A tall man with a small bowler and a thick, drooping mustache stalked toward him carrying a short, double-barreled shotgun.

"Did you need to talk to me?" Robert called out.

The man stopped about twenty feet away. "If you're lookin' for a fight, it might as well be right here!" the man declared.

Passengers waiting to board the train scurried back into the depot. Those onboard peered out from the temporary safety of glass windows.

Robert strolled toward the man with the square jaw and angry eyes. "Mister, I don't even know you. What's this all about?"

"I'm Riagan Moraine, and I don't take lightly to Irish-hating. You said you were goin' to settle this matter once and for all. Well you're totin' a gun and so am I. Let's settle it right here and now."

"Mr. Moraine, I have never, in any way, insulted the Irish. The finest men I served with in the army were all Irish. This is so ludicrous, it's almost funny. Put your gun away and go home."

"Go home, you say?" The man's voice was loud enough for all the platform to hear. "That's because you didn't think I'd show up armed, did you?"

"What are you talking about?"

"That letter you sent me. You think I'd come begging?

You Fortunes ain't nearly as important as you think you are."

Robert rubbed the bridge of his nose, then the wrinkles in his forehead with calloused fingers. "I didn't send you a letter."

The shotgun in his right hand, Moraine whipped out a piece of paper with his left. "I suppose this ain't your stationery?"

Robert leaned close enough to see his name on the top of the Fremont, Elkhorn, and Missouri Valley Railroad stationery.

"That's my letterhead, but it isn't my letter."

Moraine crammed the paper back in his pocket. "Are you callin' me a liar?"

"Mr. Moraine, you've told the truth. You do have some kind of letter. And I told the truth; I didn't send it. I don't even know what's on it."

Moraine leaned forward until he was only a couple of feet away. "You said it would be a cold day in Hades when you couldn't do away with an Irishman."

Robert tugged on an earlobe, then scratched the back of his neck. "I do not believe that way. That is not my letter."

"You sayin' that ain't your signature?"

"That's what I'm saying," Robert insisted.

"It's printed on a typewriting machine, and I know you got one in your office."

"If you know that much about my office, you'd know I've never used it—ever."

Moraine shook the gun barrel at Robert. "Well, you called me out. I'm here. You're here. We both have guns. Let's settle it."

"Mr. Fortune? We have to get the last passengers loaded," the conductor hollered.

"Moraine, let's talk about this in a more private place."

"We'll do it right out here in the open. I don't intend to get back-shot or bushwhacked."

Guthrie Holter sauntered up next to Robert. "You need help, Mr. Fortune?"

"You stay out of this. This ain't your fight," Moraine yelled at Holter.

"Mr. Moraine . . ." Robert walked to the side of the platform. "Let me see the letter again. Perhaps I can tell who forged my name to it."

A few passengers scurried from the depot to the waiting train cars.

Moraine scooted to the edge of the platform. "You ain't goin' to take this and rip it up. I got the evidence that will hold up in court."

"Then sue me."

"For what?" Moraine grumbled.

"Precisely my point," Robert added. "I haven't committed any crime, Mr. Moraine. Neither have any of my family."

"I read it in a book."

"The book is full of lies. It's make-believe. To believe it's true is as absurd as . . . as believing in the tooth fairy."

The shotgun went to Moraine's shoulder. "There *are* fairies, you know!"

Robert took a deep breath and pushed back his hat. "Mr. Moraine, I apologize to you for any misconceptions that might have been perpetuated about the Fortune family being anti-Irish. We are frontier people. Do you know what that means?"

"What?"

"It means we don't care who you were, good or bad, before you got here. It's what you are right now that counts. It has nothing to do with color of skin or nationality."

Guthrie Holter tapped on Robert's shoulder. "Mr. Fortune, the train's pullin' out. I'll take this one. You wait for the next."

"No!" Robert barked. "We are not changing plans. Mr. Moraine, I have apologized for a letter I did not send. My office is not locked. Anyone who knows how to use a typing machine could have walked in there and done that. When I return, I will find out who did and see that justice is carried out. Now I have to go to work. I'm getting on that train."

Robert Fortune turned and trotted toward the slow-moving train.

"I could shoot you in the back!" Moraine shouted.

"And just what would that prove about the Irish?" Robert replied. He caught the black iron railing and pulled himself into the car.

Jamie Sue watched her twin daughters fidget in front of the mirror. "You will only get one more ready-made dress and that's final," she declared.

"But Mama." Veronica twirled around so the hem of the navy blue dress would spin out from the toes of her shoes. "Grandpa Brazos said he'd buy us all the dresses we want."

"Your Grandpa Brazos would buy you two the moon, if

I'd let him. However, this is our purchase. We will buy yardage and make you two sets of identical dresses. That will give you both two nice dresses, two new everyday dresses, and one old one for doing chores. That's five dresses each, and no girl in the world needs more than five dresses." Jamie Sue's shoulders sagged a little forward as she stood and crossed her arms.

Veronica tugged her mother's hand free and put hers into it. "Amber says a girl needs seven dresses, a different one for every day of the week."

Jamie Sue squeezed Veronica's hand, then released it. "But Amber's mother owns a dress shop. I don't even have seven dresses. At least, not seven that fit."

Patricia chewed on her tongue, still staring at the dress in the mirror. "It was nice of Aunt Abby to order us identical dresses."

Jamie Sue straightened the shoulders of Patricia's dress, then smoothed the lace yoke. "It does seem to keep the peace around our house a bit better."

"It's my turn to wear the yellow dress to church," Patricia declared.

Veronica strolled between her sister and the mirror. "No it isn't. You wore it to Fern Troop's recital."

"But no one was there, but family . . . and the Troops," Patricia insisted.

Veronica curtseyed to herself in the mirror. "Quint Troop is not just family."

"Wait a minute," Jamie Sue insisted. "I thought the argument was over who wore the rose-colored dress? When did you start arguing over the yellow one?"

"Ever since we saw Curly Mac at the drugstore and he

said the yellow dress Veronica had on was the prettiest dress he had ever seen in his entire life!" Patricia admitted.

Sam Fortune burst through the front door of the dress shop and uttered muffled words to Abigail. Immediately, Abby waved for her to join them.

"Girls, I'm going up front to talk to Aunt Abby. You put on your old dresses and put the new ones in the box so we can carry them home."

Sam spoke as she approached. "Jamie Sue, is Bobby taking the morning or afternoon train?"

"I believe it was the morning train. But he won't be home until tomorrow. Why?" Jamie Sue pressed.

Sam spun on the heels of his polished stovetop boots. "Maybe it's late pullin' out. I'll try to catch him."

Jamie Sue felt her heart start to race. "What is it?"

"Abby will fill you in," Sammy called back.

Jamie Sue's sister-in-law wore dangling emerald earrings that matched her seasoned eyes. She studied them as Sam Fortune hurried out the front door. "What is it, Abby?"

"Sammy has a telephone line to install, and what with Pinch-Nose Pete gone, he talked to Keary Nolan about forming a crew. Keary would hardly speak to him. Said no Irish would work for him again."

"It's all over that novel?" Jamie Sue asked.

"No. That's why Sammy's so upset. They're mad because they were promised extra pay for stringing a line through Death Song Canyon. He paid the bonus to Pinch-Nose Pete to give to the men, but they never received it."

"What?" Her throat and neck were so tight the word shot out like a cork on a bottle of vinegar.

Abby paced behind the front counter. "Pete kept the

bonus and took off to Cheyenne."

Jamie Sue followed Abby's bustle. "And none of the crew ever complained to Sammy?"

"Pete told the crew that Fortunes hated the Irish and they had better not approach one of them without a gun in their hand."

"I can't believe it!"

Abby spun around and faced Jamie Sue. "Neither can Sammy."

"Did he explain it to Keary Nolan?"

"Yes," Abby said, "but Keary didn't believe it until he showed him his books, and Pete's signature on the receipt of the bonuses."

"That's horrible. Pete should be arrested."

"Pete's dead. He died in Cheyenne spending the crew's bonuses." Abby slapped her hand over her mouth, then murmured, "Sometimes, it is much more difficult being a Christian. There are many things I want to say right now, but none are allowed."

"I've often wished I had a deep cave to go into every once in a while to yell and scream," Jamie Sue admitted.

Abby took a deep breath, then smiled. "You could make a fortune renting it out."

"What's Sammy going to do now?" Jamie Sue asked.

"He asked Keary to call a meeting of the Irish. Sammy will explain the situation and give the men their overdue bonuses."

"Does Sammy have the extra money?"

"We'll borrow it if we have to. But those men deserve the bonuses they were promised," Abby insisted.

"Mr. Moraine said it was Hawthorne Miller's awful

book that got him riled."

"That must have added to the misconception."

"Or the conspiracy," Jamie Sue replied.

"Mama!" Little Frank sprinted into the dress shop with Quintin Troop a step behind. "Did you hear about Daddy?"

"What happened?" she gasped.

"Mr. Moraine met him at the depot and called him out!"

"He did what?"

The dark-headed Quintin Troop stared down at his dusty black boots. Quint was a year older than Little Frank but a good four inches shorter. "He tried to provoke him into a gunfight."

"When?"

"Mr. Landusky at the depot told Daddy that Moraine showed up just as the train pulled out. He wanted Mr. Fortune to face him in a gunfight."

"Has it gone that far?" Abby gasped.

"What happened?" She felt Abby's arm slip into hers.

Little Frank pulled off his hat and rocked back on his heels. "Daddy told Mr. Moraine that it was all a lie about Fortunes hating the Irish, and he refused to draw his gun."

Jamie Sue tried to take a deep breath, but it turned out to be so shallow she coughed. "Then Robert didn't get hurt?"

"No, ma'am. That's what Mr. Landusky told Quiet Jim who told Quint who told me," Little Frank explained.

"What happened after that?" Jamie Sue inquired.

"Daddy walked away from Mr. Moraine and boarded the train."

"Moraine threatened to shoot him in the back," Quint added.

"But he didn't," Little Frank consoled.

Jamie Sue clutched Abby's arm. "This whole thing is thundering out of control. It's almost demonic."

"I was thinking the same thing," Abby replied. She peered out the window, then shouted, "Be gone with you, Satan! In the name of Jesus, be gone with your lies and deceit."

Jamie Sue flinched.

Quint and Little Frank jumped back.

Veronica and Patricia scurried up front, wearing their old dresses and carrying their new ones.

"What happened?" Patricia called out. "Aunt Abby, what are you yelling about?"

Veronica headed for the two boys. "Hello, Quint," she drawled. "Did you come by to see me in my new dress?"

Jamie Sue sat on the sofa, facing Lincoln Street. She counted the stitches in the half-done, ecru-colored dresser scarf that lay in her lap. She held a small number 9 crochet hook in her right hand.

Now Lord, this is such a peaceful scene. There is no wind blowing down the gulch. The sky is a beautiful Dakota light blue. The temperature's so mild. I don't need gloves outdoors or a wood fire in here.

. . . single crochet in 2nd chain from hook in back loop only . . .

Robert is at work with a job that fits him perfectly. Little Frank is helping build a racetrack. His broken finger is healing nicely. I have a lovely home, . . . dear friends and family nearby, a sense of place and permanency.

. . . single crochet in next five stitches in back loop only. Work three single crochets in next stitch in back loop only . . .

So why on earth am I so anxious and nervous?

Besides the fact that my twelve-year-old daughters went on a carriage ride with their cousin, Amber, who loves to race horses, on a trip up the gulch to Central City and Lead? Which, of course, should cause everyone in all three towns sincere worry.

. . . single crochet in back loop of next six stitches. Skip next two stitches . . .

It is like putting on a very comfortable pair of old shoes . . . and having a stone in one shoe. Deadwood is the old shoe. It fits us well. We are at home. But something keeps causing me pain and keeping me away from contentment.

. . . single crochet in next six stitches back loop only . . .

Part of it's the animosity with the Irish.

Not just Irish in general, but the Moraines. I can't believe that we just arrived in town and we already have someone who hates us so.

. . . three single stitches in back loop of next stitch . . .

It doesn't seem fair. It should take time to make enemies. Why is it that it takes years to make new friends and only seconds to make enemies?

. . . repeat pattern from single crochet in back loop of next six stitches . . .

Jamie Sue carefully laid her crocheting aside as she spied Eachan Moraine trudging up the sidewalk in front of the house. She scurried over to open the front door.

"Eachan!" she called out. "Would you wait a moment? I have something for you to take home!"

He brushed his curly blond bangs off his forehead and shaded his eyes with his hand. "Mrs. Fortune, I'm not supposed to go in your yard."

"I'll bring it out to you."

His voice broke from high pitch to low in the middle of the sentence. "It ain't somethin' spiteful, is it?"

"Heavens no, it's a big cherry pie."

"Really?"

"Yes, would you take it to your mother for me? I'm not allowed to go in your yard, either," she called back.

A sly grin broke across his smooth, narrow face. "I reckon I could tote a pie."

Lord, I know I promised Little Frank I'd bake us a cherry pie . . . but . . . You said, "If thine enemy hunger, feed him." And that's what I intend to do.

She slipped the pie into a blue, quilted pie carrier and hurried back outside. The aroma of the pie and the warmness of the late June sun that blazed down from high above McGovern Hill seemed to clear her mind and lift her spirits. She hiked out to the sidewalk. Eachan was slightly taller than she was.

"Take this to your dear mother, and tell her to enjoy it. Tell her I'm praying that these misunderstandings end quickly so that our families might become good friends," she instructed.

Eachan scratched the back of his neck, then grabbed hold of the pie carrier. "Daddy's a good man, Mrs. Fortune," he said. "He just had some bad things happen to him when he was growin' up in Ireland. It's made him fearful. Mama says he still has bad nightmares about it."

"Mr. Fortune didn't write that hateful letter, Eachan."

The boy peeked under the quilted cloth and sniffed the pie. "Yes, ma'am, that's what Mama said. Who do you reckon did write it?"

"I don't know. It's certainly someone who didn't want our families to be friends, wasn't it?"

"Yes, ma'am. I reckon it was."

"What do you think we ought to do about it?" she probed.

"We ought to find out who they are and punch them in the nose," Eachan declared.

"Oh, dear, I think that would be letting them off too easily," Jamie Sue challenged.

"Oh, yeah? You think we should hang them?"

"Heavens no, there is something even worse than that."

His eyes widened. "What?"

"We don't know who they are, but we know the worst thing that could happen to them is that your family and ours became good friends. They are working very hard to see that doesn't happen."

"Whoa, I never thought of it that way. If we were good friends, we could spy out who's angry about it," he suggested.

"I believe you're right."

"So me and Little Frank should continue to be pals and keep an eye out for who is mad about it?"

"I think that would be a good idea."

"Maybe me and Patricia Veronica could become chums too," he added, "and see who would be upset with that."

"I can tell you exactly who would get angry about that right now," Jamie Sue grinned.

Robert Fortune slouched down in the backseat of the second and last passenger car. He had visually inspected the passengers and dismissed them all. He had checked the manifest of baggage and freight and determined the most valuable thing on the train was the diamond tiepin on the short man with a silk suit and starched, brimmed straw hat who snored away just across the aisle.

The most interesting person, though, was a well-dressed lady who was reading a book to two boys as they huddled in the front seat. Her black hair was immaculately tucked into her white, plumed hat, and she had a small beaded bag at her side.

Occasionally she glanced back toward Robert.

My guess is there's a pearl-handled sneak gun in the beaded purse. And she's not studyin' me because I'm such a handsome head-turner.

Robert leaned his head back against the leather seat. With hat pulled low, he could still squint his eyes and see everything in the car.

Is it because I'm the most suspicious-looking man in the car? I inspected her . . . and now she inspects me. I wonder if she would do that if Jamie Sue were sitting by my side. I wonder if I'd be having this thought with Jamie Sue by my side.

Robert closed his eyes. The image of an angry Riagan Moraine emerged. *I don't think I've faced anyone who hated me so since that band of Chirachuas down in the Sierra Madres. Somebody wrote that slanderous letter.*

Someone who wanted to get at me . . . or the whole family. Who would want to do that in that kind of way? If they want to shoot me, they can shoot me.

He realized his right hand was resting on the walnut grip of his holstered revolver. He let his hands drop down to the leather seat cushion.

But whoever it was didn't write Hawthorne Miller's book. It seems too amazing to be a coincidence.

Robert hadn't meant to close his eyes, but the whiff of strong violet perfume and the swish of a silk skirt forced his eyes back open. He caught a glimpse of the lady with white, plumed hat as she brushed by and shoved open the passenger car door behind him.

A flood of mild air and steel-on-steel noise flooded the railroad car. She paused for a moment with the door open.

"Is the conductor in that car?" she called out to Robert. Her voice was lower, more forceful than he had imagined it would be, but still with a musical quality.

He stood and pulled off his hat. "No, ma'am. That's the baggage car. The conductor should be up in the next passenger car." He pointed in the opposite direction.

She fumbled with the door latch and finally got it closed. Then she brushed her fingertips across the smooth, pale skin of her forehead. "Would you know if he has smelling salts?"

"I would think so, but I really don't know. Are you feeling ill?"

She dropped her chin slightly and tilted her head to the right. "Yes, I don't do well on mountain curves. Would it be alright if I sat back here in one of these empty seats in front of you and opened a window?"

"There's plenty of room. Your boys can come back here too." *Why did she ask me for permission? Does she know I work for the railroad? I'm sure I've never met her before.*

"Oh my, yes." There was a slight smile on her wide, full lips. "They've hardly left my side since my husband passed away." She started to return to the front. "I think I'll check on those smelling salts before we move back here."

"Would you like me to fetch the conductor for you?"

"Thank you, but the walking seems to perk me up. The fresh air between cars might just clear my head."

Robert plopped back down. The lady returned to the front of the railroad car. The thick bustle of the gray-and-pink silk dress waved from side to side in what Jamie Sue had once labeled the "San Francisco Strut." *I suppose some women are never too sick to wiggle a bit.*

She spoke to the boys, then exited the car and closed the door. Robert was still staring at the door when she returned, without the conductor. The door wouldn't close, and she had to slam it several times. Before she reseated herself with the boys, she nodded her head slightly at Robert.

That widow lady's flirting with me. Now, Lord, I can't get up and walk away, but I can surely keep my eyes to myself.

Suddenly, there was noise up front. The woman slumped over in the aisle. The oldest boy, who looked about ten, jumped up and yanked on the emergency brake cord.

The train abruptly slowed and the passengers lurched forward. Robert staggered up the aisle past the alarmed passengers. He struggled to lift the lady in his arms as the train came to a stop. He was placing her on the leather seat when an explosion behind the passenger car shook the train. Every window rattled. There was a chorus of screams. Robert pitched forward, almost falling on top of the lady.

The baggage car! Someone dynamited the baggage car! Robert yanked out his .45 revolver and shoved his way past gawking passengers to the back door of the train car, only to find it wouldn't open.

With the train stopped on a curve in the track, he couldn't see what was happening on the far side of the baggage car, but he heard shouting. "Get out of the aisle," he hollered. "Everyone stay away from the windows on the east side!"

Reaching the front of the car, he noticed the two boys still huddled over the woman. "Open that window, boys, and give your mama some air!" he hollered. Grabbing the handle on the front door, Robert cranked on it, but it didn't budge.

Both doors locked? How can that . . . ? How did they lock them when I didn't even see them?

The window above the fainted woman was now open. Robert shoved his revolver back into his holster and crawled over the top of the lady and out the window. Dropping on the rocks below, he limped along, sneaking up on the baggage car. He had just reached the coupling between cars when a shot was fired from behind him. It ricocheted inches from his head.

He dove under the railroad car and tried to peer back to see who fired the shot. *They have the train surrounded? And there is not one thing worth stealing. They are going to a lot of work for nothing.*

Lying flat on his belly, Robert crawled forward over the gravel and railroad ties between the railroad tracks. He felt brass buttons on his wool suit pop off, and a hole ripped in the right knee.

There were no more shots behind him. He concentrated on watching the feet of two men who were loading something heavy on the back of a farm wagon.

With the shredded remains of the baggage car door concealing him, Robert crept forward. As he started to swing out from under the car, a man shouted, "He's under the baggage car, Dunny!"

The report of a carbine sounded. An explosion near Robert's head peppered his face with shreds of granite. Wiping his eyes on his now dirty suit coat sleeve, he saw the boots of two men sprint toward the wagon.

Robert's first shot ripped into the heel of the man wearing gal-leg spurs with big Mexican rowels. As the man staggered and clutched the wagon, Robert squeezed the trigger at the other man's dirty brown boot.

There was a scream.

Then a curse.

"Shorty, I got shot in the foot!" he bellowed. He clenched the wagon as the first man shot back at Robert. He rolled behind the steel wheel of the railroad car.

"Drive, Shorty . . . drive . . . drive!" Dunny shouted, and the farm wagon lurched forward toward the trees.

Shorty and Dunny? Again? Every time I let one loose, they come back to haunt.

Robert rolled out from under the train car. He fired two shots in the rocks in front of the team of horses. The big sorrel geldings reared, then jerked the lead line out of the driver's hand and galloped straight at a slope of boulders.

Robert stood, pointing his gun at the back of the wagon. He hesitated to shoot again as he studied the large, bulky object in back. *The girls' trunk? All of this was to steal the girls' wardrobe trunk and a half-million dollars of worthless money?*

Who knew there was money in there? It's just an ordinary trunk, with the girls' scribbling on the outside. Who would know?

Besides the people the twins told . . . which was probably every man, woman, boy, girl, dog, and cat in Deadwood.

Robert jogged after the runaway wagon, then watched as the panicked horse spun to the left instead of running into the rock field. The wagon tipped on its side, propelling both wounded passengers and the large trunk onto the boulders. The trunk burst open and the money sprayed across the granite like confetti at a New Year's party. But the horses continued to drag the wagon for another hundred feet.

Neither man was moving when Robert reached the rocks.

Robert spun around when he heard a roaring shout from the passengers. They now sprinted out of both cars of the train clamoring over the rocks and boulders, snatching up the money.

Robert dragged one of the unconscious men off the rocks as the engineer and fireman reached him.

"What happened, Mr. Fortune?" the conductor asked.

"They blew the door off the baggage car in order to steal a trunk full of worthless money."

The engineer ran his finger through his sooty gray hair. "What are we going to do now?"

"Put your telegraph operator on that pole line and have him signal Rapid City. Find out if they want us to go forward, back up to Deadwood, or just wait. Tell them we have two of the culprits, and nothing of value was lost."

"What will we do with them?"

"Let's tie them up before they come to and stuff a rag in their boots so they won't bleed to death." Robert stared at several dozen people scampering and tripping over boulders and rocks. "They'll break every bone in their bodies for worthless pieces of paper."

"Help me!" Above the shouts of the crowd Robert heard a man scream. "Help me!"

"Is that coming from the railroad car?" he asked the conductor.

"I thought everyone had debarked!" the conductor mumbled.

Robert sprinted back to the car. The man with the patent leather shoes and diamond tie tack lay sprawled across the backseat, across from where Robert had sat.

He held his bleeding forehead.

Robert yanked out a handkerchief and pressed it against the man's forehead. The conductor followed him into the car.

"I've been robbed," he said.

Robert leaned back and surveyed the man's black silk tie. "They didn't get your diamond tie tack."

"That's a phony. They went right for my case."

"What case?"

"My diamond case."

"You were carrying a case of diamonds?"

"I'm a representative for Royal Dutch Diamonds. My display case contains gemstones worth over $10,000."

"And you didn't put it in the baggage car safe?"

"They blew up the baggage car."

"But not the safe." Robert glanced at the conductor. "Go find some linen to bandage his head." Then he turned back to the injured man.

"I notified the railroad in Deadwood that I'd be carrying diamonds."

"You did? I'm the railroad inspector and my office heard nothing of this. Who took your diamonds?"

"The dark-haired woman with the boys. We chatted on the train a few days ago. Now she's robbed me. After she shot at you through the window, she came back and robbed me."

"Woman? The one who fainted?"

"She seemed to recover well. She had a pearl-handle sneak gun. It's what she creased my forehead with. She shot at you, then ran back here. I thought she was going to try to shoot you out the window, so I grabbed her arm. She must have clobbered me, because when I woke up everyone was scurrying off the train toward those boulders. That's when I noticed my case was gone."

"Where did you keep it?"

"Handcuffed to my wrist."

"She unlocked your cuffs?"

"Apparently she got my key."

"Where did you keep the key?"

"In my right boot."

Robert looked down at the man who wore one boot. *She knew which boot to take off.* "When you came to, did you see what direction she was going?"

He pointed to the west. "I saw her and the boys running through those whitewood trees."

The conductor brought back a roll of linen gauze.

"Take care of this man. I'm going after the woman who robbed him."

"But you're on foot!"

"So's she . . . and she has two small boys with her."

⚜

Robert shoved more bullets in his revolver as he stalked toward the grove of trees. *I can't believe I let her get away with that. I was too preoccupied with the Moraine business . . . and the Irish thing . . . and, Lord, I know . . . with her good looks. Then the blast. It was all a decoy. But it worked. This is the very thing I warned Stillman and Guthrie about, and I fall for it. Guthrie almost came on this trip. What would he have done? No worse than the boss, I surmise.*

The sharp heel prints of a woman's boot were easy to spot. The shade of the trees ensured that the soil beneath them would hold the impression of each step.

In the cover of the trees, Robert followed the prints, one soft step after another. He crept over two tree-covered ridges and waded a shallow creek before he heard voices. Robert dropped to his knees and crawled behind a large stump.

"What do we do now, Mama?"

"Wait for Daddy," the woman replied.

What was this about being a widow? A ruse, I suppose. But what kind of man sends his wife and kids to rob a train? Surely she can't be married to one of those two that got foot-shot. She's much too classy for them. Besides, she saw what happened to them. She's waiting for someone else.

"What if someone tries to follow us?" a young boy quizzed. "What do we do then, Mama?"

If I wait, maybe I can catch the father as well.

"We'll shoot 'em."

What a lovely family.

"I don't have any gun," the littlest one complained.

"I'll shoot them," the woman promised.

Lying on his stomach, Robert inched his way over the ridge. The woman and two boys crouched in a small grove of short aspens near a dirt road.

It seemed like a half hour, but his watch showed only ten minutes until a buckboard pulled by two wide white horses rumbled down the road. Robert trained the sight of his gun on the driver, whose hat was pulled low.

The lady and the two boys ran out and waved.

"Daddy!" the oldest one shouted.

The man at the reins reached down to assist them up. His hat continued to shield his face from Robert's stare. *Lift your head up, mister. Let me get a good look.*

"As you figured, they bumbled the hold-up and wrecked the wagon," she reported, then held up a small black leather case. "But I got these!"

"Fortune didn't get shot, did he?" The man kept his head down, but at the sound of the familiar voice, Robert slumped back into the pine needles.

No . . . no . . . no!

CHAPTER EIGHT

Jamie Sue jumped when the telephone rang. Dropping her crocheting on the sofa, she scurried into the kitchen. *If I'm ever mending when that thing rings, I'll sew my fingers together.*

"I need to speak to Fortune!" The shouting voice was almost too high for a man, too low for a woman.

"This is Mrs. Robert Fortune," Jamie Sue replied.

"Are you the wife?"

"Yes. Who is this?"

"This is Raxton. I need to speak to Robert Fortune."

"Mr. Raxton, I'm sorry, but my husband is not here."

"Miss Raxton!"

Jamie Sue pulled back the receiver and stared at it. *Oh, dear . . .* "Excuse me, the, eh, telephone is a little scratchy. May I be of some help to you?"

"I doubt it. Fortune said if we wanted to come to Deadwood, he'd line up some backers for our mine."

"Yes?"

"Well, we're here!"

"In Deadwood?"

"There ain't telephones out at the mine. At least, not until that other Fortune, the one with gray hair and dancin' eyes, strings one out to us."

"That's Sammy. He should be in town. Would you like to speak to him?"

"Yep. Put him on."

"He's not here . . . this is . . ."

"How many telephones you Fortunes got?"

"Samuel owns the telephone exchange," Jamie Sue explained. "Just ring the operator and ask for number 1 or number 10."

"Where's Robert at?"

"He's on a train to Rapid City and won't be back until

late tomorrow."

"What's he doin' there?"

"Miss Raxton, that's his job. He works for the railroad."

"He said he'd meet us here. What are we going to do?"

"Where are you?"

"At the train depot. We need a place to stay."

"Why don't you register at a hotel? Is money a problem?"

"We've got enough gold to buy us a hotel, I reckon. But they won't let us register. They claim we're too dirty. Ain't that somethin'?"

Jamie Sue shifted the receiver to the other ear. *I've never heard of any hotel refusing gold-paying customers.* "Well, you will want to clean up to meet with financial backers."

"How can we clean up if a hotel won't have us? All the bath houses are for men. We ain't goin' into one of them."

"Miss Raxton, would you just wait at the depot? I'll make some arrangements for you."

"They already said we have to wait outside. I reckon we are a little rank."

"Miss Raxton, how many rooms will you be needing?"

"Two . . . Augusta and me can bunk together. Then we'll need one for Puddin."

"Who?"

"Our crew boss, Oscar Puddin. Byron, I mean Mr. Chambers, already has a room at the Merchant's Hotel, but he's up at Lead talkin' to some men about our mine. He won't be back until tonight."

"I'll make some telephone calls and then come down to the depot. I will see you shortly," Jamie Sue said.

"I'll be the one with the dirty brown dress and the trapdoor rifle."

"And I'll be wearing a straw hat with a yellow ribbon."

Jamie Sue sauntered into the entry and began tying on her hat in front of the mirror. *I'll call Abby . . . Rebekah . . . Dacee June . . . perhaps the March sisters can take the children . . . Abby will find the clothing, Rebekah the . . . and I'll . . . Lord, this is what I'm meant to do. To help others. They need me and for the first time in my life, I have a team to help me. I like that. I like that a lot.*

Patricia and Veronica reached the front door at the exact same moment and argued over who should enter first. While Veronica danced in the doorway, tongue-chewing Patricia shoved past her.

"Mama," Patricia began, "can Veronica and I go with Little Frank and the boys down to watch the horses run laps?"

"You are not going to a horse race."

"Please, Mama," Veronica pleaded. "This is just warm-up laps. The race isn't until Sunday. Everyone is going."

Jamie Sue picked some lint off Patricia's navy blue dress. "Everyone?"

"Little Frank, Quintin, Fern, Sarah, Jimmy, Hank . . ."

Jamie Sue raised her eyebrows. "Rebekah is letting Hank go off Forest Hill without her supervision?"

"Yes, Amber is going up to get him," Veronica explained.

Patricia ran her tongue all the way around her lips, then puckered them. "That's not all who will be there."

"Shhh!" Veronica said.

"And just who else is going to be there?" Jamie Sue reached over and straightened the lace collar on Veronica's navy blue dress.

"Tricia," Veronica fumed. "Why did you have to . . ."

Patricia bit her lip. "Eachan and . . ."

Jamie Sue gently lifted Patricia's chin until their eyes met. "The Moraines will let Eachan be seen in public with that many Fortunes?"

"Mrs. Moraine said he could go places with us but not come over to our house," Patricia announced.

"Well, that is an improvement."

Veronica stood in one place, rocking back and forth on the toes of her black lace-up boots. "And Curly Mac will be there too."

Jamie Sue stared into the entry hall mirror and adjusted her hat. "Curly Mac is in Deadwood?"

"His aunt sold her saloon in Central City," Veronica reported.

Jamie Sue stepped to the open doorway. *I don't think I'll need a wrap. The clouds are very scattered.*

"She's buying a saloon in Montana City," Veronica continued. "But they are going to live at the Merchant's Hotel for a few weeks."

Jamie Sue turned back and stood between the girls. "And just how did you learn all of this?"

"He told me . . ."

Jamie Sue crossed her arms and could feel a tightness in her neck. "But you two were just supposed to take the mince cookies to Grandpa Brazos."

"But Mama, Deadwood is a small town. Sometimes we see people on the street and we don't want to shun them," Veronica explained.

"Please, please . . ." Patricia chimed in.

"Yes, well . . . go on. But this is your test. If you get into trouble over this outing, it will be a long time before I'll let you do it again."

Patricia grinned. "Thank you, Mama."

"Exactly what would you consider getting into trouble?" Veronica mumbled.

Patricia grabbed her arm and dragged her out the door.

The four-car train was one hour and thirty-two minutes late getting into Rapid City. Robert rode in the open-door baggage car with two wounded prisoners, a busted trunk, and two-thirds of the original currency.

The sheriff, two deputies, various railroad officials, and Stillman Taite met him as he debarked.

"You look like you was drug behind the train all the way from Deadwood," Taite called out.

Robert tried brushing off his ripped wool trousers. "Stillman, get us two sturdy horses and a little grub. We have thieves to catch, and they have a head start. We'll take the afternoon train back as far as we can."

"Your telegraph said it was Guthrie Holter. I can't hardly believe it."

"The lady stole the diamonds, and he drove the wagon. No mistaking that part."

"What direction is Guthrie headin'?"

"Back along the telegraph road," Robert reported.

"Toward Deadwood?"

"At least, to start with."

"You didn't try to stop them?"

"A bullet could've hit the boys, and there was no way I'd catch a buckboard on foot. I figured it best if they didn't know I spotted them."

Taite rubbed his chin. "Yeah, that was probably best."

"We'll find that out soon enough."

It was two hectic hours before the afternoon northbound pulled out. Robert sent Taite to ride the passenger car. He rode with the horses in a flatcar pulled behind the caboose. He sat on the floor of the car with his back toward the engine and watched the disappearing scenery behind the train.

Lord, maybe I'm not the best one for this job. If I'd been doin' a better job, maybe I could have seen this happening. I hired a brawler in the train yard. And I hired wrong. I thought I knew the man. I instantly decided about him, and I was wrong.

All this talk about being separated from a wife and boys . . . he was suckerin' me all along. . . . He wrote that note to Moraine on my stationery. He figured I'd either get shot or delayed. It would have been easier if he was on the train. Moraine, at least, was an open and honest enemy. Better to have honest enemies than deceptive friends.

The most suspicious person in the railroad car was the one flirting with me. Lord, I'm ashamed I was so easy a target. I'll capture Holter, then resign. The railroad needs a better man for the job. I can always sell bolts for Todd or install telephone lines for Sammy.

A man who can't tell friends from enemies shouldn't be

put in a responsible job. Maybe army life isolated me too much. I suspected Stillman Taite but hired him anyway. I trusted Guthrie . . .

Lord, I don't know if I'm more disgusted with Guthrie Holter . . . or me. But I'll catch him. And he'll face a just punishment.

And the woman too . . . I'll . . .

The Cokesburg siding was water and wood only. There was no building. No platform. And no loading ramp.

Robert and Stillman mounted the horses while they were still loaded on the flatcar.

"We going to jump them off the side?" Stillman asked.

Robert pointed to the opposite direction. "Let's try the uphill side."

"If we run them toward the back maybe we could leap over to that embankment. It wouldn't be any worse than jumpin' a crick."

"You're an optimistic cuss, Taite. Let's do it."

Stillman Taite stood in the stirrups, then shoved his hat back so that one lone tuft of hair lapped down across his forehead. " 'Course, if we slip down between the flatcar and that embankment, the horse will kick us to death."

"Then I suggest we don't slip!" Robert sunk his silver rowels into the flanks of the black horse. At the same time he slapped Taite's chestnut with his hat. Both startled horses bolted in terror toward the back of the flatcar, their hooves thundering panic on the rough wooden floor of the car. As if a team pulling a carriage of fear, they turned in unison and leaped for the embankment.

Robert thrust his full weight on the balls of his feet. As he rode the stirrups, his knees flexed, his head leaned over the horse's neck.

Taite's chestnut staggered, but Fortune's mount didn't. They let both horses run the "scared-to-death" out of them. When they finally reined up at least nine hundred yards from the track, Stillman Taite yanked off his round bowler and wiped the sweat off his forehead.

"Mr. Fortune, remind me never to do that again."

Robert could feel his white shirt soaked with perspiration. "I trust that's the last stupid thing I do today."

Taite slipped off his horse and began to tighten the cinch. "Where do we go from here?"

"We follow that telegraph road."

"How can we follow tracks on a road?"

"I have a clue."

"Oh?"

"When they pulled out, I went down and looked at the tracks. One of the right wheels was repaired by three carriage bolts."

"That would be a bumpy ride if you was in a hurry."

Robert yanked the latigo tight on the Texas saddle, then remounted. "I figure if they head northeast, they don't have to be in a hurry."

"Why northeast? There's nothin' up there."

"Precisely."

Robert rode on the east side of the telegraph road, Taite on the right. They had ridden at a medium walk for an hour and a half when Robert shouted, "Here it is!"

"Is that a road?"

"It's a wagon track with three round-top carriage bolts sticking through the rim."

"He must have a four-hour head start. He could be in Wyomin' by now."

"Why leave the cover of the Black Hills and wander out on the prairie? Those boys will get tired. They'll spend the night in the hills for sure," Robert asserted.

"You think they'll head for Myersville or Diamond City or one of those other gold camps?"

"If I was them, I'd just hole up in one of those limestone caves. Todd says there's dozens of them up here."

Taite fingered his thick handlebar mustache. "It will be hard to find them then."

Robert spurred the horse into a trot. "But not many of them will be accessible to a wagon," he called back.

The sun slipped down to the west. The ponderosa pine shadows now blended into night shadows. Robert and Stillman continued to scour every coulee and draw wide enough to drive a wagon through.

"Boss, I can't see ground clear. We should stop," Taite insisted.

Robert reined up and rubbed the black horse's neck. "I reckon you're right. Did you find any grub?"

"Six pork chops and a dozen cold biscuits," Taite reported.

In the shadows Robert glanced down at his open, now-buttonless vest. *Jamie Sue, if you could see Captain Fortune now.* "Cold pork chops and biscuits? Then it's time to stop. Let's ride up this little creek until the water is running clean."

Miss Sandra Raxton was, without a doubt, the dirtiest woman Jamie Sue Fortune had ever seen.

That is, until she spied Miss Augusta Raxton.

Lord, how does a sane, civilized person ever get that bad? I don't know whether to cry or get the smelling salts. I trust I know what I'm doing. If You sent me to a primitive land, I suppose I'd do the same. It could be worse . . . but not much. I'm not sure the others knew what they were getting into.

After polite introductions from ten feet away, Jamie Sue led the Raxton sisters up the alley to the back of the Paris Dress Shoppe. Two nicely dressed women waited at the top of the rough wooden stairway. An elegantly dressed woman stood in the dress shop's back door.

"Miss Sandra Raxton, and Miss Augusta Raxton, this is Abby Fortune. She's Sammy's wife . . ."

"No wonder he's as happy as a pup with a new bone!" Sandra chuckled.

"She owns the dress shop and will be selecting some ready-made dresses for you," Jamie Sue announced.

"Don't reckon we've ever had ready-mades," Augusta added. "Not since we was little girls."

"We haven't had any new dresses since we were little," Sandra added. "Mama died when we were young. We're payin' for these dresses. We got gold." She glanced up and down the alley, then leaned so close that Jamie Sue had to cover her mouth to keep from coughing. "I've got eight thousand dollars worth of gold on me at this very minute!"

Jamie Sue watched Abby roll her eyes. She tried to smile at Sandra Raxton. *Where in the world does a woman that thin hide eight thousand dollars worth of gold? I don't think I want to know.*

"We're kind of tall, and skinny as a post. You don't have somethin' that would make us look fluffed up, do you?" Augusta asked. "Not like you two, of course. We don't expect miracles."

Abby stepped back a bit to take a breath of air, then smiled. "I might just have something. Now that I know your sizes, I'll see what we can do. Undoubtedly there will be some alterations needed."

"Alterations in what?" Sandra Raxton demanded.

"Why, in the dresses, of course. Ready-made dresses never fit anyone just right." Abby slipped back into the store and closed the door behind her.

Jamie Sue led the sisters up the stairway. "Now, this tall, stately lady is my sister-in-law, Rebekah Fortune."

"Which one is she married to?" Sandra Raxton asked.

"Todd. I don't believe you've met him yet," Rebekah reported.

"Ain't you got none that aren't married?" Augusta asked.

"Augusta Raxton, you told me you already picked out a beau!" her sister chided.

Jamie Sue scurried up a few more stairs. *A beau? My word, I hope he lost his nose in the war . . . Lord, how shameful of me. I'm glad Your love for us isn't dependent on our looks . . . or our smell!* "Ladies, this young woman is my sister-in-law, Dacee June."

"You mean there's four Fortune boys?" Miss Sandra quizzed.

"No," Dacee June grinned. "I'm their sister, Dacee June Fortune Toluca. We've got two tubs ready. One in the room on the left and one on the right."

"Private baths? Unused water?" Sandra added. "Ain't we actin' nobby?"

"Rebekah is in charge of washing your hair and fixing it. She's very good at that!" Jamie Sue reported.

"I don't know that it's time to wash my hair," Augusta protested.

"Nonsense, I can still see the gold dust from the mine stuck to it." Rebekah stepped to the side and took three deep breaths. "When was the last time you washed it?"

"Last summer," Augusta declared.

"No it wasn't. It was the summer before, in Miles City," Sandra challenged.

"How about that time we got thrown out of the coach in the middle of the Yellowstone River?" Augusta reminded her sister.

"That don't count for hair-washin'. Does it, Mrs. Fortune?" Sandra huffed.

"Certainly not," Jamie Sue declared. "Dacee June is in charge of hauling hot water for you, Miss Sandra. And I'll do the same for Miss Augusta. We'll help you scrub up too."

"We don't need no help takin' a bath," Augusta announced.

"Oh," Dacee June added, "it's what all the rich ladies do. They have bath attendants. We're volunteering this one time to give you a taste of being wealthy mine owners. You'll have to get used to it sooner or later."

"Well, if this is what the rich do . . ." Sandra grinned,

revealing perfectly straight, very white teeth. "I reckon we'll jist have to get used to it."

"Are you ready for this?" Jamie Sue whispered to Rebekah.

"I feel like Michelangelo trying to discover the beauty in a hunk of rock," Rebekah whispered back.

Jamie Sue watched Rebekah and Dacee June tug the Raxton sisters toward their baths. *Lord, this feels good. The Fortune ladies . . . working together . . . helping others. . . . For fifteen years it has been just me. My goodness, if we can pull this off, we can do about anything!*

With the pork chops and biscuits already cooked, Robert decided against building a fire. He hobbled the horses, then settled in with his back against the jagged trunk of a lightning dwarfed pine tree. Stillman Taite sat across from him, cross-legged.

"What do you think causes a man to go bad like Holter?" Taite asked.

Fortune gnawed on a pork chop bone and could feel shreds of sweet meat stick between his teeth. "We're all born sinners, Taite. I suppose it's no surprise that we do bad. The real question is why folks ever do good."

"You sayin' all of us are like Holter?"

"Seems to me very few of us are as bad as we could be."

"I reckon a lot of folks is as good as they can be."

Robert Fortune brushed some biscuit crumbs off his neatly trimmed dark beard. "Yes, but without the Lord, that's a mighty low standard. God doesn't want us as good as we can be. He wants us perfect."

"Shoot, I never met a perfect man." Then a smile broke across Taite's face. "But I knew some women who were mighty close."

Robert's voice was low, as if talking to the dark itself. "All of us sin. That's why we need a Savior."

"Are you theologizin' me?" Taite complained.

"Probably. I just got lulled into thinkin' I could easily tell the good from the bad. I was surprised about Holter. I thought I had him judged different. He wasn't the one I was worried about."

"You thought I was the one that was goin' to give you trouble. Right?" There was a chuckle in Taite's voice. "I saw misgivin' in your eyes that day you hired me."

"I thought . . . well, to be honest . . . I didn't expect trouble from you, but I didn't know how you'd adapt to this job. I thought maybe you stretched your qualifications a bit."

"How's that?"

"When you mentioned working for Pappy Divide in Cheyenne."

"That part's the truth."

"I know. I checked it out."

"Did you telegraph Cheyenne?"

"No, Tap Andrews and his wife, Pepper, were at the hardware last week. My brother Todd mentioned your name to him."

"What did he say about me?" Taite asked.

"Said he didn't know you but he followed you, and everyone said you were a good deputy."

"See, there . . . I was tellin' the truth." Taite picked his teeth with a dirty fingernail. "What time we leavin' in the mornin'?"

"We're leavin' in about an hour."

"We cain't track at night."

"Sure we can. The full moon'll be up by then, and the trail is well marked. It doesn't take much to follow three-studded iron-rim wheel tracks."

"We got time for a little nap, don't we?"

"Let's rest the ponies an hour, then see what we can find."

Taite stretched out on his back in the evening shadows with his hat pulled over his face, his head on his saddle.

Robert Fortune stared at the awakening night sky.

I'll let Stillman sleep. I can't. Just too many things on my mind, Lord. I thought life up here would be simple. Routine. Just family things. 'Course nothin' in my family is ever routine.

A big prairie moon crept up in the east. One lone bright star hung above it. Robert leaned back against the tree trunk and closed his eyes.

Maybe I was wrong, Lord. I do like this job. It's near the front line of right and wrong. It's keeping men, women, families safe. Well . . . not all women and boys. I can't believe they're using their sons like this. What are they going to be like when they grow up? That's wrong, Lord. Way wrong.

If there is goin' to be violence on the train, . . . then someone needs to be here to stop it. The hold-up proves they need security. Maybe it validates my being hired.

But I have to catch every criminal. If I can't catch them, then I'm not doin' my job.

If I can't catch the Holters, then maybe I'm the wrong one. . . . But if I do catch them, . . . then perhaps I am exactly the right one. Lord, I do want to be somewhere I can be in the battle of right against wrong.

Both horses were saddled and Stillman Taite stood near his feet when Robert opened his eyes again. His forehead and neck felt sweaty even though there was a slightly cool breeze. "Guess I needed a rest more than I thought," he admitted.

Taite brushed back his mustache. "Worryin' does that to a man, I reckon."

"I wish we were tracking just a man, or a gang of men. Having a woman and children along is troubling." Robert took the reins of his horse and checked the cinch.

Taite mounted up in the moonlight. "You mean, if Holter or his wife were to start shootin' at us?"

"I don't know if I want to shoot back or not." Robert stuck his left foot in the stirrup, then grabbed the hard leather saddlehorn with his right.

"I've been thinkin' the same thing."

Fortune pulled himself up into the saddle. "You a praying man, Stillman?"

"When I git scared enough."

Robert could feel the cold leather of the saddle in the places where his pants were ripped. "Well, let's pray we can capture them without a shot fired."

The wagon trail broke into a clearing. Even in the moonlight, Robert could see it stretch straight ahead of them for almost a mile. Then it seemed to lead up into some white rocks or cliffs.

Fortune and Taite rode their horses side by side at a slow

walk as they traveled across the clearing. The moon was high enough now to project slight shadows from the horses and riders and reflect off the limestone cliffs.

Taite's voice was low. "You reckon there are some of those caves you was talkin' about up in the white rocks?"

"Seems like a natural site."

"They could be up there right now watchin' us come across this clearin'. They could take a shot at us before we even see them."

Robert kept his eyes focused on the rocks ahead. "That might be. But if I were them, I wouldn't give away my position until I knew for sure someone was trailing me."

Stillman Taite scratched the back of his neck. "Mr. Fortune, you ever shoot buffalo at nine hundred yards?"

"Nope. I got meat for General Crook a few times with my trapdoor carbine, but I was a lot closer than nine hundred yards. How about you, Stillman?"

"I spent a month skinnin' for old Rum McNair. He could drop them at nine hundred to a thousand yards, when he was sober."

"Taite, where is this leading?"

"If Holter had a long-barreled Sharps in those caves, they could pick us off in this bright moonlight."

"Are you always this optimistic, Taite?"

"Yep. Born that way, I reckon."

They crossed the wide clearing and stopped their horses near a grove of pine seedlings no more than six feet tall.

"Which way now? These tracks are going to disappear in the shadows," Taite commented.

Robert Fortune climbed down out of the saddle and squatted next to the wagon tracks. *Lord, he's right, this is crazy to go barging off into the darkness. I can barely see the tracks now.*

A faint cry caused Robert to stand straight up.

"Did you hear that?" he whispered.

"A coyote . . . or what?"

"No, it was a child cryin' 'Daddy.' "

Taite pulled off his hat and brushed the hair back off his ears. "You're hearin' things."

"You don't have any kids, do you?"

"Nope."

"Then you might not hear it. It was a child's voice," Robert declared. "Let's tie off the horses and hike up there by foot. I heard one of the boys. He must have woke up from a bad dream."

Taite leaned close, then whispered back, "And I only heard a hoot owl."

Robert led them up toward the rocks. The slope of the mountain and the rocks increased, but there was still a wide enough trail for a buckboard. He pulled out his revolver but refused to cock the hammer. *How in the world do you arrest train robbers in the dark without firing a shot? But I'm not doing those boys a favor letting them think it's alright to rob and steal without getting caught.*

The trail leveled out near the front of a twenty-foot cliff. In the moonlight Robert spotted the buckboard parked parallel to the cliff. One horse was tied behind it; he couldn't see the second horse. *They may be under the wagon, in the wagon, behind the wagon, or in a cave . . . cave. . . . The boys are in a shallow cave. . . . That's why the voice echoed all the way down the mountain.*

Robert reached out and tugged on Taite's wool coat sleeve to get him to stop walking, then raised a finger to his lips.

Holter isn't with the boys because they had to call him. Mama will be with the boys. But why didn't they call for Mama? If it was me, put mama and the kids behind the wagon, and I'd sleep under it as first line of defense . . . if it was me.

Robert motioned Stillman Taite to stay back by the rocks. He crept forward toward the wagon. *Someone's lying under the wagon. But is it mama or daddy . . . or just an empty bedroll?*

Robert trained his revolver on the object under the wagon. Squatting down on his haunches, he leaned low to get a clear view. Without opening his lips, he hummed a faint "Daddy!"

There was no movement.

Again he hummed "Daddy." This time it was louder.

Someone stirred, then raised up on one elbow, looked around, then flopped back down.

That's Guthrie Holter. His wife doesn't have a mustache!

Robert glanced back at Taite and beckoned him to move up a little closer. Then he dropped down in the dirt and began to crawl on his stomach closer to the wagon.

Jamie Sue is right. I should wear duckings on this job. This suit is ruined from crawling under the train anyway. Holter, you are either snoring, or faking it to get me nearer.

Robert crawled closer . . . past the sleeping horse . . . past the wagon wheel. His gun hand led the way, the revolver pointed straight ahead of him.

With his left hand he reached out and grabbed Holter's hair, just as he cocked the pistol and shoved it in the sleeping man's ear.

"What the . . ." Holter tried to raise up, but Fortune slammed his head back down.

"It's me, Holter," Robert whispered. "You knew I'd come after you. It's all over."

Holter didn't try to raise his head but glanced over toward the cave entrance. His voice was low, resigned. "I didn't know you had figured it out so soon. I was goin' back to Deadwood tomorrow to turn myself in."

"You expect me to believe that?"

Holter's voice was almost too soft to hear. "I suppose not."

"Is your wife sleepin' over by the boys?" Fortune pressed.

"She's gone."

"What do you mean, she's gone?"

Guthrie Holter waved a hand back at the front of the wagon. "You don't see the other horse do you?"

"No. Where did she go?"

"Who knows . . . Denver . . . San Francisco . . . anywhere to sell the diamonds and spend the money."

"Without her sons?"

Holter's voice was barely audible. "It ain't the first time. She took off when I was putting the boys to bed. She knew I wouldn't leave them and follow her."

Robert kept one hand on Holter's hair, the other on the revolver. "Are you telling me a mother would just ride off and leave her children?"

"I wanted to turn myself in at Deadwood. Thought there'd be a better chance to find someone to look after the boys up there."

"This is crazy, Holter."

"She's crazy, Mr. Fortune. And I love her. That's all I have to say about it. Can we let the boys sleep before we load up?"

Robert reached down and pulled Holter's gun out of the holster, then dragged him out from under the wagon. Stillman Taite met them beside the wagon.

"Well, Mr. Taite," Holter said. "Looks like you're on the winnin' side."

"I don't get it," Taite replied. "Why did you do this?"

"You ain't married," Guthrie Holter shrugged.

"Go get the hobbles. We'll bind his hands and feet until the boys wake up," Robert instructed. "Did you hear about his wife taking off?"

Taite nodded. "Are we goin' after her?"

"Not right now. We have to take Holter and his boys in."

"She knew that . . ." Holter said. "She knew if you trailed her, the boys would slow you down. She figured you'd shoot me but then be stuck with the boys."

Robert rubbed his bearded chin. "She figured all of that?"

"She said when she saw you dive out that window above her, she knew you were a driven man."

"And then Curly Mac said, 'I'm going to tie a ribbon on your wrist so I can tell you from your sister!' " Veronica giggled to her mother. "So he tied a yellow ribbon on my wrist. Isn't it pretty?" She held up her wrist. "I am never, ever going to take it off."

"I don't think a twelve-year-old girl should be ribboned by any boy," Jamie Sue said.

"Oh!" Veronica's hand went over her mouth. "Is it naughty?"

"No, it's just that . . ."

Patricia held up her wrist with a rose ribbon. "It's just to tell us apart, Mama. We didn't pledge to marry anyone."

Jamie Sue sighed. "I'm certainly glad to hear that. Did young Mr. Curly Mac ribbon you too?"

"Of course not!" Patricia gasped. "It was Eachan."

"I'm pleased that some members of the Moraine family can tolerate some members of the Fortune family."

"I thought Uncle Sammy talked to the Irish and settled the matter," Veronica replied.

"It seems settled to everyone but Mr. Moraine."

"I don't know how anyone can hate Daddy. He's the nicest man I know!" Patricia declared.

"It's a Fortune men tradition," Jamie Sue declared. "All Fortune men are nice."

"What's the Fortune women tradition, Mama?" Veronica asked.

"To find the world's nicest men and marry them," Jamie Sue declared.

"Curly Mac's kind of nice. But his aunt runs a saloon, and sometimes he goes in there to carry out the trash and sweep. I suppose that's not very nice." Veronica managed to get out the whole sentence with one breath.

"Niceness comes out of the heart, girls. You have to

know a boy's heart before you know if he's nice or not," Jamie Sue schooled.

"How do we get to know a boy's heart, Mama?"

"Girls, this is a conversation that we should have when you're fifteen or sixteen."

"It ought to be quite a year," Veronica replied. "I have a list of things three pages long of things you promised to tell us when we are sixteen."

"You write them down?"

"Yes, they're in my . . ." Veronica took a deep breath . . . "in my diary!"

"We lost our diaries!" Patricia moaned.

"We won't know what questions to ask!" Veronica whimpered.

"Trust me, girls, you will know."

Jamie Sue pulled her long hair tight to the back of her neck and wrapped it on the back of her head for pinning.

"Mama, how come you took a bath and washed your hair in the middle of the afternoon?"

"I got a little dirty."

"I thought you went to help some ladies buy some dresses."

"I did. But they needed baths first, . . . and they were quite dirty."

"Did they run into skunks like Little Frank that one time at Camp Verde?"

"Something like that." *Skunks would have been an improvement.*

Little Frank burst through the back door. "I rode him, Mama! They let me ride him. He is the best horse I ever rode in my life!"

"Go back and close the door, young man."

"Yes, ma'am." Little Frank slunk back through the kitchen to the back porch and pulled the white, painted wooden door closed.

"Now just which horse did you ride?" she asked.

"Little Traveler."

"Which one is that?"

"His grandpappy was General Lee's favorite mount."

"The white one?"

"Kind of gray, actually," Little Frank said.

"I'm not sure I like you riding a racehorse. I trust you just exercised him."

Little Frank dropped his head. "Mr. Meyers wanted to time him on the new track."

"You galloped him around the track?"

"Oh, yes! I had the fastest time, Mama."

Veronica's eyes lit up. "Really? Wait until I tell Eachan that my brother has the fastest time on Little Traveler!"

"He already knows."

"How?"

"He was on Cincinnati Joe, the other horse. I beat him by a nose," Little Frank said.

"I can't believe this Mr. Meyers let you boys race the horses. I'll have your father talk to him."

"He paid us, Mama."

"Paid you? You've worked for him a month for free and he paid you for racin' the horses once around the track?"

"Five greenback cash dollars each." Little Frank pulled out the bill and unfolded it. "Look."

"Eachan has five dollars too?" Patricia asked.

"I'll bet Curly Mac makes more than that cleaning his

aunt's saloon," Veronica replied.

"Mama, it isn't sinful to ride a horse fast," Little Frank declared.

"No, but it's dangerous. And I will not have my son hanging around a bunch of racetrack sinners."

"Where can I hang around where there are no sinners at all?" he asked.

Robert Fortune, this is not a good time for you to be gone. You have a son to talk to . . . right now! "We will discuss it with your father when he gets home tomorrow."

"Tomorrow? But, when tomorrow?" Little Frank groaned.

"The afternoon train about 4:30 P.M. if all goes well."

"But the race is at 1:30, and I promised Mr. Meyers that I'd—"

"The big race isn't until Sunday, and I absolutely forbid my son to be at the racetrack on a Sunday afternoon and so does your father."

Little Frank jammed his hands in the front pockets of his ducking trousers. "Tomorrow they're runnin' the local races. The two racehorses separate against all comers. And the only way to get people to enter is to have hometown boys ride their horses. Nobody wants to compete against professional jockeys. Mr. Meyers chose me and Eachan since we've been ridin' them."

Jamie Sue gently placed her hand on her son's shoulder and was surprised at how muscular it felt. "You've *been* riding? I thought today was the first time."

"It was the first time we raced them, Mama. We exercise them every day, of course."

"I don't remember you telling me that before."

"'Nica and Tricia knew," he reasoned. "I didn't try to keep it a secret."

"You knew that Little Frank was racing horses?"

"Exercising them, Mama," Patricia corrected.

"Of course we knew," Veronica sighed. "Everyone in town knew."

"Well, I didn't know. And I don't think your father knew. And you will not race them again until your father comes home. Is that understood?"

"But Mama . . . I promised. I can't break my word. Fortune men never ever break their word. Grandpa Brazos taught me that," Little Frank pleaded.

I can't believe this. I'm boxed in by a fourteen-year-old imploring family tradition. Somehow, Brazos Fortune, you're behind all of this. "Perhaps your father will come home on the early train and we can discuss it with him."

"Let's send Daddy a telegraph and tell him we need him home by noon."

"I refuse to spend our money on a telegram," Jamie Sue insisted.

"Can I spend my money?" Little Frank asked, as he held up the greenback bill.

She studied the waiting blue eyes of a young man who had the affable Fortune men smile and a dance in his eyes. "It is your money, and you may spend it as you please. But that doesn't . . ."

Little Frank grabbed her neck and kissed her cheek. "Thanks. I'm going to the depot to send a telegram right now. Do you girls want to come?"

Patricia's eyes widened. "You mean, you don't mind being seen with us?"

"I want all the boys to know you have a big brother and they better treat you good," Little Frank announced.

"Is it alright if we go, Mama?" Veronica asked.

Jamie Sue pressed her fingers against her temples and nodded her head. "Go on. Don't run. Come straight home. And don't let Grandpa Brazos buy you a new dress or anything else!"

CHAPTER NINE

"Thanks for not bindin' my hands and feet in front of my boys," Holter told them.

Guthrie Holter rode next to Robert Fortune as the buckboard headed back up the dusty, narrow dirt road to Deadwood. His two boys, James and Paul, rode double on Robert's horse beside Stillman Taite, a good fifty feet behind the wagon.

"I don't get it, Guthrie. I pull you out of a railroad yard beating, give you a job, a room, a purpose, a good salary . . . and you treat me this way. I thought you were on the square," Robert said.

"It's hard to explain," Holter admitted.

"We've got all morning. Give it a try."

"Belinda, that's my wife, always lived fast and likes money. But I loved her. Shoot, I still love her. And don't ask me to explain that. But the reason I left was 'cause I just couldn't make money fast enough for her."

"She didn't live in Sidney, did she?"

"We were only there a while. She was a travelin' woman. So James and Paul ended up stayin' with their grandma a lot in Rawlins, Wyomin'. I came north to find a better job.

I kept thinkin' I could find something that would satisfy her. But I got in trouble in that Rapid City train yard over a card game. That's when you showed up."

"Why'd you lie about your family bein' in Sidney?"

"I wanted to sound more stable than I am. I wanted the job."

"You wanted a job so you could rob jewelry merchants?"

"Yeah . . . well, it don't matter, I reckon, but it was Belinda's plan."

Each bump the buckboard took jarred the pain Robert still felt from diving out the train window. "And just how is that?" *Lord, this guy double-crossed me, stole jewels, and put my life in danger . . . yet . . . there's something about him I like. Friends and enemies aren't that far apart sometimes.*

Guthrie turned around, waved to his boys, then took off his hat. "I heard she was back in Rawlins, so I listened to your advice. I decided we ought to give it another try. I sent her a telegram to get her and the boys to move up here. She said they'd come up to Deadwood and look around if I sent them the fare but wasn't promisin' nothin'."

Robert reached though a rip in his trouser leg and rubbed a raw spot above his knee. "How come you didn't tell me that?"

"'Cause I never know if she will show up or not. If I make a big deal and she don't show, well it's humblin' to say the least. Sometimes she just spends the travel money I send her and don't follow through. Anyway, by the time Belinda got to Deadwood, she had cooked up this scheme to rob the diamond man. I guess she visited with him on the train comin' up. Belinda gets along real well visitin' with men, if you get my drift."

Robert refused to look at Guthrie. "Why not rob him in an alley in Deadwood?"

"That salesman is the most cautious man in the world. When he's in town, he keeps his samples in a safe in his hotel room. He has the jewelers come up and visit him to see the display. She said the best place to rob him was on the train. Catch him with his defenses down. I said I had me a good job and wanted no part of it. She says she'll do it anyway, and take the boys with her and not come back. Said if someone chased her and started shootin', it would be all my fault if any of them got injured. And I knew you'd be the one to go after her."

Robert listened to the somber drone of Holter's confession. *Lord, it's getting harder and harder for me to like that woman. What drives a woman to be that way?*

"I tried to tell her it wouldn't work what with you, me, and Stillman ridin' the cars. She don't listen much. She said if I'd help this time, we'd buy us a house in Rawlins next to her mama's and she'd settle down."

"Did you believe her?"

"Nope, but I wanted to."

Robert rubbed his beard. "So, that's why you wanted to take my place on the train, so the jewelry theft would go easier?"

"To tell you the truth, Mr. Fortune, I wanted to take your place so I could be sure you wouldn't get shot."

"She did shoot at me, you know."

Guthrie Holter leaned forward, his elbows on his knees. "But she didn't hit you. Belinda used to be a trick-shot expert in Major MacGrueder's Wild West Show. She don't miss. Ever. For once, she followed my advice."

"How's that?"

"I told her if she shot you, your brothers would track her down anywhere on the face of the earth for as long as it took them."

Robert stared out over the ears of the one horse pulling the buckboard. "You're right about that part."

"Anyway, the diversion was my idea. I figured no matter who was on the train . . . you, me, Stillman . . . we'd go after the baggage car robbers. I thought that she and the boys wouldn't as likely get hurt if the security was busy else-where."

"How did you arrange that part?" Robert asked.

"It was easy. Last time I was in Rapid City, I hollered across the platform to the agent that a trunkload of paper money was coming down in a big green wardrobe. I knew the train yard bums would hear it. We had no idea where they would try it. But we knew they would."

"Someone could have gotten killed in that robbery."

"I know . . . but they are so dumb I figured you and Stillman would have no problem. If they wanted to be safe, they wouldn't have tried it."

"What would you have done if they hadn't provided a diversion?"

"I told her to forget the diamond man. But she would have thought of somethin'. She was convinced those dia-monds should belong to her. She don't change her mind much."

"You're stringin' me along with this tale, Guthrie. But how about the letter to Moraine?" Robert pressed. "Did you write the hate letter?"

"It was my idea to try to keep you off the train. I stole the paper, of course. But I cain't run one of them typing machines." Holter glanced back at his boys, rubbed his chin, and shoved his hat back on. "Belinda clerked for a judge for a while and learned a lot . . . includin' how to operate one of them. The judge called her the best operator he'd ever seen."

And I wonder how much that wisdom cost the judge? "So she typed the note?" Robert asked.

"Yep. I told Belinda to tell Moraine something about a meeting with you to work things out. I figured I'd just take your run. I swear I didn't know until he showed up screaming what she had typed on that paper."

Robert kept shaking his head. *Lord, I don't even know what to say. This man deceived me before. How do I know he's not deceiving me now?*

"So, what happens to me now, Mr. Fortune?" Holter asked.

"You face Judge Bennett's court, of course. You didn't blow up the baggage car. You can't be tried for shouting information at a depot. You didn't assault the jewelry merchant, but you drove the escape rig and helped plan the whole thing. No one got killed or seriously injured. I suppose a year in the state prison. What about James and Paul? What happens to them now?"

"I've been ponderin' that ever since Belinda took off last night." Guthrie rubbed the back of his neck and stared off at the tree-covered horizon. "You're the only friend I've got around here."

Friend? I just arrested you at gunpoint.

"I'm goin' to ask the biggest favor of my life and one I

don't deserve. Could you and your wife take the boys until the judge decides, then see that they get to their grandma's in Rawlins? She loves them as much as I do. Belinda loves them too, you know."

"We'll help if we can, Guthrie. But your Belinda rode off in the night and left you all."

"She has a good heart even under all that. It's like a disease sometimes that makes her do things she regrets later on."

"It's called sin, Guthrie . . . sin. And there is a cure."

Guthrie Holter lowered his voice. "You going to start preachin' Jesus at me?"

"Can you think of anyone who needs it more?"

"Only Belinda . . ." Holter murmured. "Only my darlin' Belinda."

Robert closed the front door of the house and returned to Lincoln Street where Guthrie Holter waited in the wagon. Stillman Taite, James and Paul Holter were on horseback.

"No one's at home. I don't know where they are," he said as he crawled back into the wagon.

"Ain't you goin' to change that dirty torn suit?" Taite called out.

"Not until I get the boys situated. We'll go by the hardware. Someone there will know where my wife is."

Robert drove the buckboard down the steep slope of Lincoln Street and turned right. They rolled past the Merchant's Hotel. "Can't remember when the front porch of the Merchant's was empty like that," Taite called out.

Robert pulled the buckboard up in front of a huge brick building that read "Fortune & Son, Hardware." On the front on the tall oak-and-glass doors was a hand-painted sign: "Closed."

"What do you mean, closed?" Robert grumbled. He stood up in the buckboard and pushed his hat back, then looked around town. "Do you see any smoke, Guthrie? Last time this store was closed in the middle of the day, the lumber mill was burning down. How about you boys?" he called to James and Paul. "You see any fire or smoke?"

The older, James, with dark hair parted in the middle and slicked behind his ears, called back, "No, sir, we don't see any fire."

"Have you told them what's about to happen?" he asked Holter.

"Nope. Kind of hard to figure the words."

"Tell them you did wrong and when a man does wrong there's punishment, just like there's punishment when a boy does wrong."

"Where we headed now?" Taite called out.

"I suppose I should try the phone company or Abby's dress shop . . . or maybe the doctor's office. If Daddy took sick . . . every family business will be closed."

He slapped the lead line and the single horse trudged north. "I been thinkin' about your preachin'," Guthrie said. "I think when I get out of jail, I'm going to give it a try."

"Give what a try?" Robert asked.

"Like you said . . . Jesus."

"It won't work, Guthrie."

"What do you mean, it won't work? You said He'd forgive me of everything I did wrong."

"That He will."

"Then why won't it work?"

"Because you're approaching it like a new system to win at Faro. You're going to try it out and see if the results are better. He wants everything and He wants it right now, not later."

"All or nothin'?"

"That's about it."

"That's what I figured you'd say."

"And what do you say?"

Guthrie pointed across the street. "I'd say the telephone exchange is locked up tight."

The telephone exchange business office had all the blinds drawn. *Lord, not Daddy, not while I was out of town. I moved all the way to Deadwood to be with family, and this can't happen with me out of town!* "This is crazy!"

"You want me to go into the grocery and ask?" Taite called out. "Looks like it's open."

"And tell them that I've lost my family and has anyone seen them?" He looked up to see the long black queue of an oriental man in a red-flowered silk shirt scurry across the street. "Mr. Chin!" Robert called out.

The short, older man stopped in the middle of the street and turned toward the wagon.

"Young Fortune!" he called out.

"Mr. Chin, have you seen any of my family?"

"Oh, yes, big horse!"

"What do you mean, big horse?"

The old man smiled and scooted across the street.

"Mr. Chin . . . I'm lookin' for Sammy. Have you seen him or his wife?"

The wrinkle-faced man once again smiled. "Ah, yes . . . big horse!"

"Mr. Chin, have you seen Daddy Brazos?"

The smile stiffened. "I tell you, big horse! I go now." He ran down toward China Town.

"A big horse? Daddy rode off on a big horse? Was run over by a big horse . . ." Robert mumbled.

"If your daddy was injured, where would they take him?" Guthrie Holter asked.

"Up to Dacee June's or Todd's. They live next door up on Williams Street on Forest Hill. I've got to go up there."

Guthrie Holter pointed to the large brown horse. "This one tired pony will never pull us up there. He's been doing extra duty all mornin'."

Robert stood in the buckboard and surveyed the street. "James and Paul, come sit here with your daddy. Let me ride that black horse up to Forest Hill."

He put his hands on Guthrie Holter's shoulder. "Tell them what's going on. Tell them the truth. They need to hear it from you."

"What do you want me to do?" Taite called out.

"Shoot him if he tries to escape."

"You're joshin' me."

"He won't try."

"How do you know?"

Fortune pointed back to Guthrie Holter huddled with his two boys. "He has too much to lose."

The sorrel still had some spring in his step after packing the little boys all morning. But what strength he had dissipated when Robert spurred him straight up the steep incline of Shine Street. The horse was lathered and breathing hard when he rode up in front of the mirror-identical Williams Street houses at the top of seventy-two steep city steps.

Robert was surprised to find both front doors locked.

And no one responded to the knocking.

Dacee June took those three babies somewhere? And Rebekah's five? They're all gone? And my family too . . . like they were plucked right up into heaven . . . but I'm still here.

Robert stared over the tops of the buildings of Deadwood's Main Street, toward the flat area across Whitewood Creek, near the old site of Claim #1.

Half the town must be at the racetrack . . . but the race isn't until Sunday afternoon! What are they doing there?

He wandered across the porch of Todd and Rebekah's house and gawked at the throng of people at the long, skinny racetrack that ran parallel to the creek.

"A speech? Did the governor come to town? Or the president?" he mumbled aloud. *It's some kind of political rally, and the entire Fortune crowd is there. Except me.*

Shine Street was too steep to ride the tired horse down, so Robert walked him back down the hill and across Main Street.

"What did you find out?" Taite called out as he approached.

"No one's home, but there's some big doin' at the racetrack."

"The local races," Taite answered. "I lost a day with this all-night chase and plum forgot it. Today is them local races!"

"What local races?" Robert asked.

"Anyone who wants to challenge the big gray or big

black horse can do so . . . up to eleven other horses each race. But it's local riders only. Even on them racehorses. I reckon everyone's over there."

"Not the Fortune family. We don't go to horse races. Well, Sammy might be there. He used to race horses down in the Territory, but not the rest of the family."

"Findin' one of 'em is better than none," Taite suggested.

Robert mounted the sorrel and glanced over at the wagon. Two teary-eyed boys clutched their father's arms.

Robert tipped his hat at Guthrie Holter. "I see you told them what was going to happen?"

Holter nodded.

"Have them ride there with you. We're going down to the racetrack to see the commotion."

Taite rode up beside Robert. "You ain't exactly dressed for the occasion."

"It doesn't make any difference in the world what I look like. I'm not going to stay. I'm just looking for Sammy."

Wagons, horses, carriages, hacks, military ambulances, and several bicycles were crowded around the racetrack and out into Sherman Avenue. Holter parked the wagon by a willow tree that had been permanently dwarfed by the snow heaps of winter.

"You wait here. I'll go find out what's going on," Robert said.

"I'd surely like to get close enough to see them races," Stillman Taite declared.

"I'll go find Sammy and then come right back. Then it will be your turn. You can have the rest of the day off."

"From the sounds of the yellin' and screamin', we both might miss the races," Taite surmised.

It seemed more like a parade crowd than a racetrack gathering as Robert pushed his way through men, women, and children, inching his way closer to the rail.

He could hear the roar of galloping hooves on the back side of the track. He scooted up to the rail next to a well-dressed lady and a man in a wheelchair. No one paid attention to him as the twelve horses thundered toward the finish line! The whole crowd shouted as they crossed!

When the race was over, the man in the wheelchair glanced up. "Bobby! I don't think I've ever seen you so tattered."

"And I don't know that I've ever heard you holler, Quiet Jim."

"Hello, Robert," the lady nodded. "Isn't this exciting?"

Fortune tipped his hat. "Yes ma'am, Columbia. But I see the black professional horse won."

"Did you see who finished second?" Quiet Jim asked.

"Eh . . . a buckskin . . . was that Sammy's buckskin?"

"Yep," Quiet Jim replied.

"And did you see who was ridin' him?" Columbia asked.

"No . . . but he was too small for Sammy."

"It was our Quint," Columbia announced.

Robert glanced down at the immaculately dressed Fern, Sarah, Jimmy, and Brett. "Big brother was on that horse?"

Fern nodded. "Yes, he did very well, don't you think?"

"He did wonderful, darlin'."

"Did you notice who was mounted on the black horse?" Jim asked.

"Am I going to like the answer?"

Quiet Jim chuckled. "The Moraine boy."

"Eachan? I thought they had professional jockeys?"

"Not today," Columbia said. "It's local entry day. All jockeys have to be local."

"The kid must be a good horseman," Robert said.

"They wouldn't let him ride such an expensive horse if he wasn't," Quiet Jim explained. "Next race it will be time for the tall gray horse."

Robert turned to Mrs. Troop. "Columbia, have you seen Jamie Sue today? I just got into town and no one's home."

She pointed to the east. "They are up at the finish line."

"They're here?"

"Every Fortune and most ever' fortune is here today," Quiet Jim drawled.

Two men in silk suits and top hats blocked his progress as Robert scooted along the rail. Two well-dressed ladies in bright satins and white lace stood at their sides. He glanced at the man with the round face.

"Oscar Puddin? Is that you?"

A wide smile broke across the man's face. "Oh, howdy, Mr. Fortune! Ain't this something. I got me a shave, a haircut, and a bath. I even shaved off my mustache and chin whiskers!"

"I noticed."

"And this is a fine suit."

The man next to Puddin turned around. "Mr. Chambers, are you responsible for Oscar's refinement and culture?" Robert asked.

"Fortune! My word, what happened to you?" Chambers sputtered. "Did you get run over by a train?"

"Actually, I crawled under a train. Fortunately for me, it wasn't moving at the time."

"Quite an exciting race, wasn't it?" Chambers probed.

"Yes, it was . . ." Robert stared at the two women, dressed in satins, who stood next to Puddin and Chambers.

He had to choke out the words. "Miss Augusta? Miss Sandra?"

"As you can see, we took your advice," Sandra Raxton gushed. "We came to town and arranged an investors' meeting for tonight."

"And we scrubbed up a bit," Augusta added.

"A bit? You two look clean as a new gold eagle coin."

"Which is more than we can say for you," Miss Sandra chided.

"I ran into a train hold-up and had to chase down the culprits."

"Did you catch them?" she probed.

"Half of them." He stood back and looked the Raxton sisters over more carefully. "I can't believe how nice you look all cleaned up."

"Well, don't get to starin' too long," Miss Augusta challenged. "You are a married man, and we've made prior commitments."

"You have?"

Miss Sandra Raxton slipped her hand in Oscar Puddin's arm. Miss Augusta put hers in Byron Chambers's.

"We took your advice about other things too," Miss Sandra added. "The part about seekin' what the Lord wants in our lives."

"And what does He want in your life?"

"He wants us to be rich and married," Miss Sandra announced.

"But not," Augusta giggled, "necessarily in that order."

Robert stood on his toes and tried to stare over the top of the crowd. *I wonder how long it's been since they were clean . . . and giggled.* The multitude rehuddled as different horses were led out on the track. Robert had to talk loud to be heard. "You know my brother Sammy. Have you seen him?"

"He's over there with his beautiful wife, Abby," Miss Sandra pointed.

"You know Abby?"

"We know all the ladies in your family. Who do you think picked out these dresses and made us scrub up?" Miss Augusta explained.

"You Fortune men exhort us with your words," Miss Sandra added. "But them women of yours do their preachin' with their actions."

"Ain't never met a family like yours, Fortune," Miss Augusta said.

Robert pushed his way through the crowd. *Nor have I met anyone quite like the Raxton sisters!*

Sam and Abigail stood at the rail watching the horses being led onto the track. A teenage girl, carrying a four-year-old boy, stood next to them.

The boy spotted him first. "Hi, Uncle Bobby!"

"Howdy, Garrett. Are you going to ride one of those horses?"

"No, Uncle Bobby!" he squealed.

The teen girl looked around. "Uncle Bobby, it isn't fair. They wouldn't let me ride one of the horses! They said girls were not supposed to straddle horses. I think they made that up because they know I'm better than they are!"

"Well, Amber, darlin', you might be right."

"Bobby, what in the world happened to you!" Abby gasped.

Sam turned around. "Little brother, you been out playing with coyotes again?"

"It's a long story. There was a train robbery, and I had to track them down."

"Did you have to do it on your belly?" Sam chided.

"Some of the time. I hear your buckskin came in second."

"We all conceded first to the black horse. We were really competing for second. That was Quiet Jim's boy up on top. When they wouldn't let Amber ride him, Quint volunteered."

"Have you seen Jamie Sue?" Robert asked.

Abby pointed down the rail. "I think she's on the other side of Dacee June and Carty." Sam pointed down the rail.

A big sorrel stallion reared up and dumped his rider, then broke down the track in a panicked gallop. Everyone ran to the rail to watch as Robert pushed his way to Dacee June.

"Oh, good! You arrived just in time for the second race," Dacee June announced as he approached. "Even if you are slightly . . . disheveled." She wore a crisp, starched, purple gingham dress with white lace collar, cuffs, and hem. Her straw hat was tilted to the side. The baby in her arms wore an identical dress.

"You and little Gracey look pretty," he said.

"Robert Fortune, her name is Ninete!"

"I never was too good with French," he grinned.

"Look at the others . . ." She pointed to Carty, who packed three-year-old Elita in his arms. An older woman carried two-year-old Jehane.

He tipped his hat to the lady. "Mrs. Edwards, nice to see you."

"Robert Paul Fortune, your mama, rest her soul, would never let you out of the house looking like that," Mrs. Edwards lectured.

"No, ma'am, she wouldn't. I just captured a sneak thief, and haven't had time to change. I need to talk to Jamie Sue. I didn't know this was going to be such a social event."

Twenty-six-year-old Carty Toluca shifted Elita from one arm to the other.

"Carry me, Uncle Bobby!" the little girl begged.

Robert took the toddler in his arm. She hugged his neck and gave his beard a slobbery kiss, then instantly jerked back and rubbed her mouth.

"Like kissing a wooly sheep, isn't it, darlin'," Robert laughed. "Sorry about that."

"Did you see that first race?" Carty asked.

"Caught the end of it."

"Sammy's horse sure is fast, isn't he?" Carty added.

Dacee June handed the one-year-old to her husband. "You know, of course, Amber pitched a fit to ride the horse."

"That's what she said," Robert said.

"I thought Daddy would shoot that race promoter for not letting her ride."

Robert bounced the toddler on his hip. "He's a might protective of his girls."

"You know what Stella down at the telephone exchange said?" Dacee June took the squirming Elita from Robert's arms. "She said all the single women in Deadwood wish that Daddy Brazos would adopt them so they could be one of the Fortune women."

"There sure are lots of Fortune women around already."

"These three are Toluca girls," Carty declared.

Dacee June scowled at her husband.

"Well . . . sort of . . ." Carty mumbled.

Robert leaned over and gave Jehane a kiss on the fore-head. "Whether Fortune or Toluca, you are 'God's gift,' young lady. You remember that."

Two men now had ropes on the big sorrel's neck. He yanked them off their feet and dragged the men around to the back of the track. The crowd cheered, but it wasn't clear whether they were cheering for the men or the horse. He pushed his way down to a picture-perfect family, each standing quietly at attention, under the orchestration of Rebekah Fortune.

The next-to-the-youngest child broke rank and ran to him.

"Hi, Uncle Bobby. What happened to you? Did a horse run over you?"

Robert grabbed up six-year-old Stuart and carried him back to where Todd, Rebekah, Hank, Camillia, and Nettie stood.

"Stuart's right, Bobby," Rebekah called out. "You look quite horrid."

Robert put his hand on seven-year-old Nettie's head. "Your mama speaks her mind, doesn't she?"

Nettie pulled down Robert's hand and placed her little fingers in his. "Mama always tells the truth," she explained.

"Little brother, Stuart looks identical to how you did when you were that size," Todd reported.

Robert set the six-year-old down. "You and me are partners, aren't we?"

Stuart mashed his lips together and nodded his head.

Thelma Speaker strolled up holding a four-year-old's hand. "You tore your trousers, Uncle Bobby."

"Yes, I did, Casey."

"You aren't supposed to play under the porch."

Robert laughed and shook his head. "I know. I'll try better next time. Now, where have you and Mrs. Speaker been?"

"To the privy!" Casey shouted.

Thelma Speaker's face turned beet red.

Robert leaned over and kissed the older lady's cheek. "Blush-red looks good on you, Mrs. Speaker."

"Robert, dear, Sarah Ruth would never approve of you coming to a public event so attired," the gray-haired lady replied.

"No, ma'am. Your sister has already reminded me of that." He glanced around the crowd. "Actually, I just need to talk to Jamie Sue, then be gone. I've still got work to do."

"She's on the other side of Daddy." Todd pointed through the crowd.

By now two more ropes had been thrown around the sorrel stallion's neck, and they were trying to coax him off the racetrack. Suddenly he yanked his neck back, lifting one of the men off his feet and tossing him over the rail into Whitewood Creek.

The crowd hurrahed.

The rest of the racehorses and riders were milling around the starting line.

Robert spotted his father leaning against the rail, his .50

caliber Sharps carbine over his shoulder, talking to a very fat man who wore a round straw hat.

Robert weaved through the crowd. His path was cut off by a rugged man in dirty shop clothes.

"Did you get beat up?" Riagan Moraine asked.

Robert pushed his hat back and let his hands slip down to his hips, but he purposely avoided his holstered revolver. "Not yet. I've been trailing a lady jewel thief who robbed a man on the train. She's the one that typed that letter on my stationery, Moraine."

"Why did she type it?" Moraine demanded.

"She didn't want me on the train when the robbery took place. She thought she could talk you into stopping me."

"She was almost right."

"But you found you couldn't shoot a man in the back, could you?" Robert challenged.

Moraine glanced down at his boot tops. "No . . . no, I couldn't."

Robert took a deep breath and could feel his muscles start to relax. "Now about that novel . . ."

Moraine rubbed his chin. "Your daddy already explained that to me."

"He did?"

"He and that fat man over there."

"Who is that man?" Robert asked.

"Hawthorne Miller, the one who wrote the book. Your daddy marched him up to the shop at gunpoint and made him tell me everything."

Robert shook his head. "Yep, that sounds like Daddy."

"Turns out that Fortune in the book isn't your kin after all," Moraine declared.

"I'm glad to get that worked out, Riagan." Robert held out his hand for the Irishman to shake.

Moraine hesitated. "Just one thing. We were born Catholic, and we die Catholic. I don't want you tryin' to change that."

"I'll leave that up to the Lord. Fair enough?" Robert replied.

"That's fair." Moraine reached out and shook his hand. "Did you see my boy on that black stallion?"

"Eachan did a great job on that horse."

"He's a natural at it, you know." Moraine put his hand on Robert's shoulder. "I hear your boy can ride too."

"Little Frank's learning. It comes from hanging around cavalry soldiers all his life."

"Maybe I should give them a hand with the sorrel." Moraine ducked under the railing. "Or the second race will never begin."

Robert strolled up to the rail and leaned his elbows against it next to his father.

"I knew you'd make it," Brazos said, without looking at Robert.

"Daddy, I'm glad you feel like getting out a little."

"There's no way on earth I'd miss this race." Brazos motioned at the man next to him. "This gentleman is that famous author, Mr. Hawthorne Miller."

All three men leaned against the rail and watched a dozen men yank the sorrel out of the track into the corral at the north end.

"Mr. Miller, I hear Daddy talked you into explaining things to Mr. Moraine."

"Yes . . . well . . . your father is very persuasive," Miller huffed. "I never thought anyone ever believed any of my stories."

"I believe the one about Todd's 'flying fist of death'," Robert said.

Brazos cleared his throat and pointed the carbine in Miller's direction. "All of them books about Stuart Brannon are true, aren't they?"

Miller pulled his hat off, wiped his sweating forehead, then cleared his throat. "Eh, yes definitely. . . . All the Brannon books are true."

Brazos brushed his hand against his thick, sagging, gray mustache. "I met him once, you know . . ."

Oh no, I'm going to have to listen to those "me and Stuart Brannon" stories? "Daddy, I need to talk to Jamie Sue. Why don't you tell Mr. Miller about the time you and Stuart held off that renegade Confederate veteran army down in Sonora, Mexico."

Brazos's eyes lit up. "That was a day, wasn't it!"

"Yes," Miller said, "but before you leave the track I need to talk to you about a book on how the 'Fortune Family Foils the Fearsome Five.'"

"What?" Robert gasped.

Miller shrugged. "It's just a working title."

"For what?"

"For how you, Jamie Sue, and the kids busted up that Wild Bunch gang on the train," Brazos laughed. "I reckon it's your turn."

"We don't want a book written about us," Robert insisted.

"I'm going to write it anyway. It's a matter of whether I get the story straight from you or have to make all of it up."

"Give him the facts, Bobby," Brazos said. "We don't want any more make-believe stories about Fortunes."

Robert pointed over to where Jamie Sue and the girls stared out at the racetrack. "I'll have to talk it over with my family."

He pushed on through the crowd, which was intently watching as the horses formed a crude, dancing, prancing line, nervously waiting for the signal gun to fire.

Patricia wore the rose satin dress, Veronica the yellow.

Veronica spotted him first and ran and grabbed his arm. "Daddy! Isn't it exciting! Curly Mac is riding that bay mare! I think he'll finish right behind the gray, don't you? It's like first place. Everyone knows the gray will win."

Patricia grabbed the other arm. "Daddy, did you see Eachan? They let him ride the black racehorse. He is really, really good."

"I can't believe you two got this dressed up just to see a local horse race." He stepped up next to Jamie Sue and put his arm around her waist.

She stepped back away from him and studied him boot to hat. "Robert Paul Fortune, what happened to you?"

"Chasing train robbers. I'm fine. I'll explain it all later."

Veronica held on to the rail, dancing from one foot to the other. "The race is about to start, Daddy!"

Patricia chewed her lip. "This is the most exciting day of my entire life."

"Darlin'," Robert began, "we're going to need to keep Guthrie's two boys until . . ."

"Certainly, helping others is what I do best. You know that." Jamie Sue put a soft finger against his lip to silence him. "But tell me later. There's the gun!"

"I'm trying to tell you something important," Robert hollered above the crowd. "What is so important about a horse race!"

"Because our son is on that big gray racing horse!" she shouted back.

Robert looked up to see Little Frank spur the big gray past the first turn.

My son . . . riding a professional racing horse? But he didn't . . . I didn't . . . Jamie Sue must have . . . I can't believe . . .

Veronica was bouncing clear off the ground with each jump.

Patricia chewed on her lip like it was candle wax.

Jamie Sue yelled, "Go, Little Frank!"

Robert stared. He stared at his wife, his daughters, and most of all his son who had a full-length lead on the bay mare on the back side of the track and was starting to pull further away.

"Go, Little Frank!" he screamed. "Go!"

The big gray thundered across the finish line three lengths in front of the big bay mare. The crowd roared approval.

Robert studied the crowd. *Are they cheering for the gray horse? Cheering for Little Frank? Cheering for the mare. Cheering for all the horses . . . Or just cheering because it's summer in Deadwood, South Dakota, in 1891 and it's a great time to be alive!*

Most of the crowd, including the twins, moved down to the finish line to greet the winners. Robert and Jamie Sue stayed at the rail.

"He did very, very well," Jamie Sue declared.

Robert took Jamie Sue's hand and laced his fingers in hers. They felt very soft. Very warm. Very right. "I can't believe you let him do it."

"Me? It was how you answered his telegram."

"I didn't answer any telegram. I was out chasing train robbers."

"Yes, I know." She put her hand in his arm. "I believe it said: 'Train robbery. Delayed. Go ahead with plans.' "

"Well . . . yes, I sent that when I left Rapid City, . . . but it didn't have anything to do with a horse race. I meant go ahead with the plan I told you about the Raxton sisters."

"We thought you meant go ahead with Little Frank riding the horse."

"Well, it's over now," he mumbled.

"Oh, Bobby, there is a naive statement if I ever heard one. Look at your daughters visiting with those boys. It's not over, Robert Fortune."

Robert looked around at the milling crowd. "Look at all these people. They all saw Little Frank ride to victory."

"Did you notice the entire family is here? Dacee June even brought the sweet little girls."

"That's funny," Robert added. "When we moved to town, no one was at the depot. This is like our welcoming. The entire family is all dressed up and gathered together."

"Not everyone is dressed up," she said.

"I think maybe I should wear duckings on this job."

"And take an extra pair with you on every trip. I will not have my husband look abandoned."

"Abandoned? Look at this crowd. Every friend we have in this town is here."

"And every enemy," Jamie Sue cautioned.

Robert noticed Patricia visiting with Eachan Moraine. "I suppose we will spend a lifetime trying to tell which is which."

He looked up to see Daddy Brazos walking along with one arm around Little Frank's shoulder. His other hand carried his carbine.

"I saw you in the crowd, Daddy!" Little Frank shouted as he approached. "I told Mama as soon as you read my telegram you'd be here. I just knew you'd make it back in time! Is that the fastest horse you ever saw?"

"I'm proud of you, son. You did a fine job, didn't he, Daddy?" Robert replied.

Brazos continued to keep his arm on his grandson's shoulder. "I've never seen anybody that good since we buried Big River Frank up there under a Dakota cross." He pointed at the graveyard on Mt. Moriah. "Now I've got a present for my oldest grandchild, Frank," he announced.

Jamie Sue glanced over at Robert. "Frank? No longer Little Frank?" she murmured.

Brazos glanced back up at Mt. Moriah. "Well, Big River won't mind. He was always too big a man to let petty things bother him." He turned to his grandson. "Frank, this carbine has been with me from Brownsville to today. Except for when I sent it to bring your Uncle Sammy home. It's like a member of the family. It's put meat on the table and driven all sorts of wolves from our door. Don't ever sell it. Don't ever trade it. Don't let it rust. It's yours." He handed the gun to his stunned grandson.

Tears ran down Little Frank's cheeks. "Really, Grandpa? . . . Really . . . it's mine?"

Robert put his hand on his father's shoulder. "Daddy . . .

you don't have to . . ."

Brazos held up a slightly shriveled but still-calloused hand to quiet Robert. "Yes, I have to, Bobby. It's somethin' I've been plannin' since the day Frank was born." He scratched the back of his neck, reset his hat, and stared up at the cloudless, blue Dakota sky. "Isn't that right, Sarah Ruth?" he mumbled. He took a deep breath, then patted Frank on the back.

"And now, Bobby," Brazos cleared his throat. "I have to go buy me a horse."

"Which one, Grandpa Brazos?" Frank called out. "Which horse are you goin' to buy?"

Brazos winked at Robert. "Why, that big sorrel stallion, of course."

Center Point Publishing
600 Brooks Road • PO Box 1
Thorndike ME 04986-0001 USA

(207) 568-3717

US & Canada:
1 800 929-9108